MV

You'll
Always
Have
Tara

Also by Leah Marie Brown

Dreaming of Manderley

The It Girls Series

Faking It

Finding It

Working It

Owning It

LEAH MARIE BROWN

You'll Always Have Tara

LYRICAL PRESS
Kensington Publishing Corp.
www.kensingtonbooks.com

LYRICAL PRESS BOOKS are published by

Kensington Publishing Corp.
119 West 40th Street
New York, NY 10018

All Kensington titles, imprints, and distributed lines are available at special quantity discounts for bulk purchases for sales promotion, premiums, fund-raising, educational, or institutional use.

Special book excerpts or customized printings can also be created to fit specific needs. For details, write or phone the office of the Kensington Sales Manager: Attn.: Sales Department. Kensington Publishing Corp., 119 West 40th Street, New York, NY 10018. Phone: 1-800-221-2647.

Lyrical and the Lyrical logo Reg. U.S. Pat. & TM Off.

First Lyrical Press Mass-Market Paperback Printing: May 2018
ISBN-13: 978-1-5161-0114-6
ISBN-10: 1-5161-0114-6

First Lyrical Press Electronic Edition: May 2018
eISBN-13: 978-1-5161-0117-7
eISBN-10: 1-5161-0117-0

10 9 8 7 6 5 4 3 2 1

Printed in the United States of America

Chapter One

"You are not classically beautiful, Tara." Truman Barton holds his champagne flute aloft as if giving a toast, drawling his vowels as if they were drops of bourbon rolling around on his tongue. "You're as pale as freshly peeled whiteleg shrimp, your bottom lip is too big, and you wear cowboy boots with your dresses."

Truman and Tavish Barton, known around Charleston as *Those Barton Boys* (usually said in an exasperated tone), are two of my dearest friends, despite their shared predilection for keeping me humble.

"It's true," Tavish chimes in. "Now, that you have gone and dyed your hair that ridiculous shade of blazing nutmeg—"

"Warm cinnamon," I correct.

"Whatever, dahlin'," he says, sniffing. "Cinnamon. Nutmeg. All's I'm saying is a girl shouldn't dye her hair the color of a nut."

I have been dying my hair a darker shade with more

brown tones because I think it makes me look more so-phisticated on camera.

"Cinnamon doesn't come from a nut."

"It doesn't?"

Tavish frowns at his brother. Truman shrugs.

"No," I say, laughing. "Cinnamon comes from the bark of a tree. You peanut brains would know that if you stayed in college long enough to graduate."

"Don't worry your pretty little tree-bark head about us, dahlin'. We're not chained to the kitchen, forced to bake six zillion crab-filled puff pastries just so we can pay for our John Lobb loafers."

"Hush," I hiss, looking over my shoulder. "I don't want Grayson to know I've been doing catering jobs."

Grayson Calhoun is my usually, sometimes, not right now, but will be again soon, boyfriend. We have been on-again, off-again since he pulled my ponytail in Miss Treva's third grade class. He is from one of the oldest, most respectable families in South Carolina. He just graduated from Harvard Law School, but one day he will be governor of South Carolina. I know it in my bones. Grayson's momma and daddy have been groom-ing him for a career in politics pretty much since Miss Treva named him third grade class president (despite his deviant hair pulling). The Calhouns are obsessed with politics. I guess you could say it's in their blood since they are related to John C. Calhoun, the seventh vice president of the United States. Only, Grayson is quick to point out he isn't a *direct* descendant on ac-count of John C. having been a slave owner and all. *Third cousin, four times removed. We share ancestors, not ideologies.*

"Don't fool yourself, Tara. It don't matter how many damn snowbirds build their nests out on Daniel

Island and Cainhoy way, Charleston is still a small town. Grayson knows your daddy died owing the IRS a heap of back taxes. The whole town knows you don't have a pot to piss in, dahlin'."

"I have a pot!"

Truth is, I *do* have a pot. It's just not a big pot.

Two months ago, my daddy and aunt died in a freak boating accident one hundred miles off the coast of Sullivan's Island, leaving behind a mountain of debt and years of unpaid taxes we knew nothing about. If it weren't for the trust fund my momma left me, and my job filming cooking segments with our local news station, I would be as broke as my little sister Emma Lee. I have been doing catering jobs to earn money just so I can keep up appearances. Otherwise, I would not have been able to afford the new floral silk Erdem dress I am wearing.

"Hey, Tara."

I recognize the sweet-as-a-box-of-Moon-Pies voice and have to choke back a groan.

"Hey, Maribelle."

Maribelle Cravath, my archrival in all things (including, occasionally, Grayson's affections), has joined our little gathering beneath the branches of a knobby old live oak covered in twinkly fairy lights.

"Love the dress. Is it the Erdem I saw in RTW?"

"Yes."

She widens her falsely lashed eyes and gasps, but I see right through her surprised routine. I know what she is going to say before she says it and I mentally brace myself.

"But, I thought RTW only carried that particular Erdem in size four?"

Bitch.

I smile through the former chunky girl pain.

"That's right."

She lets her gaze make a slow, deliberate journey over my gown, from the boat neckline to the full, frilly skirt.

"Oh," she finally says, her lips forming a perfect pink O—the same shade of pink as the big, bold begonias on her Lilly Pulitzer skirt. "Good for you, sweetie. Good. For. You. We all know how hard you've struggled with your weight through the years."

It doesn't matter how many pounds and years separate me from my pudgy, fudgy middle-childhood, comments about my weight still sting something fierce. Beneath my size-four (unvarnished truth: six) designer dress, I am still an insecure, eating-for-comfort fat girl, hungry for love. Not that I would ever let anyone—especially Maribelle Cravath—know that. I am a Southern girl born and bred, which means I am an expert at artifice, from the application of cosmetics to the camouflaging of unpleasant emotions. So, I smile and keep up a steady patter of polite, meaningless chitchat until my best friend arrives.

Callie takes one look at my face and *knows*. She knows Maribelle has said something to hurt my feelings and that I am mentally gorging on a box of Fiddle Faddle, burying the pain beneath handfuls of buttery, toffee-flavored popcorn and peanuts because my need to be pleasing is greater than my desire to tell Maribelle what I really think of her. Callie has super-developed bestie intuition. She can read my thoughts and feelings across a department store or polo field.

"Hey, Maribelle." Callie gives Maribelle one of those artificial Southern girl smiles. "Cute skirt. Lilly, right? My mom stopped wearing Lilly Pulitzer after they collaborated on a line of dresses for Target, but I love that you aren't letting the porcelain-teapots-and-doilies set dictate your style. Brand loyalty. Good for you."

Maribelle smiles as if she just took a bite of a biscuit made with curdled buttermilk, but doesn't want anyone else to know; a tight, eye-crinkling kind of smile.

"Oh, look," she says, pointing in the direction of the barn. "There's Shelby Drayton. I haven't seen her in weeks."

"Better go say hello," Callie says.

"By-ee." Maribelle waggles her begonia pink lacquered pointy fingernails at us. "See y'all later."

I want to waggle my own lacquered fingernails at her and say, *By-ee. Don't let the door hit you where the good Lord split you, miserable viper in Lilly Pulitzer Kristen wedges.*

But I don't.

I don't because I learned long ago that swallowing the pain of rejection is best done quickly and quietly, without artificial sweeteners. Smile, swallow, keep on smiling. People misinterpret my silences as arrogance, like I am impervious to slights and barbs because I think I am high and mighty. Believe me, I've never thought of myself as high or mighty.

Truth is, I've never liked Maribelle Cravath. She's the Helen of our group. You know the beautiful, stylish, highly competitive antagonist in the movie *Bridesmaids*? Maribelle is a Helen. She silently circles, assessing the field, waiting for the perfect moment to swoop in and feed on the carcasses of weaker women. In the movie, Helen was transformed from a heinous, uppity antagonist to a moderately enjoyable sidekick before Wilson Phillips started singing the exit music. I am still waiting for Maribelle to have her character-redeeming scene.

"Don't tell me," Callie says. "She brought up your weight?"

"Yes."

"Forget Maribelle Cravath," Callie says, slipping her arm through mine. "We all know you were more than a few RC Colas away from being able to kick it in Paula Deen's knickers."

Say what you want about Paula, but I love any woman clever enough to think of six dozen different ways to prepare macaroni and cheese. Granted, it is a shameful, secret love—like my love for boiled peanuts and Goo Clusters—but it is abiding.

"Tell her, Truman," Callie says, nudging the twin with her elbow. "Tell Tara she is a beautiful slender goddess."

Truman chuckles.

"You are beautiful, Tara."

"Classically?" I tease.

His lips quirk.

"Maybe not classically, but you could run a whole mess of circles around Crawdad Cravath, even in those godawful boots."

I laugh.

Truman started calling Maribelle "Crawdad" a few years ago, but he refuses to tell me what she did to earn such an unfortunate moniker. Callie and I have spent more than a few brunches at Poogan's Porch, sipping mimosas and thinking up devilish, delightful stories about how it might have happened. With her long, pointy fingernails and round bug eyes, it's an apt nickname.

"Damn skippy," Travish says, nodding his head so hard his thick, slicked-back chestnut curls fall over his eye. "Maribelle is just jealous because she knows half of Charleston would close their doors to her if she weren't Beau's sister."

Beauregard Cravath III—B. Crav to his friends—is a member of Charleston's ancient elite. The Cravaths are an influential political family with roots going back as far as the seventeenth century. In fact, B. Crav's ancestor was a relative of one of the Lords Proprietors— overseers appointed by King Charles to colonize Charleston. B. Crav is an enthusiastic polo player. His Whitney Turn Up is *the* social event of the polo season, a raucous, Moët-fueled party with a guest list comprised of bluebloods from all over the world. B. Crav has serious connections that stretch far beyond our magnolia shaded borders.

He's also a philandering playboy who has tried to bed or wed practically all of the women under thirty from the Mason-Dixon to the Florida-Georgia line, including my baby sister, Emma Lee.

"Beau is a dirty dog," Callie mutters. "So it's no wonder his sister.is a b—"

"Callie!"

"Let's change the subject," she says, brushing an imaginary fleck of lint from her dress. "Talking about the Cravaths always riles me up."

Talking about the Cravaths riles her up because she was sweet on Beau, and she thought he was sweet on her, too, until he tried to get her liquored up and suggested they have a three-way with his Swedish masseuse. (B. Crav has a live-in masseuse he met at a ski resort in Vail.)

"How is Manderley?" Callie asks.

Manderley is my big sister. She is the perfect Southern lady: calm, clever, generous, reliable, and terribly responsible. She's my polar opposite and everything I strive to be.

"She's fine."

"Is she still in France?"

"Manderley is in Cannes with her best friend, Olivia Tate, the famous screenwriter. Olivia's movie, *A Quaint Milieu*, was nominated for the Palme-d'Or. A glamourous job in Hollywood. Summers in the south of France. My big sister is efficiently and admirably directing her destiny. I am happy for her. Honest, I am. I just wish her destiny wasn't leading her farther and farther from Charleston."

"Yes."

"Has she seen Matthew McConaughey yet?" Callie asks. "Never mind! I don't want to know the answer to that question. If you tell me little old Manderley Maxwell is sipping champagne with Matthew McConaughey I will just die. I will! I will keel over right here at the Whitney Turn Up. They would haul my body to the coroner's office, he would do an autopsy, and say I died from an overdose of toxic putrid green envy."

Truman snorts.

"You don't still have a crush on *that* old dog, do you?" Tavish asks.

"He's not old!"

"Alright. Alright. Alright," Tavish says, mimicking the actor's Texas drawl. "Whatever you say."

"He's not old."

"He's ancient. When was he born?"

"1969."

"1969!" Tavish whistles. "Lawd, he's as old as Moses."

"You're just jealous."

"Jealous? Of Grandad McConaughey?" Tavish clucks his tongue. "Please, girl. That old man ain't got nothing on me."

"He's rich."

"So am I."

"He's famous."

"Who hasn't heard of the Barton Boys? We're notorious in three counties."

"Damn skippy," Truman agrees.

Callie rolls her eyes.

"He's married to a model."

"I'm sorry for him."

"Sorry?" Callie narrows her gaze. "He's married to a beautiful woman and you're sorry for him?"

"Sure," Tavish says, crossing his arms and leaning back against the oak. "I don't care how beautiful the cow is, why would I buy her when I can get the milk for free? Grand Daddy McConaughey is stuck drinking milk from the same tired old cow when there are millions of cows out there."

"You're disgusting."

"I'm serious," Tavish argues. "Do you know how many breeds of cattle there are?"

"Eight hundred," Truman interjects.

"Eight hundred breeds of cattle?" Tavish cries. "That's a lot of milk to enjoy."

"I can't even deal with your"—Callie puts her hand up to stop Tavish from saying anything else—"just hush."

Tavish laughs. He isn't the chauvinist in expensive loafers and fashionably rumpled linen suit he makes himself out to be. He likes riling Callie up. I think it is because he is in love with her.

"I saw Emma Lee chatting up some woman on my way over," Callie says, changing the subject. "How did you get her off the couch?"

"Do you really think Emma Lee Maxwell would miss *the* social event of the season?"

If my baby sister were dying of tuberculosis, she would use her last ragged breath to drag herself to a party. She is the most social and popular girl in Charleston, but ever since we received the news of our father's death and deep debt, she has taken to spending her days on my couch watching crap reality television shows and eating Raising Cane's chicken combos. I swear if I find one more Cane's special sauce container on my salvaged wood coffee table, I am going to—

"Has she decided what to do with her life?" Callie interrupts my musing.

"Nope," I say, twirling the stem of my champagne flute between my fingers and watching the liquid spin around my glass like a golden tornado. "She was all fired up to be a fortune cookie writer until she bingewatched *Below Deck*, and then she was positive she would make a brilliant stewardess on a super yacht. Last week, she caught a segment that ran before my review of that new French-influenced, low-country fusion place on King Street. It was an interview with a woman who works as a professional stand-in bridesmaid."

"I saw that interview!" Callie cries. "The woman actually gets paid to be a bridesmaid for brides that don't have enough friends. Can you imagine?"

"I can't, but Emma Lee could. She emailed Manderley and asked for a loan to buy bridesmaids dresses and build a website."

Truman chuckles.

"Uh-oh," Callie says. "What did Manderley say?"

"You know Mandy. She asked Emma Lee if it was a growth industry and whether Em thought she had the initiative and discipline to run an entrepreneurial business."

Callie laughs. "That sounds like Manderley."

"Then she lectured Emma Lee on the need to be fiscally responsible, now more than ever, and rattled off a checklist of things Emma Lee needed to do, like find health insurance, call Clemson's professional development center to speak to a counselor about grad school, make a budget . . ."

"Poor Emma Lee," Truman says, shaking his head.

"Poor Emma Lee? You mean poor Tara!" I exhale at the memory of the days following Manderley's practical response, Emma Lee's tantrums, and the flurry of emails that flew back and forth between them. "Do you know what Mahatma Gandhi, Eleanor Roosevelt, and Václav Havel have in common?"

"No, what?" Truman says.

"Who is Vatzel Hovel?" Tavish asks.

"Seriously?" I roll my eyes. "Writer, philosopher, first president of Czechoslovakia."

"Czechoslovakia? Petra Némcová," Tavish fires back. "Czechoslovakian model."

"Yes, brother," Truman says, raising his fist for Tavish to bump. "*Sports Illustrated*, 2003."

"Fun in the Sun!" Tavish says. "Hottest Models—"

"Coolest Places—" Truman chimes in.

"Around the World," they say in unison.

Callie rolls her eyes. "Go on, Tara. What were you saying about Eleanor Roosevelt and Václav Havel?"

"I was going to say they dedicated their lives to bring peace, love, and harmony to the world, but they were never awarded the Nobel Peace Prize."

"Robbed," Truman cries in mock outrage.

"I know their pain," I say, sniffing. "Lawd, how I know their pain! I've spent most of my life brokering truces between my sisters. People laud Gandhi for his efforts to promote nonviolence, but that's only because they've never watched me trying to negotiate peace between Manderley and Emma Lee!"

"You're a saint, Tara," Callie says.

"Yes, I am."

"That's one of the reasons Grayson loves you so much," Callie says. "Do you think tonight is the night? Is that why you pulled out the Erdem?"

Truman and Tavish exchange confused glances.

"Grayson asked me to meet him at our spot after the Turn Up. He said he has something important he needs to say to me." *Our spot* is a rickety old dock on Horlbeck Creek, halfway between his parents' home and the home where I grew up. We used to sneak out at night and sit on the end of the dock, dangling our feet over the water, talking about nonsense while the breeze rustled the swamp grasses. "I am pretty sure he is finally going to ask me to marry him."

"You know I love you"—Truman grabs my hand— "despite your freakishly large bottom lip, and Lord knows I would give up my entire collection of bow ties if you would promise to run away with me, but Grayson Calhoun is not going to ask you to marry him."

"Nope." Tavish shakes his head. "Never gonna happen."

"Hush, Tavish," Callie hisses.

"I'm just sayin'—"

"*I'm just sayin'*," Callie mimics. "You don't know what you are saying, so just hush."

Truman is still holding my hand. I look up at his face and my stomach does an anxious little flip. Even in the dim glow of the fairy lights I recognize the smudge of pity in his eyes.

"How do you know Grayson isn't going to ask me to marry him? Did he say something? Is he seeing someone else?"

"I don't know if Grayson is seeing another girl. I just know he isn't going to ask you to marry him. Not tonight." He squeezes my hand gently before letting it go. "Not ever."

"Why not?"

The air between us is heavy with humidity and thoughts Truman does not wish to express, thoughts my friends and neighbors have only shared in low whispers after I left the room.

"Don't make me say it, dahlin'."

"I'll say it," Tavish says. "Grayson isn't going to marry you because your daddy owed so much money to the government they seized your family home and all of his assets. He won't want to attach himself to your family's scandal."

"Scandal?" I cry. "I hardly call my daddy's minor financial difficulties a scandal. Besides, what politician hasn't been involved in some scandal or other? Thomas Ravenel, Bill Clinton, Richard Nixon, Teddy Kennedy, and what about Anthony Weiner, the congressman from New York who resigned after being involved in several sexting scandals?"

"Yes, but those scandals happened *after* the Weiner was elected, not before. South Carolina is the seventh most conservative state in the country. Grayson knows if he marries you, he won't even be elected to the Charleston County Mosquito Control Board." Tavish smiles sadly. "No offense."

"I hate it when people say that."

"Say what?"

"*No offense.*" Heat flushes my cheeks. "It's the verbal equivalent to stabbing someone and then slapping a Band-Aid over the wound."

"I wasn't trying to—"

I wave my hand. "I think you're wrong about Grayson. He isn't the sort of man who would let his heart be ruled by public opinion."

Tavish and Truman give each other the twin look and I want to reach over and knock their identical chestnut heads together. I don't know why I am letting them get under my skin. What South Carolina's most sophomoric bachelors don't know about love could fill the Charleston Harbor. Truman is more committed to his prodigious bow tie collection than he has ever been to a woman and Tavish is too busy high fiving himself over his latest one-night stand to think about settling down.

"I am hardly about to let two prep school dropouts educate me on matters of love."

"You don't need to graduate magnum cum laude to know a man as obsessed with his image as Grayson Calhoun isn't going to marry the daughter of a tax evader." Tavish makes the sign of the cross. "God rest your daddy's soul."

If common sense was measured in dollars, the Barton Boys would be hard-pressed to scrounge up fifty cents worth. They could look under the seats in their matching Porsche 911 Carrera Cabriolets and through the cushions on their sofa, and between them, they might make it to fifty-two cents. Might.

"You don't know Grayson the way I do," I say, tossing my hair over my shoulder. "And it is *magna* cum laude, not magnum. You would know that if you had spent more time in classes and less time playing beer pong in your frat house."

"Ouch," Tavish says.

"That was unnecessarily harsh, dahlin'," Truman sniffs. "Even for you."

There's a short silence between us all and I consider apologizing to the twins, when Callie suddenly turns to me and says, "Do you even want Grayson to ask you to marry him?"

"Of course I do! Why would you ask that?"

Callie shrugs.

I expect the Barton Boys to question my desire to walk down the aisle with Grayson, but not Callie. Callie is a head in the clouds, hopeless romantic. She's had a subscription to *Martha Stewart Weddings* since she was twelve. Her favorite movie is *Father of the Bride*. I want to shrug off Callie's question as easily as she just shrugged off mine, but I am not very good at shrugging things off.

"Callie?" A little voice inside of me is whispering: *Let it go, Tara.* "Why did you ask me if I wanted Grayson to ask me to marry him?"

"Do you see yourself marrying Grayson and settling down to have a plantation full of little Calhouns? Why Tara, why do you want to get married now?"

I stare at Callie, a breeze lifting a lock of hair from my forehead, and swallow back the words, *what a ridiculous question.* Callie has been my best friend forever. When Grayson pulled my hair in Miss Treva's class, it was Callie who came up with the idea of putting crushed up chalk in his milk to get even. She's been with us through every break-up and make-up.

"Grayson just graduated from law school and is taking the summer off to study for the bar exam. I have a good job and am financially independent-ish. Now is the time."

"That's why you want to marry him? Because now is the time. What about love?"

"Love?"

"Yes, *love*."

"Of course I love Grayson!"

"Why?"

"Why?" I roll my eyes. "What a ridiculous question."

"Is it?" She narrows her eyes in that all-knowing, all-seeing best friend way that says: *you can pretend you really like that rocket-and-pine-nut salad but I know you really want a cheeseburger with extra chipotle aioli and truffle fries.* "If it is such a ridiculous question, why are you hesitating to answer?"

"I am not hesitating! Why do I love Grayson Calhoun?" I search the crowd gathered around the barn until I find Grayson, the gingham J. Crew shirt I gave him for Christmas tucked neatly into his khaki pants, his thick brown hair combed to the side. I shift my gaze back to Callie. "Because he is intelligent, affable, ambitious, steady, reliable, conservative, and . . . well, I can't remember a time when I didn't love him."

"I love my granddaddy's Boykin spaniel—that old bitch has been around since I was still in short pants and she can still track a wild turkey around the Wateree River Swamp—but I don't want to marry her," Tavish says. "Just because you've grown accustomed to someone doesn't mean you should spend the rest of your life with them."

There's quiet, except for the distant hum of laughter and the clinking of champagne glasses. The sky is a beautiful shade of bruised blue and the fairy lights are twinkling on the branches over our heads like hundreds of tiny stars, but I feel a twinge of sadness. It's the same sort of twinge I feel after church each Sunday, when I suddenly realize I won't be spending the evening eating roast chicken dinner at my daddy's house. Strange that I should be feeling the Sunday sadness now, on a Friday night, surrounded by friends.

It's funny. I never felt like I fit in with my family. Growing up, I couldn't wait to leave home and find my place in the world, that one spot in the puzzle where I belonged, where my unique, jagged edges fit. I thought maybe Austin, Texas would be that spot, but it wasn't. I felt as out of place in Austin as I always have in Charleston.

It frightens me, this pervasive feeling of not belonging. When I close my eyes, I imagine myself as a stray dog, lost and disoriented, plagued by a sense that I belong somewhere, but baffled as to how to get there. Maybe I can build my forever home with Grayson. Maybe all I need to belong is someone who wants me to belong to them.

Chapter Two

"What do you mean you asked Maribelle Cravath to marry you?"

Grayson thrusts his hands in his pockets and leans back on his heels, his lips turned down in a sheepish expression. We are standing on the rickety old dock on Horlbeck Creek. The full moon is barely hidden behind gossamer-thin clouds and a blanket of mist hangs over the black, still creek. The air is heavy with the sweet scent of magnolia blossoms. I am wearing my beautiful (size six) Erdem gown and the toe-pinching stiletto heels I couldn't afford. It's the perfect setting for a Carolina boy to ask his childhood sweetheart to marry him.

I close my eyes and dozens of memories flicker to life in my brain, forming a sappy-sweet, romantic film montage. Ten-year-old Grayson sitting at the end of the dock, his baseball cap on backward, his jeans rolled up to his knees, holding my fishing pole while I skewered a worm on the end of my hook. Slow dancing in the moonlight with Grayson after freshman year home-coming dance. Lying side-by-side, our arms behind our heads, staring up at a cloudless summer sky, listen-ing to each other's dreams. Kissing each other good-bye and swearing we would still love each other *no matter what* just before we went off to college. The next picture should be Grayson getting down on one knee and asking me to be his wife, a diamond engage-ment ring in his hand.

I open my eyes, half-expecting to find Grayson holding a ring box with a big old *gotcha* grin on his face, but he's still standing there, looking like a kid who got caught stealing coins from the Sunday school offering plate.

"Maribelle Cravath? You're serious?"

Grayson nods his head. "Completely."

"Why?"

"Excuse me?"

Why on God's glorious green earth are you marry-ing boring old Maribelle Crawdad Cravath? She's one of a million Lilly Pulitzer–wearing, flat-ironed blonde lemmings scampering around the South.

"Why?" I take a deep breath to steady the wobble in my voice. "Why are you marrying Maribelle?"

"Maribelle comes from one of the oldest, most respected families in the United States. She's smart, socially-adept, well-connected, and philanthropic."

"Sounds like the perfect running mate."

He grins. "She does look great on paper."

I see his mouth moving, but it's as if I am watching a video with out-of-sync audio. Something in my brain is malfunctioning and it takes me a few seconds to as-sign meaning to the words I see his mouth forming.

Grayson.

Crawdad.

Engaged.

"You're really engaged?"

"Yes."

"To Maribelle Cravath?"

"That's right."

"When?"

"When?" He frowns.

"When did you ask her?"

"Tonight, just before coming here."

A thick, bitter lump coagulates in the back of my throat. I listen to the tree frogs chirping and the katy-dids buzzing. The trilling night critters seem to be mocking me. *Eh-eh-eh. Eh-eh-eh.*

"I-I thought when you asked me to meet you here you were going to . . ."

"To what?"

He dips his head and stares at me through his wide puppy-dog brown eyes and for a second I almost forget that we're not two teenagers sneaking out to steal kisses in the moonlight.

"It doesn't matter."

"It matters to me," he says, reaching for my hand. "You will always matter to me, Tara."

I want to snatch my hand away. I want to snatch Maribelle Cravath bald! Instead, I smile real pretty as the love of my life absentmindedly strokes the back of my hand with his thumb and tells me how much he hopes I will attend his wedding to my oldest frenemy.

. . . a spring wedding, when the azaleas are in bloom. Maribelle wants her bridesmaids to wear azalea pink gowns. Five hundred or so . . . in the gardens . . . plantation . . . oyster roast . . .

A spring wedding. Pink bridesmaid's gowns. Traditional low-country fare. So cliché. So Maribelle Cravath! Twenty bucks says she will serve spiked blueberry mint lemonade in mason jars and ask her bridesmaids to release live butterflies during her father-daughter dance.

I look down at my overpriced designer gown and my heart begins to ache something fierce. I splurged on the Erdem because it is a swoon-worthy, fairytale dress, the kind of dress that looks fabulous in photographs ten, twenty, thirty years after they are taken. I imagined myself with silver hair, lifting the lid of a heavy cardboard box, removing layers of scented tissue paper, and showing the neatly folded Erdem to my granddaughter. *This is the dress I wore the night your grandad asked me to marry him.* My dream is dissolving like tissue paper blown into a swimming pool.

Maribelle Crawdad Cravath has jacked my Prince Charming and my fairytale granddaughter bonding moment. When the lid of the heavy cardboard box is lifted, future generations of Calhouns will gasp and sigh over a perfectly precious (and uninspired) begonia pink Lilly Pulitzer sundress.

I want to grab Grayson's shoulders and shake him until the nonsense falls from his brain like acorns from a tree. He can't want to marry Maribelle Cravath. He just can't. He must be joking.

That's it! Grayson is teasing me. The Barton Boys must have told him I was expecting him to propose and my perpetual frat boy decided to have a little fun.

Bubbles of laughter stream up from my belly, bursting out of my mouth. Grayson stops talking and frowns at me.

"Tara?"

Like the endless stream of bubbles in a glass of champagne, the laughter keeps bubbling and bursting, bubbling and bursting. The more I think about it, the more I laugh. Maribelle and Grayson. Engaged.

"Tara? What is it? What's so funny?"

I try to speak, but imagine Grayson on bended knee, presenting one of those enameled flower rings with the stretchy bands sold at the Lilly Pulitzer store to Maribelle Cravath and a new stream of laughter erupts from my lips. By the time I am finally able to catch my breath, I have laugh-cried away most of my mascara and splotchy grayish-black teardrops stain the front of my gown.

"You . . . you almost got me, Grayson Everett Calhoun! You almost had me believing you asked old bug-eyed Crawdad Cravath to marry you. Good joke."

He frowns. "I am not joking, Tara. I asked Maribelle to marry me."

"Yeah, right," I laugh, wiping the mascara from beneath my eyes. "And you're going to have a *Gone with the Wind*–themed wedding at your family's plantation and eat barbecue beneath the magnolias, and dance waltzes, and—"

"Stop it, Tara," he says, grabbing my hand and squeezing it hard. "Don't be like that."

"Be like what?"

"Petty and biting."

Petty? And biting?

I pull my hand away and take a step back, the residual bubbles of laughter floating in my belly turning leaden, creating a sickeningly metallic taste in the back of my throat.

"You think I am petty and biting?"

"Not usually, but . . ."

"But what?"

"You've changed."

"Changed? How? When?"

He shrugs.

"I haven't changed, Grayson. I am the same old Tara Maxwell who likes to go fishing and eat Goo Goo Clusters."

"Be serious, dahlin'," he says, sighing. "When's the last time you ate a Goo Goo Cluster?"

I shake my head. What is he saying? He's not going to marry me because I don't eat Goo Goo Clusters like an overweight, insecure pre-teen?

"You want me to eat a Goo Goo Cluster? I will eat a carton of Goo Goo Clusters. Just tell me you aren't going to marry Maribelle Cravath."

He smiles sadly and shakes his head. "What happened to you, Tara? You used to be so audacious and original. You weren't like the other girls. I don't know why or when it happened, but you changed into this eager-to-please Southern girl with your buttermilk baths and starvation diets. Underneath it all—the perfectly styled hair and designer dresses—I sense a sad, tired woman who just wants to kick off her heels and go back to being real. The effort it is taking for you to pretend to be the woman you think you need to be is taking its toll, dahlin'."

Grayson's words pierce my heart like an arrow shot from a compound bow, lacerating deep. It takes me a few seconds to catch my breath.

I shake my head. "I am confused. You say you want to marry someone audacious and original, but you asked Maribelle Cravath to be your wife? She's the most unoriginal girl in all of Charleston."

"This isn't about Maribelle."

"Isn't it?"

"Did you think I asked you here because I was

going to ask to get back together?" He smiles sadly and shakes his head. "We've tried to make it work for years, Tara, but we always end up apart."

"That's just the way we are."

"It's the way we were, but it's not the way I want to be. Every decision I make from here on out will move me closer to, or further from, my end goal. I need someone on my team who wants to help me move closer to that end goal."

"What are you saying? I have always encouraged you to go after your dreams."

He looks down at his feet.

"Haven't I?"

"Yes, but . . ."

"But what?"

"Jesus, Tara," he sighs, running his hand through his hair. "I don't want to hurt your feelings. Can't we just wish each other well and go our separate ways?"

I am burning up from the inside out. My core is radiating heat, my skin aches, and my hair is plastered to my neck. It's as if I swallowed fire. Once, I snuck a sip from a bottle in my Aunt Patricia's liquor cabinet and felt the way I do now, hot and sickly. It turned out to be a bottle of Irish Poitin, a potent, illegal, home-distilled alcohol made from potatoes, malted barley, sugar.

"Go our separate ways?" The words come out strangled. "We've been in each other's lives for as long as I can remember and you just want to go our separate ways?"

"We'll always be friends."

"Friends? What does that even mean? We will exchange Christmas cards, click like on each other's Instagram photos, say *hey* when we run into each other at Poogan's Porch?"

"Sure, that's what childhood friends do, isn't it? We had a great childhood together, Tara, swimming at Folly Beach, fishing off this dock, catching fireflies in your daddy's backyard, but it's time to grow up and pack those childish times away. Grown-ups are honest about what they want, what they need, who they are, and who they want to spend their lives with."

"And grown-up Grayson Calhoun doesn't want to spend his life with Tara Maxwell. Is that it?"

He dips his chin low and looks at me through his thick brown eyelashes and I realize with nauseating certainty that Grayson Calhoun is about to become a ghost in my life, relegated to the darkest, dustiest shelf in the basement of my memories. Out of sight, but not out of mind.

"That's about it."

Chapter Three

What's the worst part about being a television broadcaster in the nation's ninety-fifth largest designated market area? You can't have a sweatpants and T-shirt day. You can't pile your hair into a baseball cap, slip your feet into a pair of ugly old Uggs, and call it a rotten, miserable, no-good, feeling-cranky, leave-me-the-hell-alone kinda day. Not even when your first love tells you that he's outgrown you. Not even when your little sister announces she is moving to the Cotswolds to become a matchmaker.

Not even then.

You have to put on your suit, slip on your heels, spackle on your face paint, and smile big as you film a segment about the Great Charleston Crab Cook-Off. One hundred and thirty-two local chefs and crab connoisseurs competing for the title of Crab Whisperer with recipes like crab nachos, artichoke and crab dip, crab and mango chutney, and Asian fried crab balls. It doesn't matter if it is an unseasonably hot eighty-two degrees, you're being devoured by a swarm of sand flies, and you've got rancid crab balls in your mouth. You have to smile through the pain.

I sometimes wonder why I applied for a job as a television broadcaster. I am not as naturally composed and graceful as my sister Manderley, nor as sociable as Emma Lee. Truthfully? It takes a lot of effort for me to be as sweet as tea, especially today when I feel as salty as a boiled peanut.

I never wanted to be a corporate drone, crammed into a cubicle, subsisting on cold vending machine sandwiches and Folgers, withering under the harsh flicker of fluorescent lights, but today that sort of cloistered, anonymous existence appeals to me. I would rather be staring at my *When Pigs Fly* screensaver than swallowing tepid crab soup or falsely complimenting the ingenuity of a Summerville housewife for combining chocolate, apples, and crabs into a sweet and savory cake. (*No, I don't think Entenmann's would consider mass producing your Crabby Apple Cake, but I am pretty sure it could replace ipecac syrup to induce violent vomiting.*)

By the time my cameraman has shot the B-roll to pad my piece and I've recorded the voice over, I want to crawl into my bed, pull the covers over my head, and nurse a bottle of ipecac until Grayson, Crawdad Cravath, and the Great Nauseating Crab Cook-Off are distant memories. But I promised Emma Lee I would meet her for dinner at, ironically, The Folly Beach Crab Shack.

Located just two blocks from the beach and with a chill, laid-back, walk-in-barefoot kinda vibe, The Shack is *the* off-season gathering spot for locals. Grayson and I used to meet at The Shack when we were home for Christmas break. We would eat oysters on the half shell and sip cold beers and then walk hand in hand to the beach to watch the sunset behind the pier.

Emma Lee is waiting for me when I arrive. She is perched on an orange painted stool and surrounded by a throng of admirers. That's Emma Lee. Life-of-the-Party Barbie. *Fashionably dressed in ankle-breaking high heels, white skinny jeans, and a floaty, frilly off-the-shoulder top, with her long blonde hair styled straight, she completes her glam look with silver bangles and the perfect bag! Life-of-the-Party Barbie makes everyone's guest list! Cannot stand alone. Accessories sold separately.*

She squeals when she notices me and I feel as rotten as a mouthful of fried Asian crab balls for comparing my sweet, if aimless, baby sister to a plastic doll. Maybe Grayson was right. Maybe I have become petty and bitter. *Petty-and-Bitter Barbie comes in a jaded gown sprinkled with bitchy dust. A tiny pitcher of Haterade completes her pretty petty look!*

"Yay!" Emma Lee claps her hands when she notices me approaching. Her bangles clatter together. "You're here!"

She hops off her perch and runs over to me, throwing her perpetually toned and tanned arms around my neck. A cloud of vanilla scented perfume floats around us and I feel my miserable, rotten, no-good, leave-me-the-hell-alone mood lift. Emma Lee has that effect on people. Spontaneous and joyful, affectionate and optimistic, spending time with her is like getting a potent shot of dopamine, serotonin, oxytocin, and endorphins. She triggers people's happy neurotransmitters. It came as no surprise when Clemson offered her a cheerleading scholarship.

By the time she stops hugging me, her admirers have dispersed and we are alone at the small cobalt painted table. She hops back up on her stool, tilts her head, and looks at me through the platinum fringe of her long bangs.

"Love the suit. Love the shoes. Love the bold blush. *So* on trend. Is it Nars Orgasm?" She squints. "Did you have a good day? How was the Cook-Off? You look *saaaad*. Did something happen to make you sad?"

One of Emma Lee's less than endearing habits is her anxiety-driven, rapid-fire prattle. She shoots comments, critiques, and questions like a tommy gun. *Rat-a-tat-tat-tat.* Without blinking, taking a breath, or waiting for a response.

"I am not sad," I say, shrugging out of my jacket.

"Liar." She raises her hand and waves it in a circle around my face. "You're wearing a lot of sad with that fab sheath dress. It's like '80s frosty blue eye shadow. Bam! Can't miss it."

"This coming from the girl who has spent the last few weeks eating fast-food fried chicken and watching crap reality television shows on my couch."

"I am done. Done. I can't *even* do that Annie routine anymore."

"Annie?"

"Little Orphan Annie, that sad, down-on-her-luck girl with the ginger 'fro who gets adopted by the crazy rich Daddy Starbucks."

"Warbucks."

Emma Lee frowns.

"The man who adopted Annie was Daddy Warbucks, not Starbucks."

"I am pretty sure his name was Starbucks"—she waves her hand and her bangles clatter together—"but

Annie's bald benefactor isn't really the point. The point is that *It's a Hard Knock Life* is a tired tune. Played out. I can't be an Annie, moping around feeling sorry for myself because I am an orphan."

I rub the vein throbbing at my temple and resist the urge to ask my little sister which version of *Annie* features a self-pitying orphan adopted by a coffee mogul, because every version I have ever seen featured a plucky and optimistic girl.

"Does this mean you took Manderley's advice and set an appointment with one of Clemson's career counselors?"

"What? Why would I do that?"

"You need to get a job, Emma Lee. The counselor will help you choose a career path based on your interests, abilities, personality, and educational achievement."

"I've already chosen a career path."

"You have?"

Please God, don't let her tell me she wants to be something ridiculous like a Cirque Du Soleil performer or the girl who walks around Disneyworld in the Sleeping Beauty costume. Please let her finally be serious.

Before Emma Lee can regale me with her plans, a waitress arrives. I order the grilled shrimp and avocado salad and a basket of hush puppies with honey butter. Emma Lee orders the most expensive thing on the menu: shrimp and oysters. Of course. Emma Lee has caviar taste on a Cane's Chicken budget.

If people could read my harsh thoughts, they might think I don't like Emma Lee. They would be wrong. Terribly wrong. I love my sister something fierce. I just get mighty vexed by her *I-am-the-baby-of-the-family-so-*

you-have-to-take-care-of-me mentality. Then again, she was a baby when our momma died. Poor Emma Lee doesn't possess a single memory of our momma. She also doesn't have a cushy trust fund to fall back on. Momma left generous trust funds for Manderley and for me, but she died before she could set one up for Emma Lee. As far as I know, my practical big sister has been sitting on her trust fund like a hen waiting for her chick to hatch, patiently and prudently watching her nest egg grow. I am not as prudent as Manderley so my egg isn't as healthy as hers. Still, at least I have an egg! Poor Emma Lee is a hen without an egg.

Daddy always took care of Emma Lee, buying her everything her spoiled heart could desire, but Emma Lee's silver spoon was pulled painfully out of her mouth when the IRS seized Daddy's assets, including the car he leased for her. She's had a hard time adjusting to life without her silver spoon.

The waitress takes our menus and hurries off to place our orders. I rest my forearms on the edge of the table and patiently wait for Emma Lee to tell me she is going to be an Instagram model/YouTube sensation/Wine taste tester. Her phone vibrates against the blue-painted table. Emma Lee reaches for her phone.

"Don't you dare," I say, snatching the phone and sliding it into my jacket pocket. "You're not answering a text, email, or FB notification until you tell me about this exciting new career path you intend to blaze."

She flips her hair over her tanned shoulder and grins. "It's more than a career path. I have developed a new life plan."

"Ooo-kay," I say, narrowing my gaze. "Does this new life plan involve performing acrobatics in a feather covered spandex body suit?"

"What?" She laughs. "No! Whatever gave you that ridiculous idea?"

"It doesn't matter," I say, smiling. "Tell me all about your new life plan."

"I am moving to the Cotswolds!"

"The Cotswolds?"

"A rural area in south central England."

"I know where the Cotswolds are located, Emma Lee. I just don't know why you are telling me you plan to move there or what you would do once you get there."

"I am going to be a matchmaker!"

"Drink some iced tea, Emma dahlin'." I push her sweating glass closer to her. "The heat is getting to you."

"I am perfectly fine!" She slides the tea away from her and leans her forearms on the table. "Mrs. Nickerson said she thinks I would make *a bloody brilliant marriage broker*. She's even agreed to pay me money—serious money—if I make successful matches for her sons."

"Wait! Are you telling me you already have a client?"

"Yes!"

"Okay, stop. Before you get carried away with your magical, fairy dust, wishful thinking—"

"Magical fairy dust? You make me sound like a flake." I stare at her. Hard. She rolls her eyes. "Tell me one flaky thing I have wanted to do."

Only one? She's making this way too easy.

"You tried to talk Daddy into buying you a Christmas tree farm so you could have *Christmas all year round.*"

"Who wouldn't want Christmas all year round? Fresh air, the scent of pine trees, happy people."

I look at Emma Lee's beautiful beaming face, see the starry, naiveté reflected in her wide blue eyes, and all I can think is, *Bless her heart*. She lives in a dream world, floating from one fabulous diversion to the next, unencumbered by pesky practicalities like developing a life plan, sticking to a budget, following rules, adhering to a schedule. She is, quite literally, the dreamer. She took the Meyers-Briggs test in her college psychology class and was classified an ENFP. ENFPs are called The Dreamers.

By contrast, my sister, Manderley is a responsible, hardworking, practical, punctual ESTJ. ESTJs are called The Executives. They're the ones who plot the paths on how to reach the far-off dreamlands.

And I am the diplomat between the two, forever bridging the gap, acting as interpreter, and brokering deals for peace. I am Jimmy Carter. Jimmy friggin' Carter, stuck between Egypt and Israel. I am that U.S. senator who facilitated the peace treaty between Northern Ireland and England.

"Gee, Emma Lee," I say, employing my age-old sandwich technique by sticking constructive criticism between two compliments. "You are charismatic, intuitive, and social, the sort who sees the best in people and helps them to see the best in themselves. I think you would make a fantastic matchmaker—"

"You do?" she squeals, clapping her hands.

"Yes, I do," I say. "Especially if you spend some time pondering the steps you need to take to be a successful matchmaker."

Emma Lee frowns.

"You don't want to be a Vermeer."

"A Vermeer?"

"Johannes Vermeer was a Dutch painter who only

produced two to three paintings a year, not enough to support his wife and eleven children. He died in debt at a young age."

"That's *saaad*."

"Yes, it is—"

"Wait a minute!" Emma Lee says, brightening. "Didn't he paint *Girl with a Pearl Earring?* And didn't that painting inspire a movie starring Scarlett Johansson?"

"Yes, but—"

"Vermeer might have died in debt, but he died doing what he loved *and* they made a movie about him, starring ScarJo! That's pretty amazing, don't you think?"

"My point, however, is that dreams alone won't pay the bills. Where do you plan on living while you are making matches for the English gentry?"

"Wood House."

"You aren't serious?"

"I am! Aunt Pattycake left me her home in the English countryside, so why shouldn't I live in it?"

"I just assumed you would sell it."

"Is that what you plan on doing with Tásúildun? Selling it?"

Aunt Patricia left me her home in Ireland, a small medieval castle on the coast. Until my senior year in high school, I spent my summers there.

"I won't inherit Tásúildun until I spend three months living in it with two relative strangers. Did you forget?"

Aunt Patricia added an unusual proviso to her will: in order to claim my inheritance, I must first spend three months living in the castle with Rhys Sinjin Burroughes, her nephew by marriage, and Aidan Gallagher, the son of one of her tenants. At the end of the three months, I have to choose a co-inheritor from either Rhys or Aidan.

I met Rhys once, when he came for a visit during one of my summer stays. He was a quiet boy with a thatch of thick black hair that fell over his forehead and tortoiseshell glasses meant to correct a slightly lazy eye. He spent most of his time in the library. As a child, I played with Aidan Gallagher practically every day of every summer. Grayson never knew it, but Aidan was my first kiss. I was twelve. Aidan was thirteen. We were on the beach below the castle. He leaned in to kiss me, I leaned away, and he ended up kissing my chin. Ever the persistent one, he tried again. So, I guess you could say he was my first *and* second kiss.

"I didn't forget the proviso," Emma Lee says. "When are you leaving for Ireland?"

"Winter said I am supposed to complete my stay within a year of the reading of the will. Otherwise, I lose my claim."

Winter V. Hastings was the lawyer who handled the execution of both my father and aunt's wills.

"Well you better get crackalackin, sister! It's been two months since the reading of the will. That means you only have ten months to get your booty to Ireland and pick a man."

"I can't go to Ireland."

"Why not?"

"Because I have a job and a life here in Charleston." Emma Lee snorts. "Gimme a break!"

"What does that mean?"

"It means you hate Charleston. You couldn't wait to go off to college and get away from here. Isn't that why you chose the University of Texas at Austin instead of the University of South Carolina or Clemson or Duke?"

I chose to go to school in Texas because I was plumb worn out from trying to get my daddy to notice me. I am not as clever as Manderley, nor as beautiful as Emma Lee. Both of my sisters have our daddy's blonde hair and blue eyes, but I inherited my momma's red hair and hazel eyes. Too green to be blue and too blue to be green. In between. Always in between. I know my daddy loved me, but he often overlooked me. I don't blame him. He was probably tired from encouraging Manderley, the over-achieving academic, and soothing Emma Lee, the high-maintenance baby.

"I don't hate Charleston, Emma Lee."

"But you don't love it, either. So why stay? Life is too short to spend it being a squatter in the Land of Mediocre. If you're not happy where you are, move. If you're not happy with your boyfriend, dump him. If you don't like your dress, charge a new one!" She draws a smiley face in the condensation on her iced tea glass with her finger. "You've been searching for your place for a long time, Tara. Maybe your place is in Ireland. You won't know unless you go."

What is this? Life advice from my baby sister, the girl without a job who has spent the last two months avoiding her responsibilities by watching reruns of *Millionaire Matchmaker*?

"Besides," she continues. "You don't want to forfeit your claim on Aunt Pattycake's castle. You always loved going there."

"What am I going to do with a rundown old castle in Ireland?"

"What are you saying, Tara Maxwell?" She speaks

with the comical sort of Irish accent usually reserved for cartoon leprechauns hawking sugary cereal. "Don't you know that land is the only thing worth fighting two strange men for?"

"What was that?"

"I was imitating the speech Scarlett O'Hara's father made to her at the beginning of *Gone with the Wind*. It's your favorite movie, isn't it?"

Gone with the Wind isn't my *favorite* movie, but it was one of our mother's favorite movies and when I watch it I imagine her sitting beside me, sighing over Clark Gable, sniffling when Scarlett falls down the stairs. My mother loved *Gone with the Wind* so much, she named me after the O'Hara's plantation.

"I thought we were talking about *your* life plan."

"We were. You were telling me not to be a Vermeer—though I don't see how being like a talented and famous artist is a bad thing—and you were going to pull a Manderley and ask me a zillion pointed questions meant to pop holes in my happy, floaty balloon."

I reach across the table and grab Emma Lee's hand.

"Is that how you see me, as a balloon popper and dream crusher? If it is, I am sorry. I don't mean to pop your balloon."

She squeezes my hand and smiles. "You're not a balloon popper, Tara, not usually. Lately, you've been ratcheted up, stressed out, and sad is all. I know you and Manderley feel responsible for me, especially now that Daddy is gone, but I am going to be fine. You'll see."

I squeeze her hand back before letting it go.

"Can I ask you one question?"

"Just one?" She chuckles. "Sure. Ask away."

I have half a zillion questions, like: Are there a lot of

lonely singles knocking around the Cotswolds willing to pay money to be matched by an amateur matchmaker from America, a matchmaker whose longest romantic relationship lasted three months? Does she realize she will have to pay an inheritance tax if she keeps Aunt Patricia's cottage? Has she applied for a work visa? Instead, I toss a softball her way.

"How will you pay for your ticket to England?"

"I am selling Momma's ring."

The bile in my stomach rolls back and forth, like a storm tossed wave, until I can taste the acid in the back of my throat.

"You can't be serious."

"I am totally serious."

"But Emma Lee, Daddy gave you that ring because he wanted you to have something that belonged to Momma. You can't sell it. You just can't!"

The waitress arrives, a massive dinner plate balanced on each hand. She puts the plates down on our table, asks if we need anything, and hurries back inside.

We eat our food in silence. Emma Lee fiddles with her shrimp while I dunk my hushpuppies in the honey butter and then practically swallow them whole. I am stress eating. I know it, but I don't stop until I have devoured every small, savory, deep-fried ball of cornmeal.

Emma Lee is the first to break the silence.

"Mrs. Nickerson says inheriting Aunt Patricia's cottage is a sign."

I dab the greasy cornmeal crumbs from my lips before responding. "Who is Mrs. Nickerson again?"

"Isabelle Nickerson is only the sweetest, smartest, most encouraging woman I have ever met. She was at the Turn Up. We got to talking and it turns out she knows, like, practically everyone. She's friends with the Cravaths and she knew Aunt Patricia."

"Aunt Patricia? How did she know Aunt Patricia?"

"They went to boarding school together. She knew Momma, too. And get this . . . she lives in the Cotswolds!"

"That's quite a coincidence."

"I know, right?" Emma Lee picks a lemon wedge off her plate and squeezes it over her shrimp. "Mrs. Nickerson said she would introduce me to everyone in the village and start spreading the word about my matchmaking skills."

I don't want to be a balloon popper, but . . . matchmaking skills? Did listening to Patty Stanger instruct gold-diggers on how to land a sugar daddy really give Emma Lee skills? I mean, really?

"What else did this Mrs. Nickerson say?"

"She said I should follow my dreams or I will spend the rest of my life working for someone who followed theirs." Emma Lee pins a shrimp tail to her plate with her knife and draws the pink meat from its shell. "She said I should be fearless in the pursuit of what stirs my soul; that to do anything else is cowardly and a waste of a life."

Of course Mrs. Nickerson is going to tell Emma Lee to chase her dreams, because she won't be the one picking her up when she stumbles and falls head first into failure, poverty, homelessness. Mrs. Nickerson sounds too good to be true, like the fairy godmother sort that pops up in children's books. I imagine an older woman toting a carpetbag in one hand and a parrot handled umbrella in the other. I want to warn Emma Lee to be wary of strangers dispensing officious advice, but Mrs. Nickerson has clearly made an impact on my baby sister, motivating her to step away from the Cane's fried chicken and reality television shows. Poor Emma Lee. When our daddy died, she not only became an orphan, she became a homeless orphan, tossed out of the only home she has ever known.

The first night at my condo, she padded into my bedroom, climbed into my bed, and curled beside me like she used to do when we were children.

If Mrs. Nickerson has appointed herself Emma Lee's fairy godmother, who am I to complain? Truth be known, I could use a fairy godmother myself. A plump, sweet-faced old woman to wave her magic wand and take away the bitterness and pain losing my daddy . . . and now Grayson . . . has left in my heart.

Chapter Four

Text from Emma Lee Maxwell, Matchmaker:
Did you order my wellies yet? Mrs. Nickerson says it rains a lot in the Cotswolds and owning a pair of 'proper rain footgear' is essential. Don't forget to order the shine kit. Must keep my proper British footgear shipshape in Bristol-fashion, right?

Text to Manderley Maxwell:
Has Emma Lee told you she is moving to England or is she avoiding it because she knows you will try to talk some sense into her?

Text from Manderley Maxwell:
She told me about her scheme to live in Aunt Patricia's cottage and open a matchmaking business. She asked me how she would go about obtaining a work visa. She sounds quite serious.

Text to Manderley Maxwell:
Well? What did you say?

Text from Manderley Maxwell:
I told her I think the idea rather absurd, but youth is the time one should pursue absurd schemes. And then I wished her a hearty and heartfelt *Bon chance.*

Text to Manderley Maxwell:
Did Emma Lee ask you to buy her rain boots? She tried to get me to buy them for her by saying "everyone wears wellies in the Cotswolds." Are you sure we should be encouraging her matchmaking scheme?

Text from Manderley Maxwell:
Yes.

I am sitting in Friday evening traffic on the Ravenel Bridge, a towering, futuristic, cable-stayed suspension bridge spanning the Cooper River. The Ravenel Bridge, an eight-lane superstructure built to withstand the hurricanes that frequently batter the South Carolina coast, was opened in 2005. It replaced the Cooper River Bridge, an outdated cantilever bridge that simply couldn't handle the traffic created by Charleston's rapid growth.

The logical part of me knows the Cooper River Bridge needed to go, but the sentimental side of me mourns the loss of the charming, if antiquated, structure. The Ravenel Bridge is symbolic of what has occurred in my hometown: painfully rapid growth that has permanently altered Charleston's face, physique, and personality. It doesn't feel like a small Southern town anymore.

There used to be a roadside stand when you came

off the Cooper River Bridge on your way to Mount Pleasant, a rickety wooden shack where a toothless old woman named Ida Mae sold ham-boiled peanuts. She had a big old cast iron pot out back she filled with water, peanuts, and ham hocks. Sometimes she would let me use a wooden paddle to stir the boiling nuts and the salt scented steam would tease my bangs and cause them to curl all up like a pig's tail.

The shack was torn down so they could put up a Walgreens. My daddy told me Johnnie Dodds Boulevard, the main thoroughfare through Mount Pleasant, used to be a sleepy country road lined with towering oaks dripping Spanish moss. Today, it is a car-clogged nightmare of a road lined with strip malls and fast-food restaurants. I would trade a dozen Moe's Southwest Grills for one Ida Mae's Boiled Peanuts shack.

Everything has changed. The Cooper River Bridge. Johnnie Dodds Boulevard. Mount Pleasant. My family home. My family.

Daddy and Aunt Patricia are gone like the wind, if you will pardon the obvious theatrical reference. Manderley is working in Los Angeles and jetting to fabulous places like Cannes, Hong Kong, Berlin, and Melbourne. Emma Lee is about to start a new, if absurd, life in England. Grayson is marrying Maribelle Cravath.

It's too much. Too damn much, I say.

Winter told me the government will auction off my daddy's home and some Japanese hotel conglomerate will probably want to turn it into a luxury boutique hotel. It's hard to imagine Black Ash Plantation as anything but a stately, historic low-country home, and the day I drive by and see a parking lot where the rose gardens once stood, a part of me will die, I think.

The car in front of me begins to move. I shift my

Mercedes out of neutral and put my foot on the gas, but only make it a few car lengths before traffic stops.

My phone chimes. I look at the screen. It's Callie asking if I want to meet her at Pawpaw's for dinner and drinks. Even though my soul is aching for a little comfort food, like Pawpaw's mac and cheese made with sharp cheddar, English peas, and smoked pork, and topped with biscuit breadcrumbs (dying!), I am bone weary. Meeting Callie at Pawpaw's would mean getting off the bridge, whipping a U-turn, and heading back across the wretched Ravenel into downtown Charleston.

Text to Callie Middleton:
Stuck on the Ravenel. Raincheck?

My phone chimes again, only this time it is another text from Manderley. It's a picture, actually, of Mandy in an old wedding dress, her head resting on some guy's shoulder. The guy is tall, dark, and hot as boiling peanuts. I barely recognize my big sister. Gone are her bookish glasses, the smudges as dark as plum eyeshadow beneath her eyes, and the wistful expression I've grown accustomed to seeing on her face since she moved to Los Angeles. This Mandy looks relaxed, confident, and happy, like a woman . . . *in love.*

I move my thumb and index finger in a flicking motion over the screen, enlarging the photo on Mandy's hand resting casually on the hottie's muscular forearm.

"What the fudge?"

A ginormous diamond sparkles on her left ring finger.

Oh my sweet baby Jesus!

Text to Manderley Maxwell:
Manderley Grace Maxwell, did you elope?

I stare at the screen in agonizing suspense, waiting for Manderley's reply, but the driver behind me aggressively beeps his horn, once, twice, three times.

"Okay! Okay!"

The traffic jam must have unjammed itself while I was answering Manderley's text because the road in front of me is clear. I drop my phone in my lap and put my foot on the gas pedal, gripping the steering wheel so tight my fingernails dig into my palms. Manderley is *not* married. She can't be married. She doesn't even have a boyfriend.

There is a perfectly logical explanation for why she was photographed wearing a wedding dress and the Hope Diamond on her ring finger and it isn't that she eloped with some stranger. Manderley would never elope. Never. She's not spontaneous or daring enough.

Once—and if this isn't the gospel truth, God can shoot a big old blazing lightning bolt at my Mercedes right here and now—Mandy told me she was afraid she had become boring and predictable, so she scheduled "spontaneous time." She literally scheduled "Do Something Spontaneous" on her iCloud calendar.

I laugh remembering it.

The traffic continues to flow off the bridge and down Johnnie Dodds, a steady stream of blinking taillights. By the time I finally pull into my condominium complex, I have concocted a plausible tale to explain Manderley's unusual attire. She's in Cannes, surrounded by movie types. She was probably asked to be an extra in an indie film and the wedding gown is her costume.

I pull into my parking spot and kill the engine. I am walking up the stairs to my condo when my phone chimes again. I fish it out of my purse and read the text.

Text from Manderley Maxwell:
I eloped.

Sweet baby Jesus in heaven! Manderley is married.

I jab the phone icon next to my sister's name and hold my breath while the line connects. One ring. Two rings. *Your call has been forwarded to an automatic voice messaging system . . .*

Voicemail? Seriously?

This is *not* happening. My dependable, responsible big sister did not elope with a stranger, a foreigner with swarthy skin and shifty eyes. I look at the picture again, this time focusing on Manderley's man—the gigolo with the I-just-married-a-trust-fund-baby grin. Expensive suit. Expensive watch. Expensive sunglasses. Perfectly groomed stubbly beard. Angled jaw. Square chin tilted at a slightly arrogant angle.

I jab the phone icon again.

One ring.

Your call has been forwarded to an automatic voice messaging system . . .

Text from Tara Maxwell:
This is a joke, right? Seriously. Who is that man? Why were you wearing an old wedding dress in that picture? Why aren't you answering your phone?

I finish climbing the stairs to my front porch and sit on one of the white-painted rockers I rescued from the veranda at Black Ash. I lean my head back, close my eyes, and listen to the frogs croaking in the nearby pond. Thank Jesus the frogs are still croaking in my new topsy-turvy world.

Text to Tara Maxwell:
Not joking. The man is my husband, Xavier. I got married in that beautiful old dress. I will call to explain soon.

Text from Tara Maxwell:
Married?!?! Have you lost your damned mind? You're supposed to be the responsible one. What am I going to say to Emma Lee?

I stare at the screen, watching the little flickering dots as Manderley composes her answer. The dots disappear and reappear again.

Text to Tara Maxwell:
Tell her being the responsible one is overrated.

Chapter Five

So much can change in two months. Fate can grab the snow globe that is your life and shake it fiercely, creating a maelstrom that obliterates your bucolic scene.

In two months, Manderley has gone from being my cautious big sister with no prospects of romance on her horizon, to a glamorous jet-setter who eloped with a French gigolo (she assures me Xavier de Maloret didn't marry her for her fortune, that he is independently wealthy, but I still smell a trust-fund-cheese-seeking rat).

Emma Lee has gone from being a matchless, aimless party girl to an ambitious would-be matchmaker. Emma Lee Maxwell, the consummate daddy's girl, who seemed destined to spend her life as a lilting Southern flower, carefully tended to and admired for her sweet, tender beauty. Our little flower is striking out of the hot house, letting the breeze blow her to a village nestled in England's rolling hills.

I glance over at my baby sister, sitting in the passenger seat, her long, slender legs crossed despite being confined in dark skinny jeans, her new Burberry trench folded in her lap—a generous *Bon Voyage* and *Bonne Chance* gift from Manderley (because *Mrs. Nickerson said a proper, classically stylish raincoat is a staple of every British woman's wardrobe*).

"Did you remember your passport?"

"Yes, Tara."

"What about your iPhone charger? I want you to call me as soon as you land and when you have arrived at Wood House."

"Yes, ma'am."

"And you remembered to make your train reservations from London to the Cotswolds?"

"Mrs. Nickerson said she would send Knightley to pick me up."

"Knightley?"

"Her son."

"That's awfully generous of them."

"Isabelle said it was the least she could do for the niece of one of her oldest and dearest friends. Besides, Knightley is some bigwig barrister. Apparently, he splits his time between London and the Cotswolds. So, it's not like it's a big deal for him to let me hitch a ride."

"Even so, be sure to thank him and Mrs. Nickerson."

"Please, Tara," she says, snorting. "I'm Southern born and raised. I know how to do gratitude. I went to the Candy Kitchen and bought a big old box of pecan pralines for Isabelle and a bag of Bourbon Balls for Knightley."

I slow to a stop at the intersection before the entrance to the Charleston International Airport and look at my sister, at the sophisticated, messy bun carefully piled atop her head, and the confident tilt of her pretty chin, and realize, with a painful pang, she has grown up.

It's an unusual phenomenon among siblings that no matter how old or grown our sister becomes, we continue to see her as a child. I have an image of Emma Lee stored in my mind, a bright, flickering film clip of her dressed in a floral printed muslin gown, a dainty miss sitting in the garden, picking berries with a coterie of giggling, giddy little friends.

But she's not that little girl anymore. She's a sophisticated, confident twenty-four-year-old woman who doesn't need her big sister telling her why she shouldn't pick berries that aren't fully red or how to slice a strawberry so it looks like a heart. I should quit my mother-hennin', but old habits die harder than a stubborn mule.

"Are you sure about all of this, Emma Lee? When was the last time Aunt Pattycake lived in Wood House? What if it hasn't been cleaned? What if it is infested with vermin? What if—?"

"Don't get your feathers all ruffled up, momma hen," she says, laughing. "Mrs. Nickerson said Aunt Pattycake gave her a key to Wood House years ago, so she could look after it while Aunt P. was away. Mrs. Nickerson sent her maid to clean the cottage and stock the larder—which I assume is a pantry—with staples."

It sounds as if Mrs. Nickerson has been working her wand overtime, bippity-bobbity-booing things for Emma Lee.

I turn into the airport and drive slower than molasses until we finally arrive at the ticketing and check-in terminal. I pull up to the curb and turn on my hazard lights.

"Are you sure you don't want me to come in with you, just in case you have any problems at the ticket counter or with security?" I snatch my press pass and station badge out of the cup holder and fiddle with the lanyard, nervously weaving it over my fingers. "I don't mind."

Emma Lee reaches over, unwinds the lanyard from my fingers, and drops the badges back into the cup holder.

"I'll be okay, Tara," she says, linking her fingers through mine. "I promise."

I look at her through a haze of tears.

"Are you sure?"

"I am mighty sure." She gives my fingers a little squeeze. "Are you going to be okay? You seem sad."

I consider telling her that losing so many people in such a short time has left me feeling like a threadbare quilt coming apart at the seams. I even consider throwing my arms around her and begging her not to leave me.

"Don't worry about me. I am just fine."

"You're sure?"

"Now who's being momma hen?"

We laugh. She opens the door and climbs out. I watch her walk to the back of my car and pop the trunk. I get out of the car and open the back door, reaching into the foothold and retrieving a big shiny black box. By the time I walk around my car, Emma Lee has removed her suitcases from the trunk and is waiting for me on the sidewalk, Burberry trench wrapped around her slender figure, the belt tied artfully around her waist.

I hand her the box.

"What's this?"

"A proper going away present."

She squeals and jumps up and down, before tearing

the red ribbon off the box and removing the lid to reveal a pair of tall glossy Hunter Wellington rain boots.

"Ooh!" She lifts one of the boots out of the box. "Military red wellies! How did you know this is the color I wanted?"

"Hmmm, let's see," I say, laughing. "Maybe I saw something on your Instagram, Twitter, or Facebook feeds. Or, was it your Pinterest board? Wait! I think I might have figured it out when you changed the screen saver on my computer to a collage of red rain boots."

"You're the best, Tara! The best," she says, kicking her heel off and sliding her foot into the boot.

"You said Manderley was the best."

"When?"

"When she called to make sure you got your Burberry."

"Oh!" She puts on the other boot and clicks her heels together, squealing again. "Well, can I help it if the good Lord blessed me with two wonderful big sisters? You're both the best."

She throws her arms around my neck and squeezes something fierce and we are little girls again, before those pesky puberty hormones had us bickering over silly things like shoes and clothes and makeup and boys. We are in the attic, tearing through fusty old trunks for some of our momma's clothes to play dress-up. I find Momma's cotton-candy pink taffeta ball gown—the one that looks like it tumbled out of Grace Kelly's wardrobe—and hand it to Emma Lee, even though the slender spaghetti straps are too wide for her little shoulders. *Thanks, Tara. You're the best!*

She stops hugging me as suddenly as she started. I pick up the discarded Hunter box. Emma Lee shoves her heels into her bulging carry-on.

"This is just fab," she says, grabbing the telescoping

handles of her suitcases and smiling confidently. "I've got my proper rain boots and my proper raincoat. I am ready for my new life as a very proper British broker of marriages. Seriously? What more could I need?"

A few dozen things come to mind, like a degree in psychology, dating experience, a wide social circle in the Cotswolds, a reality television show. I open my mouth to speak, but Emma Lee cuts me off.

"That was rhetorical, Tara! Stop worrying about me. I am all good."

She waves her hand and begins rolling her bags toward the terminal. I climb back into my car and look out the windshield just in time to see her disappear through the sliding doors, a whirlwind of blonde tresses, Burberry plaid, and shiny red rubber. My chest tightens. I have a new appreciation for how my daddy must have felt when I left for college. Then again, except for intermittent homesickness, I did just fine in Austin, didn't I? Emma Lee will probably do just fine in the Cotswolds. I am being a tiresome old momma hen over a simple rite of passage.

I am about to pull away from the curb when the terminal doors slide back open and Emma Lee runs out of the airport, suitcases bumping along behind her, Burberry trench flapping like two khaki plaid wings. For a wild, wishful second I think she has decided to abandon her new life plan and remain in Charleston.

Emma Lee wrenches open the passenger door and ducks her head inside the compartment.

"Oh sweet baby Jesus!" She reaches down and lifts her purse out of the passenger foot well. "Can you believe I almost forgot my purse?"

Purse. Passport. Tickets. Money. Pretty much every damned thing required for a transatlantic flight. Maybe

I have been clucking over Emma Lee because I instinctively know the baby chick isn't ready to leave the hen house. Just a thought.

"Can I believe you almost forgot your purse?" I tilt my head and look at her over the tops of my sunglasses. "Is that a rhetorical question, too?"

She laughs and sticks her tongue out at me, before closing the passenger door and racing back into the terminal.

My chest becomes tighter with each mile I travel away from the airport, until it feels as if my ribcage and heart are being crushed by a vise grip. I take several deep breaths.

Inhale. *I am fine.*

Exhale. *I am just fine.*

I keep telling myself I am fine as I drive across the Ravenel Bridge and down Johnnie Dodds Boulevard and that I am as fine as frog's hair as I am pulling into my parking spot and climbing the steps to my condo.

It's only when I walk into my living room and see a pair of Emma Lee's earrings on my end table, some of her sketches scattered over my coffee table, and a scrap of her needlework stuck between the cushions of my couch that I become the opposite of fine. I drop my purse on the floor, kick off my shoes, and sob my way into my bedroom, peeling off and discarding garments along the way. I pull my Texas Longhorn gym shorts and Keep Austin Weird tee out of the bottom drawer of my dresser and put them on, because desperate times calls for desperately tacky, but desperately comfortable clothes. I walk around my house, closing the blinds and drawing the curtains until my condo is as dark as my mood.

Sometimes a girl just needs to close the curtains,

shut out the world, and bake herself something ooey and gooey and chock full of calories, something so sweet it overpowers the bitterness of life, like a pecan pie.

That's it. I will bake myself a pecan pie. Not just any old pecan pie, though.

I walk back into the kitchen, open my pantry door, and lift a mint-green enameled box off the top shelf— my momma's recipe box, given to her by my daddy's momma and filled with handwritten recipes that have been tried and perfected by generations of my women-folk. I remove the card with my momma's pecan pie recipe printed on it in her elegant, loopy script. I know the recipe by heart, but holding the card in my hands, looking at my momma's handwriting, running my thumb over the vanilla extract brown spatter mark, has become my pre-pecan pie baking ritual, like I am summoning my momma's spirit.

I get out the ingredients—butter, sugar, eggs, a bottle of bourbon, vanilla bean paste, pecans—and neatly arrange them on my workspace. The instructors at the Auguste Escoffier School of Culinary Arts called the act of putting everything in its place *mise en place*.

I didn't actually graduate from the University of Texas with a bachelor's degree. I attended the Moody College of Communication studying RTF (Radio-Television-Film) my freshman and sophomore years and just got plumb worn out of the whole scene. Affected aspiring directors, screenwriters, and cinematographers smoking weed and debating whether it is possible for big budget films to have *soul*.

And then there were the student screenings—*sweet baby Jesus in Hollywood*—the student screenings of black-and-white films, moodily lit, about homeless people searching for donuts, or sock monkeys march-

ing through abandoned warehouses, or children staring
into the camera reciting political poetry punctuated by
long, self-effected pauses. I thought if I heard one
more person say, *Cinema is truth twenty-four frames
per second,* I would hang myself from the roof of the
Jones Com Center building with two-inch gaffer's
tape.

So, I changed my area of study to Journalism. It
didn't take me long to realize writing serious, hard-
hitting news stories wasn't my thing, either. I changed
my major again, but marketing really wasn't my thing,
either.

So, I dropped out at the beginning of my senior year
and enrolled in the Auguste Escoffier School of Culinary Arts. Seventy weeks later, I returned home with
an Associate's Degree from the University of Texas, an
Associate of Applied Science in Culinary Art degree,
and a Diploma in Pastry Making from Auguste Escoffier.

All of that and a tin of old-fashioned lemon zest tea
cakes landed me a job filming food-related segments
for WCSC-Channel 5, the low-country's News Leader.
Some of the country's most exalted culinary geniuses
tumbled out of Chef heaven to land right here, in my
little old not-so-sleepy hometown. I love filming stories about Charleston's food scene, like the Kyoto-born
chef who opened an Asian-Soul Food fusion restaurant
or the chef who sources all of his seafood from a family
of Gullah fishermen who use handcrafted nets and sing
chants over their catch, but sometimes I feel like I did in
college and I find myself wondering if TV news is my
thing.

Not knowing—I mean down deep in my bones the

way Manderley knows she is a writer—what I am supposed to be doing with my life and where I am supposed to be doing it distresses me to no end.

I take out a heavy saucepan, turn the burner on medium, and begin melting a stick of unsalted Irish butter. Momma jotted a note in the margin: *"Irish butter only. No substitutions."*

I am rubbing cold chunks of unsalted Irish butter between my fingers and smearing it into my flour-sugar-salt dough mix when I have a vague memory of sitting on a highchair and watching my momma make a pecan pie, the golden light of a Carolina summer day slanting in through the screen door. It might be a false memory planted in my brain after I found a photo of the scene in a battered humidor in my daddy's room.

Even so, I close my eyes and I *hear* my momma humming a lilting tune as she rolls out the crust. In the photo, she is standing behind the counter so the camera only captures what she is wearing from the waist up, but I *see* a ruffled apron tied around her narrow waist. I *smell* the syrupy concoction of bourbon, butter and brown sugar.

It *feels* real.

That one memory might also explain why I love baking and eating. Memories—even a single, grainy memory—hold awesome power, don't they? The power to shape. The power to push a body in a direction they never thought to move.

I press the crust into a blue glass pie dish I rescued from a second hand store in Summerville. The dish has an exaggerated scalloped edge that makes any pie look like a piece of art. I pour the ingredients in the crust, slide the dish into the oven, and set the timer.

I would be quite content to polish off half a pecan pie and call it dinner, but Beulah always said, *a body can't live on dessert alone, Tara Faith*. Beulah was our cook. Daddy used to say she could burn a bowl of cold cereal, but she made the most delicious peach jam and the fluffiest biscuits in the Carolinas. Daddy loved peach jam and biscuits the way I love Goo Clusters— only he didn't keep his love secret.

There's not much left in my fridge. Salad fixings. A bag of withered grapes. A pitcher of sweet tea. A jar of tomato chutney. A container of Icelandic yogurt. A Styrofoam box of Emma Lee's leftover Cane's.

I grab the Styrofoam box, dump the buttery, greasy contents onto a paper plate and pop it in the microwave. Forty seconds later I am schlumping on my couch in a very un-Southern ladylike manner, balancing leftovers in one hand and clutching a remote in the other. I point the remote at the cable box and scroll through the programs stored on my DVR.

Sweet baby Jesus! Emma Lee recorded ninety-six episodes of *Millionaire Matchmaker* and forty-two episodes of *Married at First Sight*. No wonder the latest episode of The Great British Bake Off didn't record— there wasn't enough space left on my DVR's hard drive.

I click on season one, episode one of *Married at First Sight*, a reality show where a sexologist (I had to google that one), clinical psychologist, sociologist, and chaplain match couples based on some complex algorithm and voodoo magic (not really). These couples meet—wait for it—at the altar, seconds before they utter the holiest of phrases, "I do."

Crazy, right? Like, crazier than a soup sandwich.

I dip a chicken strip into some Cane's special sauce and fast-forward through the intro. Before I know it, I have consumed a gut full of greasy chicken strips, picked at my pie, and watched three episodes of the surprisingly addictive *Married at First Sight*.

I'm not gonna lie, y'all. I'm secretly rooting for Jamie, the 27-year-old nurse who has given up on love, and Doug, the 31-year-old software salesman. I admire anyone willing to risk failure and humiliation in pursuit of their heart's desire.

I reach for my iPhone.

Text to Emma Lee Maxwell:

I am sorry I wasn't more supportive of your decision to move to England and pursue a career as a matchmaker. I am proud of you.

I am proud of my little sister. I still think her decision to be a matchmaker is crazy—maybe not soup sandwich crazy—but if it is her heart's desire, who am I to toss up impediments?

I wish I had a heart's desire. I thought marrying Grayson and supporting him as he pursued a career in politics was my heart's desire, but not anymore. Ever since he told me he proposed to old Crawdad I've felt my ardor for him fading like a sunset on winter solstice. If marrying Grayson Everett Calhoun isn't my heart's desire, what is?

I scroll through my recent calls until I come to Manderley's name and touch the phone symbol beside her number. Manderley answers on the second ring.

"I need to talk."

"Good afternoon, Tara. I am fine, thank you for asking. Cannes is even lovelier than Aunt Patricia's postcards. How are you?"

"I'm sorry, Mandy," I say. "Of course I want to hear all about Cannes. Are you having a good time?"

"Are you okay?" she asks, a new, slightly frantic note of worry in her voice. "You don't sound like yourself."

"Don't worry about me," I say, upping the perk in my tone. "I'm just worried about Emma Lee is all."

"Emma Lee will be fine, Tara. She is a charming risk taker who makes wild, daring leaps and always lands on her pretty little feet."

"Of course Emma Lee is a risk taker, because she has us running after her with a net. I would be a risk taker, too, if I knew someone would be there to catch me if I fell."

"Ah, I see. Is that what this is about?"

"What?"

"Are you envious of Emma Lee?"

"No!" I sigh. "Maybe. Yes, a little. I envy her courage to boldly chase after whatever shiny thing captures her interest. She sees something she wants and she just goes after it."

"Tara, dahlin', if there is a shiny thing you want to chase after, a bold leap you wish to make, do it knowing I will be there to catch you, too. I've always been there and I always will."

I sniffle and dash away a stray tear.

"Steady-On Manderley. What would we do without you?"

She ignores the compliment, because she is too humble to let praise puff her up with pride.

"If Emma Lee's heart is telling her feet to head to England to be a matchmaker or India to be a Bollywood star, let her go. All you can do is let her go and be ready to cheer her on with loud applause when she succeeds or welcome her home with open arms when she fails."

"Even if it is a big mistake?"

"It's her mistake to make, Tara. Ultimately, we are the only ones who can decide which way we will go in life, and we are the only ones who can say whether our choice to take one path over the other was a mistake or our destiny."

"You're right."

"I usually am."

I laugh.

"Tara?"

"Yes?"

"Take a leap. A bold leap."

Chapter Six

I am hungry and cold, lost in a strange place. Wild, unfamiliar rolling hills blanketed in mist as thick and gray as Irish wool. The ominous sort of mist one expects to see in old black-and-white Sherlock Holmes movies, usually when a bloodthirsty hound with eyes as red as the devil sinks his teeth into the neck of a poor, unwitting wanderer.

I stop walking and strain my ears to hear something, anything, but the world is portentously silent, save for the low, steady tom-tom pounding in my chest.

Thud, thud. Thud, thud. Thud, thud.

I begin climbing up a hill of low growing shrubs covered in forlorn, withered purple flowers and long, slender thorns that nip at my ankles. Each step I take the mist grows heavier, thicker, as if it means to smother me. Mist so thick, so densely layered, that not even the most brilliant and slender ray of sunlight is able to penetrate it.

That is, if it is indeed daytime. It could be night in this netherworld of mist and hunger and cold.

I climb and climb. The terrain alters. The thorny bushes replaced by fields of scrubby grass littered with lichen infested boulders that look like tumbled tombstones. I want to move closer to the boulders, to study them, but fear seizes me by the throat, pulls me brutally along.

Is my name etched upon one of those headstones? A voice slides through the mist, hissing in my ear.

"Remember as you pass by,
As you are now so once was I,
As I am now, so shall you be,
Prepare yourself, you will follow me."

I climb and climb, my feet sinking into strange, spongy ground, the mist growing thicker, the icy air biting my cheeks, until I am nearly blind, moving through wild country without the benefit of sight or the security of the familiar.

Hunger gnaws at my insides like the bloodthirsty hound with eyes as red as the devil gnawing on the neck of his wretched victim.

I am hungry and cold, still lost in this strange place, my hope ebbing, flowing out of me along with my strength.

I should give in now. Quit. Concede that I will never find my way out of this nightmare, never find my way out of this darkness, never find the place where I feel safe and warm and content—a contentment that invades my being and settles itself deep, down deep in my bones.

Just when I think I am lost forever, cocooned alive in an icy blanket of mist and despair, I reach the top of the hill. The mist remains at my back, like a hound, nipping at my heels, but ahead the horizon is clear, the skies an enameled cobalt.

A cobalt so smooth, so beautiful it seems to beckon me.

"Come. Come closer. Lose yourself in my vastness, in the potential, the promise of what could be. All you have to do is . . ."

I feel a presence behind me and I know I am not alone on this hill. Not anymore.

"Do you trust me?" says a deep, masculine voice.

I turn around, but the mist is too thick. I can't see his face, can't determine if the voice is that of friend or foe. Though, I feel my hope and strength returning.

"Do you trust me?" he says again.

I do. I do trust him. I trust him in the way a babe instinctively trusts their mother.

"I trust you."

"Then leap, Tara. Leap and I promise I will be waiting for you when you land."

Chapter Seven

I wake up covered in a sheen of perspiration, my cotton nightie plastered to my back and legs, breathless and disoriented, as if still trying to navigate my way through unfamiliar terrain. The nightmare haunts me for weeks. Until finally, I accept that my subconscious is grabbing me about the shoulders and giving me a good shake. *Pay attention! I am talking to you. There's something jacked-up with your wiring and you need to sort it out right quick.*

One morning I am filming a cooking segment showing viewers how to make an iconic Charleston dish, Huguenot Torte, a sludgy cake of caramel, apples, and pecans topped with an airy, crispy meringue that puffs up in the oven before collapsing into the sludge, when I have an epiphany.

Like the meringue, this illuminating discovery puffs up, takes shape in my mind, an airy notion, that then collapses and settles down in the sludge of my consciousness as something profound and true.

If I don't muster the courage to venture beyond the misty borders of my life soon, I will most certainly grow old and gray right here in Charleston, an unhappy, unfulfilled wanderer squinting at the road less traveled and wondering where it might have taken me.

It was right in that moment—as I was dicing a Granny Smith apple and making sure the carton of buttermilk I would need to make the whipped topping wasn't blocking my shot—that I decided if my practical big sister could throw caution to the wind and elope with some French guy, I could step off my well traveled road and onto a new one.

I reckon it sounds mighty vain, but sometimes a new wardrobe and a head full of fabulous highlights are all a girl needs to boost her courage.

After my Huguenot Torte epiphany, I called a property manager to sublet my condo, officially resigned my position as special correspondent for WCSC, and made an appointment at You Glow, Girl. Miss Yolanda is Beulah's cousin and she's been styling my hair since I wore it in Dutch braids and ribbons. Most of the women I know get their hair done at a high-class salon on King Street because the owner was a Hollywood stylist for a hot Hollywood minute and offers complimentary head massages and mimosas, but I've never been tempted to stray from Miss Yolanda or You Glow, Girl. She might not send embossed appointment reminder cards, but sometimes she calls and says, *Girl, when you gonna let me get up in that head of yours? I saw you on TV last night and you lookin' like a Boo Hag. I's afraid you were gonna start snatching some*

skins. You need to get down here so we can style you.
She's pretty much a hair genius.

Miss Yolanda transformed my flat-iron-tortured hair back to its more natural curly state, adding several layers so the curls are big and bouncy. "Tara girl, you can go on as many starvation diets as you want, but we both know inside that stick figure is a big, bouncy, badass girl just dying to bust out. Be big and bouncy." She kicked the color up a few notches, taking me from warm cinnamon back to my more natural blazing ginger. In a city filled with born- and bottle-blondes, it feels good to be a redhead.

I sold most of my clothes to the consignment store down on Meeting Street and then went shopping for a few new outfits, replacing my brightly colored maxi dresses, sweet-as-Southern-tea eyelet lace skirts, and statement necklaces for items that made me feel free when I tried them on in the fitting room. Black denim leggings. Thigh-high suede boots (because I have wanted thigh-high boots since I saw Gigi Hadid wearing a pair in *People*). A black minidress. Worn-out, beaten soft jeans. Slouchy sweaters. Irreverent slogan tees. And a ridiculously cute oversized flannel shirtdress. I am calling my new look Rebel Without a Cause (yet). It's edgy and unpretentious, which is more my style than the fussy, frilly, girly-girl staples found in every Southern deb's wardrobe. I'm not gonna lie, y'all. I didn't shed a single tear at parting from my pearl earrings and monogrammed sweater sets.

Some in my circle will probably say *(behind my back, of course)* that I am acting all crazy, subletting my condo, selling my wardrobe, joining the Ginger Brigade, but in for a penny candy, in for a pound cake, right?

I don't know if Ireland is that one spot in the puzzle where I belong, where my unique, jagged edges fit without alteration or force. I just know I won't find my place if I don't venture beyond my Southern comfort zone.

> *You can't leave Charleston!*
> *But why?*
> *Where will you go?*

I met Callie at Pawpaw's the day after I had the Huguenot Torte epiphany. I told her about my plan to move to Ireland over pulled pork sandwiches and sides of mac and cheese and she cried. Now, over buckets of crispy flounder and baskets of fries at The Shack, I am telling the rest of my friends that at the end of the week I will board an Aer Lingus flight out of Charleston International Airport bound for Dublin.

"That explains your new . . . *style*," Maribelle says, flipping her glossy blonde ponytail over her shoulder. "Is that the way they dress in Ireland?"

Callie leans close to Maribelle and whispers in her ear, just loud enough for me to hear. "You best be nice tonight, Maribelle Cravath, or I'm gonna jerk a knot in your ponytail. You hear me?"

"Your hair looks great, Tara," Grayson says.

"You think? Not too bold?"

"Not for you," he says, chuckling. "I've always thought you had the soul of a redhead. You really quit your job?"

I nod my head.

"What will you do?"

I shrug.

"Why Ireland?" B. Crav asks. "What's in Ireland besides bogs and booze?"

"Mary Kate Lanigan," Tavish says.

"Louise Byrne," Truman says.

"Who?" Maribelle asks.

"Instagram's hottest Irish models," the twins say in unison.

Maribelle rolls her eyes.

"Tara isn't moving to Ireland to hook up with an Instagram model," Callie says.

"I never considered Tara hooking up with Louise Byrne, but now that you mention it"—Truman looks at his brother and raises his closed fist—"I think that is a visual I need to take some time pondering."

"Yahss, brother," Tavish says, bumping his knuckles against Truman's fist. "Nice."

"I swear you Barton Boys have more testosterone than sense. If either of you ever had an intelligent thought it would die of loneliness," Callie says, swatting Truman with her napkin.

"Seriously, dahlin'," B. Crav says. "Why Ireland?"

I take a sip of my wine to stall for time, mindful that Maribelle Cravath is perched on the edge of her stool eager to hear my answer. I can't very well tell Charleston's biggest gossip that my aunt thought up some bizarre inheritance scheme that requires me to spend three months living with two men in an isolated castle because I know, I know, she will twist and pervert that story until the entire low country believes I am engaged in some sordid, Fifty Shades-esque ménage-a-trois.

I am about to put my glass back on the table when Grayson answers the question for me.

"Tara spent every summer in Ireland, remember?" He smiles at me and the warmth of a thousand Carolina days spreads through my body. The kind of warmth that comes from knowing even though the foundation of our friendship was shook, it remains intact. "I always thought she would end up there someday because she loved it so much."

"I did?"

For a minute, the noisy clatter of The Shack fades away, Callie with her sad eyes, Maribelle with her pinched expression, the Barton Boys with their fist-bumping, fall out of focus.

"Sure you did." Grayson rests his forearms on the table and leans forward, his eyes sparkling. "Don't you remember the way you would come home with your hair all wild, wearing ripped jeans and a big fisherman's sweater, your cheeks slapped pink from all those walks around the *lough*? You'd speak in an Irish accent and insist your daddy call biscuits *scones*?"

I laugh. "Quit it."

"Quit nothing." Grayson laughs. "You would grumble about having to spend the summer away from Charleston, but then you would come back and everything was *grand. Ah, Grayson, the sun is shining and the magnolias are blooming. 'Tis a grand day. Just grand.*"

We all laugh.

"You don't remember that?" Grayson asks.

I shake my head.

"Ireland was your happy place, Tara. It seems only fitting you go there now, what with your daddy being gone and your sisters living in Europe."

"First Manderley, then Emma Lee, and now you,"

B. Crav says, raising his wine glass. "Charleston might still have her towering magnolias, but she has lost three of her most genteel flowers, and is a sadder, drearier place for it."

"Here, here," Truman says, clinking his beer bottle against B. Crav's wine glass.

"To Tara"—Callie lifts her glass—"and her happy place."

Chapter Eight

Text to Emma Lee Maxwell:
How are things in the Cotswolds?

Text from Emma Lee Maxwell:
Different and bloody vexatious. Apparently, the English don't do fried chicken. I missed Cane's so much yesterday, I bought a carton of Ultimate Frozen Chicken Nuggets from Tesco, but I couldn't make Aunt Pattycake's stove work. It's a cast iron antique that runs on oil. Oil! I swear Mrs. Patmore used the same stove on *Downton Abbey*. Good luck in Ireland. I hope things are the way you remember them and without vexations.

The last time I saw Rhys Burroughes he was a painfully shy boy who hid behind his thick thatch of hair, his tortoiseshell spectacles, and his library books to avoid having to interact with others—especially other children. He was Harry Potter, but with a wonky eye and far less confidence.

Winter Hastings phoned a few days before my departure to let me know Rhys rearranged his schedule so he could pick me up at the airport and drive us both to Tásúildun Castle, so I am looking for that awkward, uncertain little boy as I stride through the Dublin International Airport, pulling my suitcase behind me, feeling badass in my black denim leggings and thigh-high boots.

I'm not going to lie, y'all. I decided to wear my thigh-high boots and thigh-hugging leggings because they make me feel empowered, and I want Aidan Gallagher and Rhys Sinjin Burroughes to know who they need to bow down to if they hope to win the right to be king of the castle. I don't know why my aunt put such an unusual proviso in her will, but I do know I need to be shrewd in how I proceed because I don't want to spend the rest of my life battling for control of my aunt's home.

The terms of my aunt's will were clear: whoever I choose to be my co-beneficiary will share the ownership and maintenance of the castle and grounds. That means Rhys (or Aidan) could be knocking around the castle when I am in my Longhorn shorts and Keep Austin Weird tee, binging on Goo Goo Clusters, and Netflix series. It also means Rhys (or Aidan) might eventually marry and then bring his wife and children to the castle, perhaps to live. I imagine a brood of Burrougheses (or Gallaghers) lurking around the castle, peering at me over their thick glasses, and . . .

Sweet baby Jesus and all the cherubs in Heaven!

I stop walking. A man is standing near the exit doors staring at me in a mighty familiar way, a hand pressed to his chest, a grin lifting the corners of his mouth. A man as tall, dark, and handsome as Rhett Butler. He's wearing a dark, expensively tailored suit that makes him look as if he just stepped out of the pages of a Dolce and Gabbana catalog.

If this is the way they grow them here in Ireland, take my passport, and file my application for citizenship because I'm staying.

I start walking again, slower, because I know any second now Mister Ireland is going to realize he is amping up the Colgate smile and feigning a swoon for the wrong girl.

"Tara!"

I stop and look around for Mister Ireland's lucky girl—who must also be named Tara—but there's only an elderly couple trailing behind me and an Italian soccer team crashed out on some gray plastic chairs nearby.

"Tara Maxwell!" Mister Ireland closes the distance between us in two long-legged strides. "You're here."

"Rhys?"

He leans down and kisses the air near my cheek in a very European greeting and I catch a whiff of his intoxicating cologne. Strong, peppery, and unapologetically masculine. I close my eyes and inhale. Cardamom. Bergamot. For a delicious moment, I am transported to a coastal village in Calabria, the sun hot on my skin, the scent of ripe lemons teasing my nose. When I open my eyes, he is staring at me with a grin on his handsome face.

"You smell good," I say, without thinking.

"Thank you." He chuckles. "You're beautiful."

My cheeks flush with heat.

"I am?"

He nods and a hank of his thick, dark, wavy hair falls onto his forehead. *Sweet Baby Jesus in Heaven!* It really is Rhys Burroughes. Little old lazy-eyed Rhys.

"You are so beautiful I thought I was having a heart attack when I first saw you walking toward me." He reaches around me and grabs my suitcase, lifting it as if it doesn't contain Aer Lingus' weight limit in clothes. "Come on. My car is just outside."

I reach into my purse and pull out my sunglasses, sliding them onto my face even though a downy blanket of fog is hanging low in the sky and blocking the sunlight. I slide my sunglasses on my face so I can check Rhys out, and you know what?

Rhys Burroughes is gorgeous, y'all! Just plumb gorgeous. He's taller than the average man, with the trim, toned body of an athlete. An image of Rhys seated in a long, narrow shell, his arm muscles rippling as he pulls an oar through the Thames flickers in my brain. Who would have thought little old Rhys Burroughes would grow up to be so blazing hot? At least . . . I think this is Rhys.

"You are Rhys Burroughes?"

He stops walking and sets my suitcase down. I stop walking. He directs the full force of his gray-eyed gaze on me and my heart trembles like a crape myrtle blossom in the breeze.

"Forgive me. It has been awhile," he says, in his proper, posh British accent, holding out his hand. "Rhys Sinjin Burroughes, at your service, but my friends call me Sin."

Sin. I nearly snort. *Sure as Beulah's biscuits go with peach jam, you are sin in an expensive suit. Sin tumbled out of heaven so fast you lost your wings on the way down. Sin stepped out of my darkest dreams and into this watery, grayish Dublin light . . .*

I shake his hand.

"It's nice to see you again, after all these years."

"It's nice to see you, Tara." He grins and my heart trembles again. "I only wish the reunion had been prompted by less mournful circumstances."

"Me too."

He lifts my suitcase and we continue walking to the carpark. Sin leads me to a stylish BMW coupe, opening the passenger door before stowing my suitcase in the trunk.

"Winter said you drove from London and caught an earlier ferry just so you could meet me at the airport," I say, climbing into his car and smiling up at him. "Thank you."

"It's my pleasure, Tara."

For a few seconds, the whine of airplane engines, the squeal of car tires on the cement parking garage floor fades away as we stare at each other. Funny. I don't remember him having such pretty eyes, fringed by the thickest lashes I have seen without use of fiber mascara or falsies. He bends down and leans into the car. *Sweet Lawd! He's going to kiss me.* He grabs the seatbelt, pulls until the belt is slack, and hands me the clip.

"Buckle up," he says, grinning. "I like to go fast."

Remember what I said earlier? About not wanting to spend the rest of my life battling for control of my aunt's home? Scratch that. I will gladly spend the rest of my life living with Sin.

A couple of hours later Sin and I *(There now, doesn't that sound nice? Sin and I?)* are speeding down a narrow two-lane road, bordered by impenetrable hedges. We stopped for lunch at a little pub in Killashandra, a charming village located near the banks of Lough Oughter, warming ourselves by the small potbellied stove and eating Irish stew with soda bread.

Sin is really quite sweet, as sweet as he was when he was a bespectacled boy with his nose stuck in a book. Sweet, but with enough spice to make him intriguing. He reminds me of the Salted Chocolate Diablo Cookies I make each Halloween, soft chocolate cookies with crunchy edges that tingle your lips with the hint of cinnamon, ginger, and cayenne.

He's a charming driving companion, too, deftly maneuvering his BMW and the conversation.

"What made you decide to go to university in Texas?"

"I wanted to get more out of my college experience than a bachelor's degree and blurry memories of nights spent playing beer pong." I study Sin's strong profile and wonder if he is a stereotypical British man: uneasy with emotional conversations. Emotions, full-stop. "I felt pinched by the poverty of my situation."

"What do you mean?"

"The neighborhood where I grew up is filled with the same, predictable types of people: old, white, conservative Christians. I felt trapped in a claustrophobic social circle. I wanted to move beyond my narrow sphere, broaden my horizons. I wanted to meet people who didn't spend every Friday night drinking mint julips at the Gin Joint, Saturdays at the Farmer's Market on Marion Square and the pier at Folly Beach, and Sundays eating after-church brunch at High Cotton."

I don't tell Sin that I was tired of being the odd tomboy out in a town full of flounce-wearing Southern belles or that I was plumb tuckered out from trying to compete for attention with my sisters. Manderley might be a jet-setter—winging her way from Hollywood to Tokyo—but she is a Southern belle clear down to her marrow, all pleasing and proper. With her grace and gorgeousness, Emma Lee puts the *deb* in debutante. I swear she came out of our momma wearing an all-white ball gown and elbow-high satin gloves.

Sin glances over at me, his eyebrow raised in question. "So if you didn't want mint julips and farmer's markets, what did you want?"

I cast my mind back to those emotionally charged days before I plucked up the courage to submit my application to colleges located north of the Mason-Dixon Line and west of the Big Muddy. It's not hard to do. That lost and searching little girl is still alive (and kickin' it in new grown-up thigh-high boots).

"I wanted to do things that would shock any well-bred Southerner, like dance with someone outside my social circle, someone scandalous, and go to subversive political meetings, and think for myself, and speak my feelings out loud, without apology." I look down at my hands, folded in my lap. "I wanted to do just about everything Miss Belle told me not to do."

"Miss Belle?"

I groan. "Miss Belle Whatling. She taught Comportment and Etiquette at Rutledge Hall Academy, the private school my daddy made us attend."

He laughs, warm and deep.

"What were Miss Belle's prohibitions?"

"Lawd! It would be easier and more expedient if I told you what Miss Belle permitted." I slide my sunglasses down to the end of my nose and glare at him, speaking in a slow, thick Southern accent, my words dripping off my tongue like molasses off the end of a spoon. *"Hell yawns before you, Miss Maxwell, as it yawns before all who are unwilling to follow the basic commandments of etiquette. Hush now. I don't want to hear your excuse for forgetting to place your napkin to the right of your plate before standing up from the table, nor do I want to hear your reason for laughing like a deranged savannah animal. Hyenas cackle. Young ladies do not. You are capable of being gracious and charming, clever and elegant. You're from a respectable Southern family. It's in your genetics."*

He whistles and I suddenly hear myself as if through his urbane British ears, gauche American girl whining because she's expected to keep her elbows off the dinner table and make pleasant small talk with strangers.

"I had a Miss Belle."

I look over at Sin.

"You did?"

He nods.

"Only mine was called Mister Greeves." He sucks his cheeks in and lifts his chin high in the air, speaking in a rumbling voice. *"An efficacious young gentleman endeavors to master the balance between cerebral and social pursuits. Get out of the library and onto the playing field, Master Burroughes. It's your only hope for developing true grit. For true grit is a prerequisite for success."*

"Yikes! Your Mister Greeves sounds as miserable as my Miss Belle."

"He was a right proper tosser," Sin says, lowering his chin. "But, he wasn't entirely off the mark. His prodding and condescension propelled me to toughen up."

"Did you need toughening up?"

He turns, his eyes wide with incredulity. "Are you having a laugh? Don't you remember what happened when Aidan dared me to swim across the lough?"

I shake my head and feign the expression of the

oblivious, all blank-eyed and slack-jawed. I remember what happened. Rhys—Sin—made it about one hundred yards before he started wheezing. Did I mention Rhys—Sin—had asthma back then and wore a rescue inhaler around his neck, secured by a bright blue lanyard? He would have drowned if Aidan hadn't jumped in, pulled him back to shore, and thrust the inhaler between his blue lips.

"Why, no," I say, lying to spare his pride. "I don't believe I do."

"Liar!" He laughs. "But thank you."

We drive along, cozy in his luxury car and our ever-warming conviviality. Rhys is a brilliant conversationalist, peppering me with questions about my life back in Charleston and my aspirations for the future. I talk until my mouth is as dry as a day-old biscuit. I realize, with a start, I haven't spoken a word about Grayson, haven't even thought of him until just this second. Guilty heat flushes through my body. I stop talking and stare out the window.

We have turned onto a single lane rural road on our final leg to Tásúildun. Out my window, St. John's Point Lighthouse looms at the end of a long, narrow peninsula and the North Atlantic stretches across the horizon like a swath of blue fabric, unfurled and undulating on the breeze. During the potato famine, millions of starving Irish immigrated to America, hoping, praying for easier lives. I wonder how many of those ships sailed past St. John's Point and how many immigrants watched the looming lighthouse shrink in size until it resembled a small white dot on the waves? Their last view of home. I narrow my gaze, peering far in the distance, in the direction of my home. Charleston.

"You're awfully quiet. Is something wrong?"

"I suppose I am feeling a little guilty."

"Guilty? Why?"

"I have been talking for the last four hours, telling you every little thing about my life in Charleston, and I just now realized I didn't mention my . . ."

My childhood sweetheart. Lifelong boyfriend. Almost fiancé. Ex-lover. What do I call Grayson Calhoun?

Sin looks over at me, his eyebrow raised in question.

"Your boyfriend, Grayson?"

"Yes! How'd you know?"

"I guessed."

"No, I mean, how did you know about Grayson?"

He looks back at the road. "In my profession, not knowing *things* can kill a deal."

What does that even mean? I am embarrassed to admit I don't know what Sin does for a living. I don't know much about him. Period. Everything I know about Rhys Sinjin Burroughes—the man—could have been gleaned from glancing at his picture in a Dolce and Gabbana advertisement. He looks amazing in a suit and has a lethal amount of sex appeal, the sort of sex appeal that drives smart women to mindlessly buy men's cologne or cigarettes or salad dressing. I am ashamed. Gone from Charleston for a day and already I'm forgetting my manners.

"What do you do?"

"I am an Independent Strategy and Financial Advisory Consultant, but we can talk about that later," he says, shifting into a lower gear. "Right now, I want to know more about your relationship with Grayson and why you feel guilty for not mentioning him in the last three hours."

"Four hours. I have been talking for *four* hours."

"You're not answering the question."

"Was there a question?"

He shifts into a higher gear. "So what if it has been four or twenty-four hours," he says, frowning. "Why the compulsion to not talk about your boyfriend?"

"Actually, he's not my boyfriend. At least, not anymore."

I give him the Twitter version of my relationship with Grayson—one hundred and forty characters or less—because, well, I reckon I have already exceeded the limits of polite conversation. Besides, a true Southern woman doesn't air her tattered old laundry. She keeps her dirty wash hidden in a pretty, pink, monogrammed hamper. She keeps a brave face and a strong back.

"You said you have been in an on-again, off-again relationship with Grayson since you were teenagers. Maybe this is just another one of those off-again times."

"It's not."

We arrive at a crossroads. Sin pulls to a stop and looks over at me.

"How can you be certain?"

"Because, on the evening I thought he was going to ask me to marry him, he proposed to someone else."

"Bloody hell!" he says, staring at me. "That's a brutal business."

I pull a Kleenex out of my purse and clean my sunglasses even though they're not dirty just so I don't have to see the pity in his eyes, so he can't see the lack of grief in mine. The driver in the car behind us honks their horn. Sin shifts into first and we are off again.

I slip my sunglasses into my purse, chew my bottom lip and wonder what Sin thinks of me, a single American girl stomping through the Dublin Airport in thigh-high, man-slaying boots just weeks after breaking up with her childhood sweetheart. Worry is gnawing at my insides, making my gut ache. I don't want Sin to think I am a heartless, unfeeling hussy.

"I am sad about Grayson, but . . ."

"But?"

"I feel as if I should be mourning the end of our relationship."

"But you're not. Why?"

I take a deep breath and hold it for several seconds. My thoughts are whirling around in my brain like cottonwood seeds on a windy day, wispy, elusive, too many to gather. Sin is British. I thought the British avoided emotional conversations and public displays of affection. Even my friends haven't asked what happened with Grayson. They've just continued on as if nothing happened. There's no rubbernecking in the South, not when it comes to someone else's personal business. *Move along. Nothing to see here.*

Why didn't I throw my arms around Grayson's neck and beg him to marry me instead of stinky old Crawdad? Why didn't I drink a bottle of wine and drunk text him, or drive by his house just so I could catch a glimpse of him, or internet stalk him like normal women do after they've been dumped? I mourned my baby sister leaving more than my man.

The wind stops blowing, the cottonwood seeds settle, and the answer materializes in my brain as clear as day.

"I guess I didn't mourn losing Grayson because I suddenly realized I didn't love him with the all-consuming, breath-stealing kind of love a woman should feel for the man she wants to marry." I am still holding my Kleenex, bunched up like a boll in my hand. "Wow. I can't believe I just said that out loud."

"You're not grieving because your relationship hasn't ended, it has simply been redefined. Grayson is your friend now." He glances over at me and smiles a broad, toothy smile. "Which means some other man is going to step into your life and steal your breath. And what a bloody lucky bastard he will be."

He returns his attention to the narrow, twisting, road. I am pretending to stare out the front window, but secretly I am studying Sin's profile out of the corner of my eye. Will he be the lucky bastard? My lucky bastard? He's definitely stolen my breath, with all of his cheek kissing and bag carrying and seatbelt adjusting attentions.

"Enough about me," I say, shoving my balled up Kleenex in my pocket. "I want to know about you. Do you have a girlfriend?"

One corner of his mouth lifts in a wicked grin and warning bells sound in my head. "*A* girlfriend? As in, one remarkable woman who has inspired me to forsake all others? No, I definitely do not have a girlfriend."

Sin indeed. If I were the betting sort, I would place all my money on Rhys Sinjin Burroughes being a major London player.

"Wouldn't you like to settle down, have kids?"

"With you?"

Heat flushes my cheeks. "You're a wicked flirt."

He laughs. "Keep smiling at me like that, Miss Maxwell, and I just might be tempted to repent."

My word. Is it getting hot in this car? I swear he turned the heat on when I wasn't looking. Probably pushed one of those little buttons on his steering wheel.

"What about your job," I say, shrugging out of my jacket. "What is an Independent Financial . . . doohicky?"

"Independent Strategy and Financial Advisory Consultant," he says, laughing. "I operate at the highest level of the consultancy market, specializing in corporate and organizational strategy, economic policy, government policy, and functional strategy."

Either he is speaking fast or I am feeling the effects of jetlag already because I swear his words blended together.

"Dahlin', you're going to have to slow that way down for me," I say, in an exaggerated Southern drawl. "In case you forgot, I'm from Charleston. We have two speeds where I come from: nice and easy."

Sweet baby Jesus in Heaven! Did I really just tell this fast driving, smooth talking London player that I like to do things nice and easy? Why didn't I just wriggle out of my panties and throw them on his dashboard? Please, please Lord, don't let him think that was a double entendre.

Luckily, Sin continues speaking as if I didn't just perform a metaphorical strip tease.

"When someone is ill, they go to a doctor. The doctor asks questions, orders tests, and, eventually, comes up with a diagnosis. I am a doctor for corporations. After ruthlessly scrutinizing every aspect of their business, I develop and recommend strategies to increase productivity and profitability."

I suddenly feel ridiculous for having spent so much time telling him about "I Do So Like That Yam," my segment on the many ways to prepare yams, inspired by Dr. Seuss' *Green Eggs and Ham*. Never mind that "I Do So Like That Yam" won the Southeast Regional Emmy for Outstanding Feature.

"I am impressed."

"Thank you."

"How will you work if you have to live in the castle with me for the three months?" I ask.

"Don't forget Aidan."

"I beg your pardon?"

"I have to live with you and Aidan Gallagher."

Aidan Gallagher. I almost forgot about Aidan.

My stomach suddenly feels rotten as curdled buttermilk. It's the same feeling I used to get right before I went on the air. Strange that I didn't feel it before now. "Have you kept in touch with Aidan?"

"No," he says, shaking his head. "I haven't talked to him in years. Have you?"

"Not since I was eighteen. That was the last full summer I spent in Ireland before going off to college. After that, I only visited for a few weeks in the summer, but Aidan had left home. I used to keep in touch with his sister, Catriona. We were thick as horse thieves when we were kids, me and Catriona."

We have left the rolling green hills and hedgerows of the middle counties behind and have arrived in the Northern Headlands, the most rugged and remote area of Ireland. A short drive up the Wild Atlantic Way and we will arrive at Tásúildun. I stare out at the sea. Memories of my summers at the castle come rushing back, like the tide crashing on the rocks below. How strange it will be to arrive at Tásúildun without Aunt Pattycake waiting to greet me.

And how strange it will be to see Aidan Gallagher after all these years. He was always energetic and sociable, ready with a good story and laugh. The Irish would say he was full of the *craic*. I had a wee bit of a crush on him that last summer, when we went rowing on the lake and he kissed me in the rain. I even thought we might have a long distance romance, visiting each other on holidays and long breaks. Then Catriona wrote telling me Aidan left home to make his mark in the world. I never heard from him again, not even a postcard.

"Will you be happy to see the castle again?"

"As happy as I can be without Aunt Patricia there," I say, pressing a hand to my churning buttermilk belly.

"I miss her," Sin says. "She was quite a character, always planning her next adventure. Sometimes I reach for my mobile to call her and then remember she is gone."

"Me too."

He removes his hand from the steering wheel and grabs my hand, squeezing it gently.

"Are you happy to be going back to Tásúildun?"

"Of course," he says, turning off the road and onto the gravel drive leading to our aunt's castle. "I love the castle. It's my second childhood home."

"Did you spend a lot of time there?"

"Every Christmas and Easter break."

I turn to look at him. "Really?"

"Really."

"I had no idea." I am astonished. "I thought you only visited the one summer."

Even though Aunt Patricia's husband died a few years after they wed, she continued to forge a close bond with her sister-in-law, Sin's mother. It makes sense—and fits with her warm, loyal character—that she would spend time with Sin. Yet, somehow, I imagined the bond between us to be unique and stronger than her bond with her other nieces and nephews. It's selfish and childish, but I am jealous of the time Sin spent with our aunt.

"Aunt Patricia knew things weren't easy for me at home, so she opened her home and heart to me. I felt more like her son than her nephew. Tásúildun became my refuge."

"Mine too."

"I know."

"You do?"

"Aunt Patricia told me a lot about you."

I am now beyond astonished. "She did?"

He nods. "She used to say she believed you and I were kindred spirits and that our life circles would intersect again someday." He makes a noise low in his throat, something between pain and disbelief. "Strangely prescient of her."

"Unless she added the proviso to her will years ago."

"Still strange."

We drive through the tunnel that runs through the middle of the medieval gatehouse in silence. I am trying to understand the logic in my aunt's bizarre request—that I choose a co-beneficiary from either Aidan Gallagher or Rhys Burroughes—when Sin turns onto the drive leading to Tásúildun. I remember Sin for the awkward, shy boy he was and wonder if that is the way Aunt Patricia saw me, a misfit.

"Why did Aunt Patricia think we were kindred spirits? What reasons did she give?"

"She told me you weren't happy in Charleston because you often felt lost between your sisters, overlooked by your father. She said when you learned your unique worth you would find your place, be it Charleston or Cairo."

I turn to look at Sin.

"What did you just say?"

"She said you would find your place in this world once you accepted that you were special and remarkable."

My place.

You could knock me over with a chicken feather. I always knew my aunt was a clever woman, but—

We reach the top of the drive and Tásúildun appears on the horizon. From this vantage point, with the sea stretching as far as the eye can see, it looks as if the tumbledown stone castle is perched on the edge of the world. It's magnificent, even if it isn't as grand as it appeared in my memory, with an outer wall and two four-story towers connected by a small rectangular main building that was once the great hall. Like Doe Castle, located up the coast, it is one of the few whitewashed castles left in Ireland.

"Okay," I say, pulling my jacket back on. "So Aunt Patricia thought we were kindred spirits. Why not just leave Tásúildun to the both of us? Why name Aidan Gallagher in her strange inheritance scheme?"

"I don't know"—he pulls to a stop in front of the southern wall—"but I think we will soon find out."

An Irish wolfhound comes bounding around the corner, a massive gray beast that could easily be mistaken for a small horse. He is galloping toward the car—as if he might leap onto the windshield and paw the glass—when he suddenly stops and whips his shaggy head around, looking back. I follow the dog's gaze and that's when I see him. A broad-shouldered, thick-necked beast

of a man with a fierce scowl on his face. He's wearing
his sandy blonde hair in an undercut, the top longer
and textured so it looks as if he just ran his fingers
through it, the sides close-cropped like the GI Joe doll
he used to play with when we were children. I don't
think I have ever seen a man with such a haircut, except on *Peaky Blinders*.

*I'm not gonna lie, y'all, he looks like he might sew
razor blades into the band of his flat cap.* I am about to
ask Sin if he thinks we should lock our doors when . . .

"Wait a minute!" I say, narrowing my gaze. "Is
that—?"

Chapter Nine

"Aidan Gallagher!"

We climb out of the car. Aidan continues walking toward us at a leisurely pace, shoulders back, head up, gaze fixed. At least, I think it is Aidan. This man is taller, bulkier than the boy who kissed me on a rickety rowboat in the middle of the lake. The muscles of his broad shoulders and massive biceps visible through his wool sweater. If he is smiling, that ready, dimpled smile, it is hidden behind his mustache and beard.

When he finally reaches us, he crosses his arms over his chest and stares down at me with an unflinching, twinkle-free gaze.

"Howahya, Tara," he says, a toothpick—or is it a wheat shaft—dangling from his bottom lip. "Welcome back to Tásúildun."

There is a high-pitched ringing in my ears. My skin is flushed and clammy. My legs suddenly feel weak, too weak to support me. I feel as if I might . . .

"Are you quite all right?" Sin reaches for my arm. "The color has gone from your face."

Heavenly Father! I didn't expect Aidan to be such a . . . man. I might have just blacked out for a second.

"I'm fine," I say, pushing Sin's hand away. "I think I just stood up too fast."

A twinge of a smile pulls at the corner of Aidan's mustache and I have the distinct impression he is laughing at me, on the inside, like he knows my near swoon was a reaction to seeing him again.

Arrogant ass. He was always arrogant, too cocky for his jeans. Lawd. That just came out wrong. You know what I meant.

"Rhys," Aidan says, nodding his head at Sin.

They don't shake hands. Tension crackles in the air like static electricity as they stand across from each other. It's as if I am watching two fighters circling in a boxing ring. *LET'S GET READY TO RUMBLE!! Good evening and welcome to tonight's boxing match, which promises to be a classic in every sense of the word. In the British corner, weighing in at approximately 190 pounds, the man known only as Sin, a highly polished specimen of masculinity. And in the Irish corner weighing in at about 175 pounds of terrifying ferocity and chiseled muscle, Aidan "The Beast" Gallagher.*

If I don't throw a metaphorical bucket of water on these two I am going to be standing on the shore of the lake, watching them engage in a grudge rematch. I move between England and Ireland and give Aidan a hug. He smells like wool, sea spray, the smoke from a burning peat fire, scents that always remind me of Ireland. I close my eyes and smile, because inhaling Aidan's scent feels warm and familiar, like stepping through the front door at Black Ash and catching a whiff of Beulah's biscuits baking.

"It's good to see you again, Aidan," I say, pulling away and smiling up at him. "You've grown several inches since the last time I hugged you."

My cheeks flush with heat as I realize how flirty my comment sounded. Thank Jesus and the saints Sin doesn't know the last time I hugged Aidan was in the old stables, when we fell in the hay and kissed until my lips were raw and I had straw sticking out of my hair. The memory makes me smile.

Aidan isn't smiling, though. *Why isn't he smiling?* The Aidan Gallagher I knew always had a smile on his face and a twinkle in his sky-blue eyes. When we were younger, I could take one look at him and read him like a well-thumbed Bible. I don't know this Aidan. His stony expression and dead-eyed gaze tell me nothing. I am about to fill the awkward silence with pleasing chatter when I see a tiny spark flicker in his eyes.

"I'm glad to see you, Tara," he says, rolling the R in my name and pronouncing you as *ya*.

We stare at each other. His gaze, flat and unreadable, mine searching for signs of the boy I once knew.

Sin clears his throat.

"Shall we go inside?"

He pops the trunk and lifts my suitcase out, setting it down on the gravel drive. He is about to lift his suitcase out when his mobile rings. He pulls it out of his jacket pocket and looks at the screen.

"Excuse me," he says. "I need to take this. Go on ahead. I'll meet you inside."

I am reaching for my suitcase, when Aiden grabs it by the handle and swings it onto his shoulder. He whistles and his dog stands up, alert, ears twitching.

"Come Ailean."

"Your dog's name is Alan?"

"Ailean," he says, pronouncing it the same way. Al-an. "It's Irish for rock."

I used to love listening to Aidan speaking Irish.

"As in Dwayne Johnson, the Rock?"

Aidan looks over at me, grimacing. He starts walking and I get a good view of the broad expanse of his back, the jagged, pink scar behind his left ear. I want to ask him how he got it, but our easy camaraderie seems to have vanished like a wisp of fog in sunlight.

I follow him through the front door and up the stairs to the second floor, my footsteps echoing in the quiet house. I can't stop staring at Aidan's muscular back and shaved head. This intense, self-contained man bears little resemblance to the Aidan who has lived in my memory all of these years, the freckle-faced boy full of mischief and laughter. The sleeve of his sweater slides up his arm a bit, revealing part of a tattoo. This Aidan is nothing like the polo playing, Bourbon at the club, ex-frat boys I usually find attractive. This Aidan is dark and dangerous . . .

. . . and sexy as all get out.

Did I really just think that?

He hoists my suitcase off his shoulder and puts it down in the hallway beside the tall-case clock, his biceps bulging with the effort.

Hell, yes I did.

"Mrs. McGregor thought ya would want to stay in your aunt's room," he says, pronouncing thought as *taut*. "Will ya be stayin' in your aunt's room, then?"

"No!"

Aidan frowns and his sandy blond brows knit together.

"Moving into my aunt's room and sleeping in her bed so soon after her death would feel wrong."

He crosses his muscular arms over his chest. "But Tásúildun is your home now."

I want to say Tásúildun is not my home, not really, not until I spend three months living with two men, and even then it won't be truly mine. It will always be my aunt's home.

"I know this probably sounds silly, but"—my voice wavers with emotion—"if I moved into my aunt's room right now, it would be like sweeping away fallen leaves. In the autumn, the leaves on the oak trees at my daddy's home would turn the most beautiful colors. When they fell off the trees, the lawn would look like a carpet of yellow and orange. I always hated it when the gardener raked them up. I just wanted him to leave them be. That's how I felt when we packed up Daddy's things. I just wanted to leave them be."

Aidan is still staring at me. The expression on his face is inscrutable, but there is a faraway look in his eyes. I feel as if we are standing on opposing cliffs, separated by an ever-widening space. I want to fill the space with words.

"I don't want to accept two people I love are gone forever, swept off the face of the earth, never to be seen again, so I keep the ghosts of them near me. Does that sound crazy?"

He blinks and shakes his head, as if an invisible hypnotist snapped their fingers to wake him from a trance.

"No," he says, his voice rough and low. "I don't think that is crazy."

I look away, embarrassed and a wee bit ashamed at myself for having dumped emotional baggage on a man I haven't spoken to in almost ten years. I listen to the ticking of the tall-case clock, counting the ticks until my shame fades, until Aidan says something to shatter the uncomfortable wall of silence between us.

One. Two. Three. Four. Five.

Aidan clears his throat.

"Which room would ya like, then? Gráinne's Room?"

The room Aidan is referring to is magnificent, with wood paneling and iron-framed casement windows overlooking the sea. It is named after Gráinne Ní Mháille, a seventeenth century female chieftain and pirate whose legendary exploits inspired countless Irish folk tales. It is believed she spent several nights at Tásúildun, hiding out. There's even a stairway concealed behind one of the panels.

"I do love Gráinne's Room, but it is so cold, especially when a gale blows off the sea and the winds howl through the window cracks." I rub my forearms. "I am starting to shiver just thinking about it."

Aidan tilts his head to one side and looks at me through narrowed eyes, his gaze moving down my body, from my wool jacket to my thigh-high boots. I can almost hear him thinking, *"Go on ya woman. Donegal is no place for a weakling."*

"I see some *things* haven't changed."

People in Donegal drop the *h* from their *th* words, a dialectic tic that makes me want to giggle each time I hear it.

"What does that mean?"

"Nothing." He lifts my bag by the handle. "Which room would ya like, then?"

"I'll stay in the Governess's Room," I say.

Located at the end of the hall, away from the other bedrooms, the Governess's Room is a cozy little nook of a room, with paneled walls painted robin's egg blue and an alcove bed hung with drapes. It has a connecting door that leads to the old school room.

"Grand," Aidan mutters.

"Which room did you choose?"

"I moved my kit into the old stables."

"The stables? You can't stay out there."

"Why not?"

"There's no heat."

"I like the cold," he says.

Aidan is not a normal Irishman. Complaining about the cold temperature is a national sport here.

"But, it's damp and dreary."

"I grew up in a cottage. I don't require satin sheets and a fecking maid to leave a piece of chocolate on my pillow to fall asleep. Besides, I've slept in far worse places than the stables at Tásúildun."

I have a hunch the maid comment was a jab at me, but I let it go because I know Aidan didn't grow up with most of the luxuries I took for granted until my daddy died.

"Wouldn't you rather stay in the castle with us?"

"No."

"So, you would rather be alone?"

He grits teeth.

"I like being alone."

"Fine!"

"Grand," he says, grabbing my suitcase.

I don't know why Aidan's choice to stay in the stables is rubbing my fur the wrong way, but right now I feel more riled up than an alley cat.

"Only . . ."

"What?"

"Aunt Patricia's said we have to live together under one roof. It was clearly stipulated in her will."

"God between us and all harm," he mutters, dropping my suitcase again.

The Irish are superstitious about many things, especially death. A true Irishman would do everything in his power to honor a loved one's last wish and I know Aidan loved my aunt. They always had a special bond.

"It was her last wish."

"Fine," he growls, lifting my suitcase and striding down the hall.

I follow him at a leisurely pace, my head held high as if I am queen of the castle, though I stop short of lifting my hand and giving one of those patronizing, cupped hand waves.

That's right, Aidan Gallagher. Who's the boss now? If I have to obey the dictates of this ridiculous inheritance scheme, so does he! After all, I gave up my job and rearranged my life to be here. The least he can do is move out of the damp, smelly old stables and live in a clean, renovated castle.

He drops my suitcase at my door.

"Thank you," I say, smiling sweetly up at him. "Who says chivalry is dead everywhere except in the South?"

"Cork?" He chuckles, deliberately misunderstanding me. "I've heard Donkey Aters described in many ways, but never as chivalrous."

"You know I was talking about the southern United States," I snap.

"Of course ya were."

"What is that supposed to mean?"

"I think ya know what it means. Ya fecking Americans think your country is the center of the fecking universe."

His accent is thicker than molasses.

"Oh, and I suppose you're going to tell me that the

Irish don't know anything about nationalism." My voice is raised to an unladylike level and my tone is dripping sarcasm like nectar from a honeysuckle. "God knows you're not a patriotic lot."

He widens his stance and crosses his arms over his chest, scowling down at me, but I won't be intimidated, not by a sinfully sexy Brit or a rude, unsociable Irishman. I mimic his stance and stare back.

"I said thank you for carrying my bag and a chivalrous, well-mannered man would say, 'You're welcome.'"

"Go way outta that," he says, which is the Irish way to brush off thanks. "Mrs. McGregor is making a special dinner. She asked us to be in the dining room by six thirty."

I open my mouth to respond, but he doesn't wait to hear what I have to say. He does an about face and marches back down the hallway.

Chapter Ten

I unpack my suitcase and arrange my toiletries in the bathroom across the hall—littering the counter with my cosmetics, face lotions, body creams, perfumes, and myriad hair products. The governess's room and the old school room are the only bedrooms in the castle that aren't *en suite*, so I won't have to share a bathroom with Sin or Aidan. Thank Jesus, Mary, and Joseph!

Mrs. McGregor must have known I would choose to stay in the Governess's Room because she left extra blankets in the wardrobe and a tray on the table in front of the window with bottles of water and a tin of my favorite homemade Irish butter cookies.

I love Mrs. McGregor! She looks like a character straight out of a Colm Tóibín novel, with a face like a baked apple, wrinkled and brown from years of living near the sea, and a head scarf knotted under her chin. She has been at Tásúildun since Saint Kevin lived like a hermit in a cave in Glendalough and is a walking encyclopedia when it comes to the castle and village. I have fond memories of times I spent with her in the kitchen, learning how to make Irish soda bread or lamb stew or corned beef.

I open the window and look out over the rolling glen glowing with golden furze. The prickly evergreen shrubs bloom all year and form many of the hedgerows around Donegal. Even though they add pops of color to the predominantly green landscape, they make hiking through the glens a challenge.

I lean out the window, hoping to catch the sweet, nutty aroma of the blossoms. When the sun is strong and the wind just right, the small yellow flowers infuse the air with an aroma that reminds me of toasted coconut. I smell only fresh, salty sea air.

I shift my gaze to the prehistoric standing stone perched on a nearby hill. It's one of a dozen standing stones in the area that form the Turas Cholmcille. Pilgrims used to travel the Turas, stopping at each stone to pray and practice their devotions. Bless their hearts. I can't imagine climbing dozens of hills and picking my way through thorny furze just to stand at a stone and say a prayer. As Emma Lee would say, "Respect!"

A cold gust of wind blows in through the open window, billowing the drapes and slapping my cheeks silly. It always took a while for my thin blood to thicken up enough to stand the colder temperatures along the Donegal coast. It's a vicious, biting kind of cold that grabs ahold of you until even your bones ache with the pain of it. I close the window, hurry over to the wardrobe, pull out a nubby wool blanket, and toss it over my shoulders. Then, I grab the stack of magazines I bought at the airport—*Food & Wine, Bon Appetite, Savuer*—and the tin of butter cookies and climb into bed, clicking on the sconce and closing the bed drapes.

I munch on butter cookies and read an article about women who turned their passion for food into lucrative businesses. I am ugly with envy when I read about the successful commodities broker who gave up her job to make organic fruit bars and is now the president of a multimillion-dollar business! I keep reading, though, about the hairdresser who put down her scissors to start making goat cheese cheesecakes, the bus driver who made a career detour and now sells mass-produced "homemade" chicken noodle soup over the internet, and a radio DJ who found her groove making chipotle aioli. Don't laugh. The former disc spinner made four million dollars last year selling mayonnaise seasoned with peppers!

I don't care what anyone says. Mayonnaise is mayonnaise, y'all, even if you give it a fancy French name, sprinkle it with chili peppers, and put it in a pretty bottle! No matter how you whip it, it's still mayo.

I read until the words blur and my eyelids feel too heavy to keep open. Maybe it is the jet lag or the belly full of butter cookies, but I suddenly need a nap something fierce.

I am buried under a mound of blankets, the empty cookie tin by my head, my cheeks and pillow sprinkled with buttery crumbs, warm in a dream world where I have become the queen of a condiment empire, when someone shakes my shoulder.

"Tara?"

I blink my eyes open and—sweet baby Jesus and all the sheep in the manger—find Aidan standing over me, his previously tousled hair neatly combed.

For a split second I am embarrassed that Aidan has found me in a most unladylike position, splayed out on my bed like roadkill.

"Ya look like ya went out on the lash and got locked out of your tree like a monkey who forgot his keys." He chuckles. "Ya are in tatters."

"What does that mean? In English, please."

"Wasn't that English, then?"

I roll my gritty eyes at him.

"American English."

"I said ya look like ya went out drinking and got extremely intoxicated, to be sure."

"Thanks," I say, pushing away the covers and sitting up. "Does that line get you far in the pubs?"

He ignores my question and reaches for the empty cookie tin.

"Jaysus," he says, turning the tin over and giving it a good shake. "Did ya eat a whole tin of Mrs. McGregor's biscuits, then? In one sitting?"

I reach for the tin.

"What I do with my biscuits"—I snatch the tin out of his hand and cradle it—"is none of your business."

"I've never seen anyone eat an entire tin of butter biscuits."

"Mrs. McGregor knows the fastest way to my heart is with butter."

His lip pulls up in a half-smile. Or is it a sneer? I can't tell with him. "I'll remember that."

My breath catches in my chest. Hold up. Is the intense, scowling Irishman flirting with me?

"Hello?" There is a knock and Sin sticks his head in the door. "There is a woman downstairs waving a wooden spoon and cursing in Gaelic. At least, I think it is Gaelic."

Sin. In my bedroom. Staring at my crumb covered sheets. I comb my fingers through my hair and climb out of bed real slow and graceful-like, as if it is perfectly normal for me to be entertaining gentlemen in my bedroom, as if I am a Victorian lady rising from a swooning couch.

"You look knackered," Sin says. "Jet lag can be a bloody brutal thing, can't it?"

I am dying inside, y'all. Dy-ing. Because I know I must look a fright, with my hair all sleep tangled, standing in a mess of cookie crumbs in my stocking feet. What would Miss Belle say if she could see me now, without a stitch of makeup on my face?

I dig down deep, mustering every last bit of my grace, elegance, and charm.

"You're terribly kind, Sin," I say, in a voice as sweet as honeysuckle. "I am feeling refreshed now that I have had a little nap. If you give me just a moment, I will join you in the dining room."

"Brilliant," he says, winking. "See you soon."

He disappears. I listen to his footsteps fade as he walks back down the hallway.

Aidan is standing with his arms crossed over his chest. He looks at me, shakes his head, and chuckles.

"What?"

"Nothing."

"Well it sure enough was something," I snap. "Where I come from it is impolite to snicker or laugh at someone."

"Thanks for the etiquette lesson, *banphrionsa*."

"What does that mean? What did you just call me?"

"Princess."

"Don't call me that," I say, gritting my teeth. "I am not a princess!"

He walks over to the wardrobe and picks up one of my crystal encrusted Christian Louboutin heels.

"Ya know what they say, *banphrionsa*," he says, tossing the shoe for me to catch on his way to the door. "If the glass slipper fits . . ."

Chapter Eleven

I was madder than a wet hen when Aidan called me a princess and walked out of my room, but Mrs. McGregor's beer braised Irish stew and colcannon has fixed my ruffled feathers.

I'm not ashamed to say I had seconds of colcannon, a traditional Irish dish that warms the belly. I pretended not to notice Aidan's grin or his raised brow when Mrs. McGregor spooned the potatoes and cabbage onto my plate. Let him judge me. See if I care. I ain't too proud to beg for colcannon.

Mrs. McGregor's butter cookies. Colcannon. My momma's pecan pie. These are my soul foods. Foods that nourish my body *and* my soul. When I eat them I feel loved and closer to the people who first cooked them for me. Besides, I plan on hiking to the village tomorrow. There's a path that meanders through the hills. A girl can work up a nice glow and burn off the colcannon calories climbing up those hills.

We help clear away the dishes and then I insist Mrs.

McGregor join us for tea and sticky toffee pudding. I close my eyes and breathe in the intoxicating aroma of ginger, dates, and dark, spicy-sweet treacle. Monsieur Museau, one of my instructors at the culinary institute, said smell is the most underrated of the senses. A good chef, he said, understands that flavor and aroma are linked. *Develop zee nose,* he would say, tapping his bulbous beak. *Exercise zee olfactory organ.*

My olfactory organ exercised, I spoon fluffy whipped cream on top of the steaming cake and watch it melt and flow like a river into the sea of toffee sauce at the bottom of my bowl.

"Thank you for preparing such a delicious meal for us," I say, remembering my manners. "I know it was a lot of work."

"Get away with ya," the old woman says, waving her hands at me.

We eat our dessert in companionable silence, the peat and wood logs crackling in the fireplace. When we finish satiating ourselves on sticky toffee, we sip our tea and make polite conversation.

"How have you been, Mrs. McGregor?"

She shakes her head. "I have been sad, mournfully sad. Tásúildun has been an empty place without herself."

"The news of Aunt Patricia's death must have come as quite a shock to you, Mrs. McGregor," Sin says softly.

"It came as no surprise!"

Sin chuckles.

"Are you prescient, Mrs. McGregor?"

"'Tis omens I read, not the future." The old woman shifts her gaze from Sin to me, but I have the strange, fearful feeling she doesn't see me. "The day before herself perished in the sea, a *snag breac* tapped his beak on the kitchen window pane . . ."

"Snog brack?"

"Magpie," Aidan says, translating the word from Gaelic to English.

". . . and that terrible morning herself perished, the *feannóga* were circling the sky over Tásúildun."

Sin looks at me and I shrug.

"Feannóga is Gaelic for crows," Aidan explains. "In Irish mythology, crows circling over a home portends death."

Mrs. McGregor nods her head.

I always knew Mrs. McGregor was superstitious—she once told me to avoid the fishermen in the village because redheads bring bad luck to seafarers—but I thought her superstitious notions were of the average, run-of-the-mill sort. After all, Ireland is the land of superstitions. *It is bad luck to put new shoes on a table. If you see a penny, you must pick it up. When you see a new moon you should bless yourself or you will have bad luck. If you spill salt on the table you will get into a fight.*

"I wish the crows would have flown over Black Ash that morning instead of Tásúildun," I say, casting my gaze down at the caramel colored residue left on my bowl. "Maybe then, I could have asked daddy not to go sailing."

Sin reaches across the table and covers my hand with his, squeezing it gently. "There was nothing you could have done to prevent the tragedy, Tara."

"I know."

Aidan shifts in his seat and Sin pulls his hand away.

"Will you be staying on at Tásúildun now that my aunt is . . ."

"Away with the fairies?" Mrs. McGregor asks.

"I thought 'away with the fairies' meant daydreaming."

"It does, but it can also mean someone who has literally been snatched from this world by The Folk."

"The folk?"

"The Fair Folk."

I stare at her blankly.

"The Good Neighbors. The People of the Sídhe."

I shake my head.

"Fairies," Aidan snaps. "She's talking about the bleedin' fairies."

Ya bleedin' eejit is what he meant to say. He might not have spoken the words, but I heard it as clear and sharp as a whistle. I want to snap back at him. Who do you think you are, you puffed-up, self-impressed bully, trying to make me feel like an idiot just because I forgot the Irish refer to the fairies as The Folk?

"Do forgive me, Mister Gallagher, for not being an expert in Irish mythology. To my everlasting mortification, this conversation has illuminated the gaping holes in my exclusive, private school education."

Sin chuckles.

"Forgiven."

Ooo! He is ruffling my feathers again.

"And I suppose you view my ignorance in matters of the fairy folk as a great deficiency?"

"Actually—"

Mrs. McGregor makes a quick, sharp noise that sounds like air hissing out of a punctured tire and Aidan stops talking.

"Go on," I prod. "What were you going to say?"

The teacups suddenly rattle against their saucers,

Aidan inhales sharply, and I realize Mrs. McGregor must have given him a swift kick under the table.

"Nothing."

I might have forgotten to mention Aidan and Mrs. McGregor are related. Aidan's grandmother and Mrs. McGregor were sisters or cousins. Whatever the connection, it's clear she has some influence over him. Thank heavens. Let her put a muzzle on the scowling beast.

Though, if I am being completely honest, I still want to know what was going to come after his actually.

"If we have to live together for the next three months, and then, perhaps, share the responsibilities of managing this estate, it is important we develop an open and honest rapport." I stare at Aidan, daring him to charge at the red flag I am mentally waving. "Please, finish what you were going to say."

"Well now, if ya insist, *banphrionsa*," he says, leaning back in his chair and crossing his arms over his chest. "Wasn't your mam born in Ireland?"

"County Kerry. What does that have to do with anything?"

"Did ya never develop a curiosity about where ya come from?"

"What are you saying? I spent every summer in Ireland."

"Until you turned eighteen."

"So?"

"Don't give out like ya don't understand," he says, piercing me with a sharp stare. "Ya spent summers here because ya had no choice, but as soon as ya were old enough to have a say in where ya went, ya turned your back on m"—he looks away—"Ireland."

I am so riled up I open my mouth before I know what I want to say. I could have sworn Aidan was going to say, "You turned your back on *me*." I close my mouth and look at him, really look at him. Could his brooding, aloof, unfriendly demeanor be a symptom of a broken heart? Maybe our last summer together—the kisses on the boat, in the stables, at the beach—meant more to him than I realized. Maybe he was in love with me.

That's actually very sweet.

"Ya can stop making cow eyes at me," he says, leaning forward and resting his forearms on the table. "If you're thinking I was in love with ya and wept when ya didn't return, think again."

"Sure and begorrah," I say, mimicking an Irish accent. "What did it matter if I came back to Donegal? It's not like I was good for a laugh and a snog. Eh, boy?"

"Jaysus! Nobody in Ireland says *sure and begorrah*. Next you'll be saying, *'Top o' the mornin' to ya.'*"

"Only if I'm eating me Lucky Charms," I say, grinning.

Sin laughs.

Aidan groans.

"Can't ya see she's winding ya up, boy?" Mrs. McGregor says, picking up Aidan's empty bowl and placing it atop the others. "To answer your question, Tara. I will stay at the castle for as long as ya need me, luv."

"Thank you, Mrs. McGregor. Can we help you with the dishes?"

"What are ya on about?"

She looks genuinely affronted as she carries the rattling bowls out of the dining room on her way to the kitchen.

"Mrs. McGregor is an ace cook," Sin says, tossing his napkin on the table. "I can't remember the last time I ate so much."

"It was a delicious meal," I say.

Aidan doesn't contribute to the conversation and an awkward silence fills the room, the sort of silence where every small sound seems magnified. The popping peat logs. The distant ticking of the tall-case clock. The soft patter of raindrops on the window.

"Perhaps we should adjourn to the living room," I say, smiling brightly.

"Brilliant idea," Sin says, standing. "I would like to have a proper chat about how we intend to sort things out."

We follow Sin into the living room. I select one of four upholstered chairs arranged around the fireplace and sit down, crossing my legs at the ankles even though I want to prop my feet on an ottoman and zone out while staring at the flickering flames. Sin sits in one of the chairs opposite me. Aidan remains standing, assuming his crossed-arm stance.

"What sorts of things did ya want to sort out?"

"Well, for one," Sin says, resting his elbows on the arms of the chair and pressing his fingertips together to form a triangle. "I thought we might discuss the running of the estate."

"Go on," Aidan says.

"According to her solicitor in London, Aunt Patricia left funds in an account to be used for Tásúildun's maintenance and upkeep. I ran the numbers and that figure is not sufficient. Economies will have to be made."

"What sorts of economies?" I ask.

"I have drawn up a list."

"Of course you have," Aidan mutters.

Sin rests his hands on the arms of the chair, tilts his head to one side, and looks at Aidan through slightly narrowed eyes, a polite smile on his handsome face.

"Are we going to have a problem, Gallagher?"

"I don't know, Burroughes," Aidan says, in a low, steady voice. "Are we?"

They continue to stare at each other like a pair of wary gunslingers confronting each other outside the saloon, six shooters drawn, and fingers itching to pull the trigger.

"Holster your weapons, cowboys," I say, forcing a laugh. "I am pretty sure Mrs. McGregor won't appreciate having to scrub blood out of the living room rug."

Aidan, the immovable object, and Sin, the irresistible force, continue their childish, testosterone-fueled stare-down. I hear the theme song from *The Good, The Bad, and The Ugly* playing in my head and consider whistling it to break the tension. Instead, I stand up and move between them, turning my back to Sin.

"Aidan, please," I say, reaching for his hand. "Sit down and hear what Sin has to say."

He looks down at me and his hard-as-granite expression softens a smidge. Just a smidge. I walk back to my chair and sit down. Aidan sits in the chair beside mine.

"For some inexplicable reason, Aunt Patricia wanted to bring the three of us together again." I look from Sin to Aidan. "We might never understand the method to her mad inheritance plan, but I feel deeply that we should respect it. The thing is, I don't have"—my voice wavers and I have to dig down to my steely magnolia core to keep from crying—"I don't have anywhere else to go. There's nothing for me in Charleston. Not anymore. I never really felt like I belonged there anyway. I don't know if this is where I am destined to spend the rest of my days, but it is where I will be spending the next ninety days and I would like them to be peaceful."

"I feel the same way," Sin says. "Tásúildun is extremely important to me."

I look over at Aidan. I expect to find him staring straight ahead, his brows knit together, a scowl pulling down the corners of his mouth, but he is staring at me with an intense gaze, studying me, really, like he has never seen me before.

"What about you Aidan?"

"What about me?"

"Why are you here? What does Tásúildun mean to you?"

He looks past me, fixing his gaze on the fireplace.

"The Gallaghers have lived in the castle's shadow for generations. When I was a wee lad, I would fall asleep staring at the lights glowing in the towers. After me mam died, Mrs. MacCumascaigh, your aunt, became me surrogate mam, and I spent most of me time here."

He continues to stare at the flames in the fireplace, transfixed, transported to another place, another time. I want to continue looking at his face, to study him in this unguarded moment, but I don't want to break the spell that has transformed him from a scowling beast into a vulnerable man. He clears his throat.

"Did ya know herself arranged birthday parties for me each year?"

Aidan looks over at me and I shake my head. There's a lot I didn't know about my aunt, it would seem.

"They were grand parties, grand." A smile lights his

face, before flickering and fading away. "When I left home, she never forgot to send a birthday gift. It meant the world to me that she remembered."

"So, we were the children Aunt Patricia never had"— Sin forms a steeple with his fingers and rests his chin on the highest point—"and as such, she has entrusted us with Tásúildun."

"You said we need to make economies," I say. "What were you thinking?"

"Companies pay me to help them cut the fat. Tásúildun is fat, obese, actually. We need to trim expenditures."

"Let's hear your suggestions," Aidan says.

"We must make significant reductions in the workforce, keeping only the essential staff members, those who perform skilled labor."

"Like Mrs. McGregor," I say.

"No." Sin shakes his head. "Not Mrs. McGregor."

"Mrs. McGregor is the heart of Tásúildun. Without her there will be no pulse, no life." I shake my head. "No, Mrs. McGregor must stay."

"A cook is an unnecessary expenditure. Mrs. McGregor is simply a luxury we can no longer afford," Sin argues.

I look to Aidan for support, confident he will join me in the cause to fight for his kinswoman, but he just stares at me with the same infuriatingly inscrutable expression on his face, all flinty-eyes and grim mouthed. I am good at reading people, but Aidan is written in a foreign language.

"If it comes down to it, I will pay Mrs. McGregor's salary out of my trust fund," I argue. "If I budget carefully, I should have enough to pay her salary and my

expenses until . . . I figure out what I am going to do
with my life."

"Be reasonable," Sin argues.

"Sometimes loyalty defies reason."

"You don't need a cook."

"I don't need a castle, but here we are."

"You're a trained chef, Tara."

I cross my arms over my chest and glare at Sin.

"Mrs. McGregor stays."

"Bloody hell! You are stubborn, Tara Maxwell." Sin
runs a hand through his thick black hair. "Fine. Mrs.
McGregor stays."

I glance at Aidan and my heart skips a beat. He is
smiling at me and—*sweet baby Jesus if he ain't handsome when he smiles I don't know who is*. Sin is talking, but I can't make out his words. All I hear is
buzzing, like the time a bee got stuck in my hair. *Buzz.
Buzz. Buzz.*

Aidan stops smiling and—just like that—the bees
clear out of my ears.

". . . you must agree with me about Fitzpatrick?"

"I am sorry," I say, turning my attention back to Sin.
"Who is Fitzpatrick?"

"Aunt Patricia's butler and part-time chauffer. He is
on holiday visiting his daughter in Boston, but he is
due to return next week."

"Aunt Patricia had a chauffeur?"

I can't imagine my aunt sitting in the backseat of her
Range Rover, being driven around Donegal like Miss
Daisy. She celebrated her fifty-fifth birthday learning
how to drive a tank at the Irish Military War Museum
in County Meath and her last birthday climbing Machu
Picchu!

"Old Fitz is a special case," Aidan says, shifting in his chair. "He lost his wife and son to cancer a few years ago and was having a bad go of it. He was wrapped more times than a bad Christmas present, that Fitz."

"Wrapped more times than a Christmas present?"

"He was a broken man. He spent his time in the Red Horse crying into a pint or making pilgrimages to the stones." Aidan shakes his head. "Dara worried he would freeze to death up in the hills, so she invented a story about needing a man to help around the castle and with driving."

"I'm sorry, who is Dara?"

Aidan shifts again, looking decidedly uncomfortable.

"Dara was what I called your aunt."

"So my aunt offered Mister Fitzgerald a job to keep his mind off his grief?"

Aidan nods.

I look at Sin.

"We have to keep Mister Fitzgerald."

"Tara!"

I don't know old Fitz, but when Aidan described a broken man mourning his lost wife with beer and tears, I instantly thought of my daddy sitting in a rocking chair, sipping his brandy, and remembering my momma.

"He's a heartbroken old man," I say, swallowing the lump that formed in my throat when I thought of my daddy all alone on the porch at Black Ash. "Where's your charity?"

I feel a thorn of guilt nettle my conscience. Who am I to be preaching like a Baptist minister? Other than fretting about what dress I was going to wear to the South Carolina Aquarium Conservation Gala or the Charleston

Symphony Orchestra League Benefit, I haven't paid much mind to being charitable.

"We can't afford charity," Sin argues.

"You can *always* afford to be charitable. Don't you remember the parable of Jesus and the widow?"

"No," Sin says, sighing. "I don't."

"It's a story in the Bible about an old woman who was poor as dirt and gave her last two coins to Jesus." I raise my brows and suck in my cheeks, giving Sin the same severe expression my Sunday school teacher gave me when I forgot to memorize the books of the Bible.

My Sunday school face doesn't seem to be working on Sin. He looks like one of the sharks on *Shark Tank*, coolly measuring my worth before telling me to follow the green not the dream.

"The household funds simply can't support redundant—"

"Redundant?" Aidan says, tensing all up like a cat fixin' to pounce. "What a cold and sterile word to describe a human being. People are not superfluous or expendable."

I look at Aidan, startled by the force and eloquence of his words. He is looking at Sin with a stone cold stare that would intimidate most people—most people, but not Sin.

"My business—the business of rescuing failing corporations—is cold and sterile. It is about calmly, honestly assessing the situation free of passion or personal agenda. It is about quickly determining the ruptures and developing ways to fix the leaks before the enterprise sinks, like talking to creditors, cutting payroll, devising aggressive reinvestment strategies." He takes a deep breath and releases it in one controlled exhalation. "As you know, Aunt Patricia donated the bulk of her fortune to *charity*. Without the dividends from her investments, Tásúildun has sprung leaks. Many leaks."

I mentally tabulate my trust fund minus my living expenses for the next year to determine if I have what it takes to keep the castle afloat.

"It will be tight, but I think I could pay Mister Fitzgerald's salary for the next several months."

"What then?" Sin asks.

I shrug my shoulders.

"I would be happy to show you the financial documents Aunt Patricia's solicitor forwarded me, but, in brief, the funds in the house account will pay the taxes and property insurance for the next four, maybe five, years, if we are savvy and less charitable. There is a small amount earmarked for the maintenance and preservation, after that . . ."

"Are you saying I am going to lose Tásúildun?"

Chapter Twelve

Lord have mercy! I don't think I could survive losing Black Ash and Tásúildun in one year. Where will I go? What will become of me?

I know what you are thinking. Poor Tara. How will she survive without her plantation and castle? (Insert #HeiressProblems) Thank God Aidan can't read my thoughts or else he would be calling me banfarista or banprintsa—whatever princess is in Irish.

"What I am saying"—Sin leans forward and the fire-light gives his skin a gorgeous golden glow—"is that we will have to come up with the funds to pay the taxes and insurance, as well as the maintenance."

"What kind of maintenance?"

"The eavestroughs need repairing or replacing."

"How much are we talking?"

"The estimate for replacing the lead eavestroughs is three hundred and sixty euros."

"That's not so bad."

"Three hundred and sixty euros *per square foot*."

"Mother Fiddle Faddle!" I slap my hand over my mouth to keep from uttering a more colorful profanity. "I am sorry. I just didn't realize it would cost so much for . . . What is an eavestrough again?"

"A gutter affixed beneath the edge of the roof," Aidan explains. "I was here when the roofer presented Dara with the estimate. He would sell ya the eye out of your head. A shyster that one. I know an old fella, Colin O'Ceallaigh, head like a bag of spuds, but hardworking and fair as the day. I'll speak to him about giving you an estimate."

"Thank you, Aidan," I say, feeling better now that we are all working together.

"Perhaps now you understand why I suggested reducing the staff."

"Some of these people have worked at Tásúildun their whole lives," Aidan argues. "They rely on the income."

"There is no other way," Sin flatly says.

"We have to find a way," I say. "Do you have any suggestions, Sin? Anything that might help plug up the leaks?"

"We have to make Tásúildun self-sufficient."

"How do we do that?"

Sin shakes his head. "I don't know yet."

"Right," Aidan says, pushing his sleeves up to his elbows to reveal elaborate tattoos from his wrists to his elbows. "Aislinn is always saying she is so racked from taking care of her wee ones she can hardly make the drive to Tásúildun and Maeve was thinking about applying at Lough Eske Castle."

"Aislinn and Maeve?"

"Two of the maids."

"Okay?" The jetlag must be catching up to me because I am having a hard time following the Brit, with his *eavestroughs*, and the Irishman, with his dropped consonants. "How will that help us?"

"Mrs. McGregor could do more of the cleaning if you were willing to pick up some of the slack in the kitchen."

"Done." I smile. "I've wanted to get back into the kitchen."

"Ya don't mind then?"

"My dance card is empty."

Aidan frowns.

"I don't mind."

"Grand," he says. "I will mow the lawn, which will save the estate a considerable amount. Since old Fitz doesn't need to chauffer Tara, he could spend the extra time gardening."

"Do you think he will mind?"

"Fitz loves to garden."

"Brilliant," Sin says. "We are cutting the fat."

"What will you do, Oxford?" Aidan asks, fixing his unflinching gaze on Sin. "Unless ya are afraid to roll up your Savile Row sleeves and do a wee bit of manual labor."

"It was Cambridge, actually," Sin says, brushing an imaginary piece of lint from his slacks. "And very little frightens me, Gallagher."

I don't know how these two aren't bone weary from all the male posturing they've been doing. I am a spectator and I am plumb tuckered out!

I look around the room—at the exposed medieval ceiling beams, the white plaster on the stone walls, the expensive Indian rug on the floor, and the rich velvet upholstered furniture—and realize it is a curious combination of rustic and refined. Rustic and refined, just like Aidan and Sin.

Then, I look over at Aidan, at his razorblade-wielding streetfighter haircut, tatted up arms, and menacing scowl, and then at Sin, at the designer watch on his wrist, smooth shaved cheeks, and easy smile. Aidan looks like the kind of man I would have crossed the street to avoid back in Austin. Sin looks like the sort of man my daddy would have encouraged me to date/fall in love with/marry.

"My daddy used to say"—I walk over to the liquor cabinet, grab a bottle of Bushmills, and tip a wee dram of whiskey into three shot glasses—"*Whiskey, women and war, Tara. Three things that have the power to bring men together or tear them apart.*" I hand both a shot glass before sitting back down. "You already look like you want to kill each other, so why don't we raise a toast to Aunt Patricia and see if this whiskey doesn't bring you together—or, at the very least, make you stop circling each other like a pair of junkyard dogs?"

Aidan doesn't wait long before raising his glass and speaking in Irish.

"Death leaves a heartache no one can heal, love leaves a memory no one can steal," he repeats, this time in English. "Thanks a million for the memories, Dara."

"To the memories," I say.

"To the memories," Sin says.

I raise my glass and take a swig. The amber liquid blazes a path down my throat, into my belly, and I cough until the burning stops. I've never enjoyed whiskey.

Aidan looks at me, one eyebrow arched in concern. Or is it judgment?

"I am sorry," I say, coughing one more time. "I just don't have the stomach for hard liquor—unless, that is, you incorporate it into a dessert, like brownies with rum sauce or maple bacon bourbon cupcakes."

"Would ya like me to see if Mrs. McGregor has any Irish Butter Biscuits left? Ya could always dunk them in your whiskey," Aidan asks, his expression serious.

"Funny." I put my half-filled shot glass down on the table between our chairs. "Very funny."

"Did I miss something?" Sin asks.

"No," I say, smiling sweetly at him while pointedly ignoring Aidan. "You didn't miss anything."

Sin smiles back at me and I swear a little bolt of electricity passes between us. A white-hot bolt that passes through my body, making me feel flushed clear down to my toes.

"If we are done here," Aidan says. "I have some things I need to do."

I tear my gaze from Sin in time to see the back of Aidan's partially shaved head as he strides out of the room, leaving me alone with Sin.

Alone with Sin.

"Speaking of memories," Sin says, filling the silence with his British accent. "Do you remember when Aunt Patricia went to Zimbabwe?"

"The safari?"

"Yes." Sin laughs. "She called me the day before she flew to Africa to tell me she was going big-game hunting."

"She called me, too," I say, sharing his laughter. "I asked her why she wasn't spending her holiday in the south of France, cruising the Mediterranean on her yacht, as she normally did and she said, *there comes a time in every woman's life when she must test her mettle, really test it, and she can't possibly accomplish that dining on lobster at Hotel Cap-Eden Roc.*"

We both laugh because we know how the story ends. When the moment to pull the trigger finally arrived, my aunt found she didn't have the sort of mettle required to kill a lion. She said she would have fallen to the ground if not for the marrow keeping her upright.

We swap stories about our beloved aunt, laughing, our eyes misting over with emotion, until the tall-case clock chimes eleven times.

"I have quite enjoyed reminiscing with you, Tara." He stands and for a crazy hot second I think he intends to kiss me, but he only flexes his shoulders. "There's nothing I would love more than to sit here with you, but I have to be up in a few hours for a conference call with our Tokyo office."

"I should be getting to bed, too," I say, feigning a yawn. "A girl can't afford to miss her beauty sleep."

He reaches over and lifts a lock of hair from my cheek, tucking it behind my ear.

"Losing beauty sleep is one thing you can definitely afford, Tara."

"Thank you," I murmur.

"You're quite welcome."

Sin just called me beautiful and played with my hair. He is standing so close I can smell his peppery cologne. And yet, I don't feel the electrifying jolt of desire I felt when he looked at me earlier. I just feel . . . pleased.

"Goodnight, then."

"Goodnight, Sin."

I walk over to the fireplace and wait, staring into the flames and listening as he crosses the foyer, climbs the stairs, and walks down the hallway, his footsteps fading away.

Pleased? A drop-dead gorgeous guy just flirted with me—at least, I think he was flirting—and the only feeling I could muster was pleased? I am going to blame it on the jetlag. What other reason could there be?

Chapter Thirteen

It's after midnight and I am sitting on the floor of my room with cotton balls stuck between my toes, painting my nails a bold, empowering cranberry. If you want to be a bold woman, the kind of bold, badass woman who convinces two men to forfeit their keys to the castle, you need bold nail polish, am I right?

I am wearing my earbuds with the built in mic because I called Callie before I started painting my toenails. She's telling me about the date she went on last night (Charleston time) with Landon, a guy she met recently.

"We met at that new taqueria," she says.

"The one on Meeting Street?"

"Yes, ma'am."

"Ooh, tell me you tried their guacamole with the grilled Mexican sweet corn spicy mayo and cotija cheese?"

"Oh, we tried it!"

"And? Delicious, right?"

Callie doesn't answer. The line crackles and I am afraid the call dropped.

"It was the best guacamole dip I ever had—"

"I told you!"

"—until Landon lost his lunch."

"Lunch?" I stop painting my big toe and press my finger against the earbud. "I thought you met for dinner?"

"No, dahlin'," Callie coos. "He *literally* lost his lunch."

"Are you telling me he tossed his cookies?"

"All over the guacamole."

"Hush your mouth!" I giggle. "You lie like a no-legged dog."

"I do not," Callie cries. "Hand on the Bible, I am telling the God's honest truth. He drank two beers, shoveled a handful of chips into his mouth, and turned as green as the guac. Next thing I knew he was heaving like a cat yakking up a fur ball."

"Oh, Callie! How awful. What did he say?"

"Get ready for this one," Callie says. "The waitress came over with a stack of napkins and Landon snatched them from her hand and demanded she tell him what was in the dip."

"Okay . . ."

"He's allergic to avocados."

"What? Are you kidding me?"

"Dead dog serious," Callie says. "He was yelling at the manager, threatening litigation because the menu didn't list avocado as one of the ingredients in guac-a-effing-mole dip, when I picked up my purse and left."

"I am sorry, Cal," I say, brushing bold cranberry onto my middle toe. "That must have been a nightmare."

"I don't know how I will show my face downtown."

"Landon? I don't know anyone named Landon. How did you meet him?"

"Happn."

"Happening?"

"Sweet Tea, Tara, you've been out of the States for one day and already you are becoming hopelessly disconnected. Happn is a dating app."

"Like Tinder?"

"Happn is so much better than Tinder! Tinder shows potential matches within a few miles, but Happn shows you potential matches based on people you actually pass in the street or encounter around town using geolocation services."

"That's creepy."

"It's revolutionary," Callie argues. "Every time you cross paths with someone, their profile pops up on your timeline."

"So Mister Lost His Lunch's profile popped on your timeline?"

"Dozens of times. I thought the Universe was trying to tell me he was my Mister Right."

"Or . . ."

"Or?"

"What if the Universe was trying to warn you that he is a serial killer with a weak digestive tract?"

She laughs.

"Enough about my sorry life," she says. "Tell me about your exciting new life in Ireland. How's the weather, the castle, the men? Start with the men."

I tell Callie about Sin, starting with his rom-com worthy greeting and finishing with his rom-com worthy compliment. I think I might have even sighed a few times.

"And what about the other one, Ian?"

"Aidan."

"Is he a rom-com hero, too?"

"Aidan Gallagher? A rom-com hero?" I snort. "If rom-com heroes are surly and contrary, then sure, Aidan is a rom-com hero."

"Is he handsome? An ugly personality is like a cheap suit, if the man is good looking enough you can look past it."

"What did Landon look like?"

"Never mind about Landon. Tell me about Aidan. Is he tall, dark and hot as Sin?"

"He doesn't look anything like Sin," I say, switching legs so I can paint the toenails on my other foot. "He's a little shorter than Sin, but a lot more muscular. He has eyes as blue as the sea and sandy blonde hair that's always messed up on top, like he just rolled out of bed."

"Yes, please."

"He's not your type."

"Is he *your* type?"

"He has tattoos."

"On his face?"

"Don't be ridiculous! On his arms."

"So, just to recap," Callie says. "You have a tall, dark and lethally handsome man who looks like he tumbled out of heaven named Sin and a gorgeous, muscular, tatted-up man who looks like he walked out of hell. Sin or Aidan? Tough choice. I'll take one of each, thank you."

"You can't have either one of them."

"Selfish."

I laugh.

"So, which one are you going to do the deed with first?"

"Callie Rae Middleton, if your momma heard you talking like that she would wash your mouth out with soap."

"Momma is at the clinic in Geneva having her eyes lifted. Now answer the question. Are you going to bump uglies with Aidan or Sin?"

"I am not bumping uglies with either of them! You're so nasty!" I say, fanning my face with my hand. "Besides, I thought I was supposed to be devising a plan to make them want to give up their claims on the castle."

"Bump uglies."

"Will you hush now? Stop saying that vulgar term."

"Pick a man and bump some uglies," she says, giggling. "If he enjoys it, he will twist himself around your little finger. If he doesn't enjoy it, he will toss you the keys to the castle and you will never hear from him again."

"You're so wicked."

Over Callie's laughter, I hear a muffled thud.

"I think someone just knocked on my door."

"Woo-who! It's ugly bumping time!"

"It is *not* ugly bumping time," I whisper.

"Come on Tara, just lie back and think of England . . . or Ireland. Do it for the castle!"

"Goodbye, Callie."

I disconnect the call, pull my earbuds out, and walk to the door on the heels of my feet so I don't smear the wet polish on my toenails. I press my ear to the door and listen. I hear nothing in the hallway except the soft, muted tick-tock, tick-tock of the tall-case clock. A chill trickles down my spine.

I pull my ear away from the door and look around the room. Behind the robin's-egg blue-painted paneled walls—added in the eighteenth century and restored in the twentieth century—are the original stone walls of Tásúildun, walls that stood witness to centuries of history, some of it gruesome.

Sweet baby Jesus! Could one of Tásúildun's ghosts have made the mysterious thud?

When I was a girl, Mrs. McGregor told me the castle was haunted by the ghost of a young woman, the daughter of one of the castle's previous owners. Apparently, Lady Margaret fell in love with a sea captain, which was a wholly unsavory match for the daughter of an important and wealthy man. Incensed, her father locked her in her room. But Lady Margaret was able to send a secret message to her lover, instructing him to anchor his ship off the shores near Tásúildun and she would come to him on the first moonless night. Dressed in an opulent black gown, a long black veil wrapped around her head to conceal her beautiful blond hair, Lady Margaret fashioned a rope out of her bedlinens and climbed out her window. But she lost her grip halfway down and would have fallen to her death if not for her veil. The fabric, which had become tangled and trapped between the makeshift rope, worked like a noose, strangling her. She was found the next morning, her lifeless body dangling like a ragdoll.

Overnight visitors to Tásúildun have said they were roused out of deep sleep by strange gurgling noises, like the sound someone might make if they were being strangled to death. Some even said they saw Lady Margaret's ghost, a forlorn figure dressed in black, standing at the window, staring out to sea. Mrs. McGregor says on moonless nights golden orbs move over the sea. She swears it is the sea captain, sailing his ghostly ship into the harbor on his eternal search for his lost lover.

I hear another thud and my heart skips a beat.

Wait a minute. That sounded like it came from the room next door. Heels up, toes still separated by cotton balls, I walk over to the connecting door, take a deep breath, and turn the knob, half-expecting to see Lady Margaret's apparition hovering in the old school room.

Instead of a ghost, I see Aidan lying on his back, knees up, elbows out, doing crunches. Shirtless.

Sweet Jesus is he muscular.

"Aidan!"

He stops crunching and looks over at me.

"Tara."

"What are you doing?"

He stands up and puts his hands on his hips, giving me a clear view of his smooth, tatted chest and rippled abdomen. *Forget the six pack, y'all, this boy has an eight pack of hard Irish Guinness.*

"Exercising."

"Obviously."

"Ya asked," he says, a sardonic smile tugging at the corner of his mouth. "Don't ask an obvious question if ya don't want an obvious answer."

"I meant what are you doing here, in the old school room?"

"You said you wanted me to move into the castle."

"I never said that."

"Ya did."

I exhale, but it comes out as a growl. "I said the terms of Aunt Patricia's will require us to live under one roof. Tásúildun is a big castle, with a big roof, you didn't have to pick the room next to mine."

"What's the matter, *banphrionsa*?" He walks closer, close enough for me to read the words circling the tattoo over his heart—not that I am staring at his chest. "Are ya afraid to be this close to me?"

"Afraid?" I snort. "Why would I be afraid?"

"Having me this close might interfere with your romantic plans."

"What romantic plans?"

"I've seen the way ya moon over Oxford."

A very unladylike laugh escapes my lips. More of a cackle, really.

"Don't be ridiculous. I do not moon."

"Ya moon." He smiles and my knees feel like bowls of wiggly, rubbery Jell-O. "In fact, ya act like a stook every time he's around."

"Stook?"

"A fool."

"I do not act like a fool!"

Standing in an oversized tie-dyed Keep Austin Weird tee and teeny-tiny boy shorts, with cotton balls stuck between my toes, I do not offer a very convincing argument. I must look like a stook.

"Ya remind me of our Catriona when she first saw Cillian, staring at him like a lovesick cow, hoping he would give her a good shifting."

"Shifting?" Sweet Jesus please don't let it mean something nasty. "What is shifting?"

He looks at my lips and his grin widens. "Kissing."

Heat flushes my cheeks. "I do not want Sin to kiss me."

"Are ya sure about that, *banphrionsa*? Because your cheeks are as red as your hair."

"Ooh." I can't stop myself from stomping my foot. "You are rude and obnoxious, Aidan Gallagher! You are . . ."

I close my mouth before I say something vulgar and unladylike, something that would have made Miss Belle have an apoplectic fit.

Aidan leans down so we are eye to eye and—sweet baby Jesus—there's that buzzing in my ears again.

"What am I, *banphrionsa*?"

"You are no gentleman."

His laughter fills the room as bold as you please, as bold and strong as his chiseled body, and for some strange reason, it doesn't nettle me. Actually, and this probably will come as a shock to you—because it sure enough comes as a shock to me—I like the sound of Aidan's laughter, low in his belly and rolling easily, melodically out of his lips. His eyes light up when he laughs and he gets cute little crinkles around his eyes. *Cute little crinkles?*

"Thanks be to God," he says, looking into my eyes. "Why would I want to be a gentleman?"

Just like that I forget about his belly laugh and eye crinkles. Ooh, he makes me mad.

"Gentlemen aren't coarse or rude. They're refined."

"There ya go again, mooning over Oxford again."

"It's Cambridge, not Oxford," I snap. "And I am not mooning over him."

Aidan stands up tall, crosses his arms over his bare chest—his heavily tattooed arms—and looks down at me with an expression that could only be described as half-smile, half-sneer.

"If being a gentleman means dressing like a ponce in fancy button-down shirts with poncey monograms on my cuffs and rattling off numbers like a machine, I am definitely not a gentleman."

"You sound jealous."

"Do ya want me to be jealous, Tara?" He winks at me. "Is that it, then?"

"Why would I want you to be jealous of Sin?"

"Maybe ya fancy us both and ya have some eejit romantic notion we will fight over ya."

I snort. "If you think I fancy you, Aidan Gallagher, you are the *eejit*! I definitely don't—"

He stretches his arms over his head, giving me another view of his naked chest, and yawns a fake-ass loud yawn.

"I'm sorry, but could ya tell me how much ya don't fancy me tomorrow? I'm shattered and I've got to get up early."

He doesn't wait for my answer. Instead, he walks over to the bed, steps out of his shorts, letting them drop to the ground in a pool of gray fabric, and climbs between the covers.

I am still standing in the doorway, mouth hanging open, eyes as round as teacups, and cheeks flaming hot, when he switches off his bedside lamp.

"Goodnight," he says.

"Goodnight," I sputter.

I am about to close the door when he says, "Tara?"

"Yes?"

"Don't worry, if I hear ya"—he pauses and I stand frozen in the doorway, staring into the darkness— "What was that phrase? *Oh, yeah* . . . bumping uglies. If I hear ya bumping uglies with Oxford, I promise not to barge in and challenge him to a duel."

I back into my room and slam the door.

Aidan laughs, the sound echoing in the old school room, taunting me even through the closed door.

Remember what I said about liking Aidan's laugh? I've changed my mind.

Chapter Fourteen

I wake the next morning to the sound of a dove crooning outside my window, a soft, hypnotic *who-who, who-who*, that gently lures me from my dreams. I stay snug under my covers, still wrapped in the downy warmth of slumber, my eyes closed, listening to the sounds of the world beyond my room stirring, stretching, greeting the new dawn. I am happy. Cozy and warm and happy in my sleep-induced amnesia.

Then, I hear it—like Lady Margaret's strangled breath coming out of the darkness—I hear two haunting words in my head: *bumping uglies*. The memories of the previous evening flood my brain in a horrifying wave. Aidan's mocking laughter playing over and over again like a broken record.

I could have died. I could have just curled up like a tired old tabby cat who has worn out all nine of her lives, when I realized Aidan overheard my conversation with Callie.

Sweet baby Jesus and all the saints in heaven! Aidan

heard me describe him as having *eyes as blue as the sea*. I feel hot all over despite the chilly morning air. Why? Why did I have to tell Callie about his eyes and his messy hair and his tattoos? No wonder he thinks I like him. Arrogant Irish ass. That's sure enough what he is: an Irish ass with an ego as big as all get out.

My plan to charm and finagle the castle away from Aidan Gallagher and Rhys Burroughes is proving more difficult than I imagined. Aidan is too grouchy to charm and Rhys is too clever to finagle.

Yesterday I said I wouldn't mind sharing Tásúildun with Sin, but that was only my lust talking. This morning, in the bright, cool light of a new day, I see things clearly. I couldn't possibly share my castle with someone who would give sweet old Mrs. McGregor the boot. Besides, if my aunt really wanted Sin or Aidan to inherit her castle she would have named them as full beneficiaries, wouldn't she? Sure, both men have compelling reasons for wanting to inherit Tásúildun, but sentimentality alone is hardly a reason to give someone a valuable estate. I felt sentimental about Black Ash, as did my sisters, but our attachment to our family home meant very little to the IRS.

I need. I need to know I belong somewhere, to something, now more than ever. I need this big old pile of rocks and all of the people who work to keep it standing.

I lost Black Ash, but I won't lose Tásúildun.

The terms of my aunt's will are clear: I, Tara Maxwell (hereafter referred to as Executor and Trustee), must cohabitate with Aidan Gallagher and Rhys Burroughes for ninety consecutive calendar days. Upon successful completion of the requisite cohabitation, Executor and Trustee must name either potential beneficiary two (Aidan Gallagher) or potential beneficiary three (Rhys Burroughes) as her co-Executor and Trustee. What wasn't clear? Who inherits Tásúildun if both Aidan and Rhys forfeit their claim.

Fortunately, I still have two months and twenty-nine days to convince Aidan and Sin that Tásúildun, with its creaky floors, drafty rooms, expensive gutters, and tortured ghosts, isn't worth *their* efforts to keep.

Mrs. McGregor is kneading a ball of bread dough when I walk into the kitchen an hour later, showered and dressed in black tights, my new flannel shirtdress, and my battered Doc Martens, a sweater tied around my waist. The warm air is heavy with the scents of simmering broth, onions and garlic, and carrots.

"Good Morning, Mrs. McGregor," I say, perching on a wooden stool. "You're making your famous lamb stew, aren't you? I would know that scent anywhere." I close my eyes and inhale. "Mmmm. You should bottle it and sell it as an air freshener."

She chuckles.

"Go on with ya, then."

"I am serious," I say, opening my eyes. "A pot of your lamb stew simmering on the stove is one of the best scents in the world. It makes me feel warm inside before I have even taken a bite."

"What a grand t'ing to say, luv." Mrs. McGregor smiles at me. "It does me old heart good to hear ya say such a lovely t'ing about me cookin'."

"You're welcome."

"Now, are ya hungry? Will ya be wantin' a full breakfast, then? Rashers, black pudding, eggs, veg, and potatoes or just oatmeal?"

"What I want and what I should have are two very different things, Mrs. McGregor," I say, patting my stomach. "I want the works, but since I wasn't able to fit my treadmill in my suitcase, I will stick with the oatmeal and a pot of Barry's."

"What do ya need an exercise machine for when ya have hills to climb and miles of beaches to walk?" She stops kneading the bread dough, wipes her hands off on her apron, and walks over to the window, pulling the lace curtains back. "Have the full breakfast, why don't ya, then go hike the pilgrim trail."

"Keep talking, Mrs. McGregor, and you just might persuade me."

"Ya know what I always say, don't ya? Eat breakfast like a queen, lunch like a princess, and dinner—"

"—like a pauper," I say, laughing. "You have mystical powers of persuasion. Aunt Pattycake always said you descended from druids."

"Herself liked to tell guests me ancestors were the Bandrúi, the druid women who lived thousands of years ago"—Mrs. McGregor chuckles and shakes her head—"she had a load of blarney in her, that one."

We slip into a companionable silence as Mrs. McGregor prepares my breakfast and I set a place at the old wooden work island in the middle of the kitchen.

"Would you like me to finish kneading your dough?"

"T'at would be grand," Mrs. McGregor says. "T'anks a million."

I wash my hands and dry them on a dishtowel, then begin kneading the dough that will eventually form a loaf of brown bread. I push the dough down and out, stretching it flat with the heels of my hands, until it is smooth, then I form it into a boule.

"Don't forget to cross the top"—Mrs. McGregor

hands me a sharp knife for slashing the dough—"or the devil and the wee fairies will be trapped inside."

I slash a big X in the dough and cover it with a large copper bowl and then sit back down on my stool to wait for my breakfast.

"Did Sin eat already?" I ask.

"Who? I don't know anyone by that name." Mrs. McGregor made her feelings about Rhys's new name known during dinner yesterday. She told him she thought it was blasphemous and warned him to stop knocking on the devil's door or he would be invited in. Then, she made the sign of the cross and left Sin sitting there laughing. "Do ya mean Rhys?"

"Yes," I say, flushing.

"He drove out of here in that fancy car of his early this morning, in a rush to his funeral, that one." She carries a plate laden with fried eggs, potatoes, sausages, and tomatoes and sets it down in front of me. "Here ya are, my dear. Don't ya know a full Irish breakfast is the cure for jetlag?"

"I thought it was the cure for a hangover?"

"That too."

I laugh. "Would you keep me company, Mrs. McGregor, please?"

"Ah, sure," she says, sitting across from me. "I could go for a cuppa."

I pour her a cup of strong Irish tea, set the cup on a saucer, and slide it across the island to her.

"Thanks, luv."

I inhale the curlicues of steam twisting up from the plate, savoring the scent of fresh sausage, before cutting my egg in half and forking it into my mouth.

"Herself told me about your important television job. Proud of ya, she was."

"Really?"

"Sure."

I know my aunt was proud of me, but it feels good to hear it again. A part of me *needs* to hear it again, the part of me that is still a chubby little girl who feels like she doesn't fit in at home or at school. Doesn't every person have a fat/skinny/lonely/shy child living inside of them?

"Are ya going to miss being on the television?"

Will I miss being on TV? Will I miss waking up before the sun to film cooking segments with other chefs? Will I miss standing in ninety-degree heat and being bled dry by mosquitos while I interview the president of the Carolina Women's League about their jam festival?

"No, ma'am," I say, dabbing my lips with a napkin. "I never felt fulfilled in that job. I never felt like it was my calling."

"What will you do with your days?"

Mrs. McGregor has spent her whole life within a fifteen-mile radius of Tásúildun. Her parents worked at the castle, her husband worked at the castle until he died. How can I explain to a woman who has such deep roots what it feels like to be suddenly rootless?

"I don't know. I feel adrift."

"What does your heart want to do? Answer with your heart, child, not your head."

"I would like to bake," I instinctively answer. "Maybe even write a cookbook or start a blog about baking. I am tired of talking about food and tasting other people's food, I want to get in the kitchen and create, lose myself in the art of it. Baking makes me happy because I take pleasure in knowing what I am creating will bring joy to others. There is too much pain and suffering in this world. I just want to spread joy, one cookie at a time. Does that sound silly?"

"I have been cooking and baking for other people most of my life. I wouldn't be in this kitchen if it didn't fill me with joy." She takes a sip of her tea. "You're welcome to join me here anytime ya want."

"You wouldn't mind?"

"Tásúildun is yours now, Tara, love." She smiles sadly over the rim of her teacup. "Besides, I welcome the company. I've been a wee bit lonely since . . ."

"Thank you."

I gather our dishes and rinse them in the sink.

"Thank you for a delicious breakfast," I say, giving her a hug. "It's just what I needed."

"Where are ya off to then?"

"I thought I would work up a glow on Donegal's treadmill," I say, walking toward the door. "I am going to take a hike."

Mrs. McGregor frowns.

"In this weather?"

I open the door and look up at the blue sky. There are only a few, wispy clouds ringing the top of the distant hills.

"What do you mean? It's beautiful."

"Mark me words, it's going to rain."

"I won't be gone long."

"Here, take a brolly," she says, pulling an umbrella off a wooden hook on the back of the door. "It will be lashing outside before you get back or me bones are lying."

Chapter Fifteen

I've barely made it to the first standing stone before I have to stop to retie my bootlaces. The toes of my boots are scuffed and the tongues are limp and floppy. My battered old Doc Martens have seen better days.

Lawd, how my daddy hated these boots. He said I was too pretty to wear combat boots, but I kept on wearing them. I was smack dab in the middle of my rebellious phase, going to school in Austin, and hiding my Southern deb roots beneath layers of grungy denim, tattered flannel, and irreverent tees. The grungy rebel was soon replaced by the cowgirl rebel. By the time I graduated from the culinary institute and returned to Charleston, I was back to being the rebel deb, a Southern girl fighting against a well-established, genteel system. When I got the job at WCSC, I packed away my chunky-soled boots and grungy jeans and filled my closet with Charleston-appropriate attire. In that way, I seem to have traveled full circle.

I finish tying my boots and continue climbing, skirting

around the thorny furze, until I reach the first stone, the one visible from my bedroom window. My boots sink in the spongy, wet ground. Water seeps in through the laces. I make a mental note to stop in at Finnegan's, a pub/general store in the village, to see if they sell rain boots.

I keep climbing until I reach the sixth stone on the trail, the most elaborately carved of all the stones. Sitting on a flat boulder across from the stone, I close my eyes and say a little prayer for Daddy and Aunt Patricia. I am about to ask God to help me find my purpose and my place when I hear someone approaching.

"The stones can't bring ya another tiara, *banphrionsa*."

Mother Mary and Baby Jesus! Aidan Gallagher is not standing in front of me. He is not taunting me as I pray. I open my eyes and there he is, towering over me, a rucksack on his back, that half-grin, half-sneer on his handsome face. Ailean is standing beside him, great tongue lolling out of his mouth.

"Don't you know you're not supposed to interrupt someone when they're praying, you arrogant—"

"You're right," he says, the grin-sneer sliding from his face. "Sorry."

He sits down beside me and the scent of apples fills the air around us. Apples and heated skin, clean and manly. I don't know what to say or how to feel about Aidan. He confuses me as much as his half-grin, half-sneer. Ailean flops on his side at Aidan's feet.

"Tara," he says, my name rolling of his tongue. "I am sorry, truly. Will ya forgive me?"

I look at him, see the sincerity shining in his blue eyes, and all the breath leaves my body. All I can do is nod my head.

We sit together, staring at the stone. I can hear him breathing, feel the heat from his arm warming my arm. I remember the way things used to be between us. So easy, like we were two peas sitting contentedly in a pod.

I look at him. "Aidan?"

"Yes."

"What did Mrs. McGregor mean when she said my aunt was away with the fairies?"

He smiles and for a second the intense, gruff man fades away and the warm, lighthearted boy is sitting beside me.

"Some people believe the voices of the dead can be heard at night laughing with the fairies. They fall silent a year after their death, when they move onto the next world."

"That's a lovely thought, isn't it? That our loved ones remain, unseen, laughing with the fairies. Do you think the dead stay behind for a while?"

Like the steady beat of timpani mallets on a kettle-drum, the sound of rolling thunder can be heard in the distance.

"Are you asking if I believe in ghosts, Tara?"

"Yes."

Something about his gaze changes. He is staring at me, but I have the strange feeling he doesn't see me.

"I think some souls stay behind because they feel they didn't finish what they were meant to do. Others stay to torture those who remain."

He has a haunted, faraway look in his eyes, a for-lorn, lost sort of look that makes me want to grab his hand and to pull him back to me. I consider telling him he sounds like an Emo girl, but I don't think it is the right moment to tease him.

"That's dark, Aidan."

"Is it?"

"Very."

"Death is dark, isn't it?" He shifts his gaze from my face to a place on the horizon where the dark sky is being fractured by bolts of lightning. "Death is the dark cloud that rolls across our skies and robs us of light. It is massively brutal, and, often, massively unfair."

I study his profile, the muscle working along his jaw-line, the way this light gives his beard a reddish cast, the jagged scar behind his ear, like a lightning bolt fracturing his smooth skin. In my mind, I see myself reaching out, tracing the puckered line with my fingertip, touching him in the easy, intimate way a woman might touch her lover.

A lover? The fairies must be playing tricks on me. "Aidan?"

"Mmm-hmm."

"Do you still believe in fairies?"

When we were children, Aidan told me the most fantastic stories about fairies, ancient fairies who lived in grand forts beneath the piles of stones found in the hills around Donegal, soldier fairies who fought a magnificent battle near Ulster, wicked fairies who snatch human babies and take their places here on earth.

He turns his strange, vacant gaze back, fixing it on me. I smile and wait for him to return from his distant place. It is like standing outside an empty house at night, staring at the darkened windows, wondering what lurks behind them, then someone lights a candle inside and the windows glow with life and warmth. Slowly, the darkness behind Aidan's gaze recedes and the warmth and spark of life in his sea blue eyes returns.

"If you're Irish, there's only one answer to that question," he says. "Besides, if Mrs. McGregor thought I stopped believing in the fey folk, she would knack me bollocks in. Why?"

"I was just wondering. You used to tell me the best fairy stories. I loved listening to your stories."

He smiles so softly, so sweetly, I almost forget he has grown into a massive snarling, tattooed beast of a man.

"Ya liked stories about selkies best."

"Selkie stories are the best," I say, laughing. "Remember how I used to look for selkie skins whenever we walked on the beach?"

"Yeah, yeah. I remember."

"Now that I think of it, most of your stories involved mythological creatures who would transform themselves into beautiful women so they could seduce men." I narrow my gaze on him. "A little pervy."

He laughs.

"Puberty can make a fella a wee bit pervy, can't it?"

My cheeks flush with heat. The world is one jacked-up, crazy-ass place, isn't it? A few weeks ago, I was standing in the moonlight with my childhood sweetheart, listening to him tell me he was marrying another woman and now I am sitting by a sacred stone, talking about pubescent desires with Aidan Gallagher.

"What are ya thinking?"

"I am wondering if any of your stories involve mythological creatures who transform themselves into mortal men so they can seduce women?"

He laughs.

"Now who's pervy?"

My cheeks flush with a new wave of heat. I look away, squinting at the distant charcoal smudged sky.

"Maybe we should go," I say. "It looks like a storm is coming this way."

"Nice try, *banph* . . . but you're not getting off that easy."

"What do you mean?"

"Ya asked me about the *gánconâgh,* didn't ya?"

I frown.

"*Gánconâgh* comes from the Gaelic word *gean-canagh,* which mean love talker," he says, his voice low. "He arrives just before a storm, appearing with a cloak of mist swirling around him. The birds stop singing and the cattle stop lowing as he roams through valleys and glens, looking for shepherdesses and milkmaids to seduce. When he finds a maiden, alone and unsuspecting, he whispers words of love in her ear, wooing her with his voice, until she yields her body and soul to him."

The air around us feels charged with unseen currents, as if our slightest movement will result in a skin-tingling jolt of static electricity.

"Why did ya want to know about the *gánconâgh*?"

Because I think you are one of the dark fairies you used to tell me about, a creature who has donned the visage of a mortal man in hopes of seducing a woman. You're certainly seducing me.

"It's starting to drizzle." I wipe a raindrop off my cheek. "If we don't hurry we are going to get wet."

A slow, naughty smile spreads across his face.

"You're not afraid to get a wee bit wet, are ya?"

I stand up quickly, but Aidan grabs my hand.

"Come on," he says, pulling me up the hill. "I know a place we can go until the storm passes."

Aidan leads me over the hill to a small stone cottage with painted shutters. The red paint is faded and chipped and a few of the windows are missing panes, but the thatched roof looks as if it was recently rethatched. The rain is coming down, steady and hard, when he batters his shoulder against the old wooden door. The wood creaks and the door swings open. We hurry inside. The inside is surprisingly tidy, with an uneven flagstone floor and a large fireplace.

"What is this place?" I ask, stomping my feet.

"A derelict shepherd's cottage."

"So, a shepherd used to live here?"

"Or a shepherdess," he says, winking.

My body begins to tingle again. I untie my sweater from around my waist and pull it over my head, shivering from the cold rain, but also eager to put another layer between me and the dark fairy.

Aidan shrugs out of his rucksack, unzips one of the compartments, and removes a thin green field blanket, rolled up tight. He sets his rucksack down on the ground and spreads the blanket out beside it, inviting me to sit. I sit on one corner of the blanket and fiddle with the strap of Mrs. McGregor's umbrella, suddenly shy.

Aidan pulls two dark bottles out of his rucksack and hands one of them to me. "Have a drink, we're going to be here awhile."

I take the bottle and look at the woman on the label, a beautiful woman with long red hair floating around her head, a tattered silver shroud hanging off one of her slender shoulders, and a scythe in her skeletal hand. Her mouth is open, as if she's about to scream.

"What is Ban . . ." I struggle with the strange word printed on the label.

"Bánánach Brew," Aidan says. "It's a craft cider."

"*Cider*? You filled your rucksack with hard cider?" I

laugh. "Silly me. I only brought a sweater and an umbrella on my hike."

I twist the cap off my bottle and take a sip. The flavor of crisp, tangy apples fills my mouth.

"Mmm, this is good."

"Ya like it, then?"

Aidan watches me carefully as I take another sip. I hold the cider in my mouth, on my tongue, before swallowing, so I can savor the flavors. The cider packs a tart, powerful punch, but then mellows, leaving a sweet, apple-y aftertaste.

"It's like taking a sip of expensive champagne and then biting into a candy apple. It's good," I say, looking at the label again. "Very good."

Aidan nods, the corners of his lips pulling up in a furtive smile, and then takes a sip of his cider.

"What is Bananck?"

"*Bánánach*," he says, pronouncing the word as if he is about to hock a mouthful of saliva. "It is a creature from Irish mythology, a female specter that haunts battlefields."

"Yikes! That's morbid."

Aidan doesn't respond. He leans back and studies the label. He's slipping away again, retreating to a place in his mind. I can feel it.

"Do you hike up here often?"

"What?" He blinks at me. "Hiking? I wasn't hiking."

"You weren't?" I say, pointing to his rucksack. "What were you doing then? Running away from home?"

"I was returning from home, actually."

I frown because the Gallagher cottage is located between the castle and the village, not up in these hills.

"I don't live with me aul fella anymore."

"Of course you don't," I say, embarrassed. "I don't

know why I assumed you would still be living with your father and sisters. I guess I froze you in my mind, where you have lived as a lanky, laughing eighteen-year-old boy."

"I'm not that fella."

"I know."

"But ya wish I was, because ya don't like Aidan Gallagher, the man."

"I don't know Aidan Gallagher, the man."

"What do ya want to know?"

Everything. Where have you been? Where do you go when you get the faraway look in your eyes? Why don't you laugh like you used to? Do you have a girlfriend? Did she break your heart? What is up with all of those tattoos?

"Did you miss me?" I say, smiling and batting my lashes at him.

"Of all of the questions ya could have asked me, that's the one that's been gnawing away at ya? Did I miss ya?"

I take another sip of my cider and feel emboldened. "Is that a yes?"

He rolls his eyes and takes a swig of his cider.

"Well? Is it?" I prompt.

"Yes."

My heart skips a silly beat. "Where do you live now?"

"I have a wee cottage on some land just over the next hill."

Go ahead. Ask him. Do you have a girlfriend? Just say it. Do you have a girlfriend?

"What does that tattoo mean?"

He frowns.

"Which tattoo?"

"The one over your heart."

"It says, *Buaidh nó Bás*. Victory or death. It's the Gallagher motto."

I set my cider bottle on the floor beside me and look at Aidan, reaching my hand out and gently touching the scar behind his ear with my fingertips.

"How did you get this scar?"

He stiffens. "Ya don't want to hear about that," he says, grabbing my hand and pushing it away from his head. "Believe me."

The unspoken subtext in his words: *Mind your own damn business, dahlin'.* Chastened, I do what any Southern woman does when she commits a social faux pas: I change the subject by making polite small talk.

"How is Catriona?"

"Grand," he says, relaxing. "Our Catriona is grand. She's in Galway on a Hen Weekend."

"Is she engaged?"

"Cat? Engaged?" He chuckles. "No, our Catriona is not engaged. Her best mate is getting married. She is probably on the tear, having a deadly time."

"How nice."

"She can't wait to see ya again."

"I can't wait to see her. It's been a long time."

I lean back on my elbows and look at the window, the beads of rain sliding down the broken panes of glass, the frames painted red, and feel as if I am in an episode of *Black Mirror*. Everything is the same—Ireland, Tásúildun, Aidan—and everything is different. Sitting in this abandoned cottage, listening to the wind howling through the stones, smelling the wet thatch over our heads, feeling the nervous excitement of being alone with Aidan, it's as if I never left Ireland, like my doppelgänger returned to America and lived my life these last ten years.

Aidan lays down beside me and puts his arms behind his head. "What are ya thinking?"

"I think someone cast a time spell on me." I look at the damp thatch of sandy blonde hair on top of his head, and I have a powerful urge to touch him again. "The Gullah believe time is a mystical thing that can be manipulated. They believe you can put a root on someone and it will freeze them at a certain point while the rest of the world continues on."

"Put a root?"

"A voodoo curse."

"A curse? Why?"

"It feels as if we have been here together forever, that time has continued around us, but we have stayed the same as we were when we were young . . . but I also feel as if I don't know you at all. I don't know myself anymore, either. Do you know what I mean?"

He turns his head, looking at me through his thick eyelashes, and my breath catches in my throat.

"I know what ya mean." He smiles. "The posh clothes, caked-up face, and fussy hair. I don't know ya, either."

"What?"

"Eat some chips and have a Guinness, will ya? You're too fecking thin."

I hear Grayson's voice in my head, *When's the last time you ate a Goo Cluster?*

Did I stand too close to one of B. Crav's polo ponies because my heart aches something fierce, like a thousand-pound thoroughbred just kicked me in the chest.

"Do you have any idea how hard I have worked to shed my pudgy, fudgy middle, how many boxes of Fiddle Faddle and cartons of Goo Goo Clusters I have had to forsake to fit into a size four . . . *ish*?" I am weeping like a televangelist caught in a sex scandal. "If I've learned one thing it's that no matter how damned hard you try; you're not going to please everyone."

He waits until I am done pitching my hissy fit and then reaches his arm out and pushes my elbow. I fall on my back beside him. He rolls over, props himself up on one elbow, and looks down at me.

"What are ya on about?" He brushes a lock of hair off my face. "You're beautiful, Tara. You've always been beautiful."

"You think?"

He smiles.

"I know it, as sure as I know me name is Aidan Pádraic Gallagher," he says, his voice low and tender.

I look up at him, losing myself in the depths of his blue, blue eyes, swimming back through time to when I was an innocent girl, holding my breath and hoping a handsome Irish fella would kiss me in a rowboat in the middle of a lough in Donegal.

Everything is different—and everything is the same.

He leans down and presses his lips to mine, a sweet, undemanding kiss that makes me forget about the years and differences between us.

I am just a girl and he is just an Irish fella.

An Irish fella with whiskers that tickle my cheeks and lips that taste like apples so sweet they make my teeth ache. That's the way I would describe what I am feeling: a deep kind of aching. I think I have been aching for a long time.

I close my eyes and let Aidan kiss me, and for a little while, I forget about the unfulfilled and unrealized dreams that have been gnawing away at me, paining me something fierce.

Chapter Sixteen

Text from Manderley Maxwell de Maloret:
I am sorry, darling, but I can't tell you what you should be doing with your life. Nobody can. It's one of those things you have to figure out for yourself. You will figure it out, Tara. You will figure it out and you will be a spectacular success, an awe-inspiring, breathtaking, beautiful success. You always are.

Text to Manderley Maxwell de Maloret:
Thank you, Mandy. I wish we were kids again. I can't believe I am saying this, but I actually miss the days of you telling me what to do. It was so much easier when you put your hands on your hips, looked at me over the tops of your glasses, and gave me what-for. I miss you, Little Miss Bossy Pants.

Text from Manderley Maxwell de Maloret:
I miss you, too.

Text from Emma Lee Maxwell:
Yay! I am so glad you traded in your sorry old Doc Martens for a pair of rain boots. I met a girl in the village and she said Hunter wellies have suffered prole drift.

Text to Emma Lee Maxwell:
What is prole drift?

Text from Emma Lee Maxwell:
A stupid term used by uppity Brits to describe when an upscale product becomes popular with the non-aristo classes. Like I care. If Hunter wellies were good enough for Princess Diana, they're good enough for us! Right?

Text from Emma Lee Maxwell:
Right?

A girl can only go on so many aimless hikes before she starts to question her purpose on this planet—even if she is taking those hikes while wearing shiny, new, prole drift Hunter wellies.

The weeks have melted away like ice cubes on hot asphalt and I haven't accomplished an apple-picking thing. I say *apple-picking,* because I am pretty sure one of my roommates has kept busy picking produce.

Aidan leaves the castle before sunrise and returns just before dinner, his rucksack heavy with squat apples with red-tinged, strawberry-flavored flesh, and dark-blue plums with yellow, spicy-flavored flesh. He delivers his bounty onto Mrs. McGregor, dumping the fruit into an ancient wooden trencher on the counter, and then climbs the narrow, twisting tower stairs to his room, returning freshly scrubbed and smelling of soap. Discovering why Aidan has developed an addiction to apples and apple products has become the riddle in my very own Nancy Drew mystery.

The Message in the Apples.

The Mystery in the Rucksack.

Sin, on the other hand, spends his days involved in more cerebral pursuits. He has claimed the Steward's Room as his own, transforming it into his office. In the old days, the steward would have been in charge of collecting rent from the tenants of the estate. The tenants offered their coins to the steward, who would deposit them through a slot on the top of his desk, where they would drop into a hidden, secured compartment. Sin cleared away the old leather bound ledgers and replaced them with dual computer monitors and stacks of black, three ring binders. He stays holed up in his makeshift office for most of the day, only venturing out for his afternoon tea. I am not sure when he sleeps—if he sleeps. Discovering how he is able to keep his body so fit and his skin so healthy with lack of apparent exercise or fresh air has become the riddle in my second Nancy Drew mystery.

Clue in the Steward's Room.

The Workaholic's Secret.

Mystery at Tásúildun Castle.

Actually, *The Ridiculous Wonderings of an Aimless Woman* would be a better title for the story of how I spend my time.

This morning is going to be different, though. This morning, I am not going to stay in bed binge watching *Cooked* on my Netflix app and puzzling over the riddle that is Aidan Gallagher. This morning, I am going to stop being the Girl Detective and start being Woman Determined (to find her purpose).

Showered and dressed, I am ready to boldly go where very few have gone before: Mrs. McGregor's kitchen. I've had this little caterpillar of an idea wriggling around inside me and I want to give it some room, see if it will develop into a big, beautiful butterfly. The idea came to me yesterday while I was sunning myself on the boulder beside the prayer stone. It was unusually warm so I took my boots off and stretched out on the rock, my bare feet dangling off the side. The sun on my face, the sound of the distant surf like white noise in my ears, lured me to that place between consciousness and sleep, where ideas pass through your brain unfiltered. I was just about to drift off to sleep when an overactive neuron in my brain fired off a memory of the article I had read about the women who gave up their jobs to start lucrative food-based businesses.

The hairdresser and her cheesecakes.

How does a hairdresser with no culinary experience become the president of a million-dollar gourmet cheese-cake company?

People love my cheesecake.

Goats. She used cream cheese made from goat's milk. Big whoopee pie. I could make a cheesecake using goat's milk cheese.

Man, this sun feels good on my face.

Did I remember to put on my moisturizer with SPF this morning? I hope so or else my face is going to be one giant freckle. Aunt Pattycake used to have a German shorthaired pointer with freckles all over his face. She called him Herr Sommersprossen, which she said meant Mister Freckles in German. He would do tricks for Cheetos. A dog that ate Cheetos. Funny . . .

. . . almost as funny as a hairdresser making goat cheese cheesecakes.

I should start selling cheesecakes. I'll bet there are loads of people in Donegal hankering for cheesecake, especially one made by a trained American pastry chef. Cheesecake made with Bailey's Irish Cream.

Ooo, I know! I could make glazed plum cheesecake using those fat, juicy plums Aidan brings home each night. I could pair the plum cake with a strong ginger tea or a delicately flavored citrus tea. I could turn the old stables into a tea room and serve—

And that's when my little wriggling caterpillar was born, while I was sunning myself on a boulder high in the hills over Tásúildun.

Mrs. McGregor is standing at the island, scrubbing a copper pot with a paste of salt and white wine vinegar, when I walk into the kitchen.

"Good Morning, Mrs. McGregor."

"Good Morning, luv," she says, smiling. "Be sure to take the brolly with ya. The clouds over the hills are trying to rain."

"I'm not taking a hike today." I grab one of the tarnished copper pots and a handful of Mrs. McGregor's paste. "If you don't mind me lollygagging around the kitchen, I thought I would do some baking."

"Of course I don't mind."

I finish scrubbing the copper saucepot and then carry it over to the sink, rinse it under the faucet, and dry it with a soft cloth until it gleams.

"Mrs. McGregor?" I place the saucepot back on its shelf. "What happened to all of those old cookbooks that used to be in the butler's pantry?"

"They're still there. Why?"

Mrs. McGregor stands quietly while I tell her about my burgeoning butterfly of an idea. I tell her about the plum cheesecakes and apple pies I want to bake, the pots of ginger tea, the cozy and inviting tea room that will beckon travelers from all over Donegal.

"What do you think?" I ask. "Don't worry. I won't pitch a hissy fit if you say you think it sounds like a completely harebrained idea."

I mean what I said. I won't pitch a hissy fit if Mrs. McGregor laughs at my idea. I am talking about creating a lucrative commercial venture even though I have no experience developing, implanting, or operating a business. It sounds as half-cocked as . . . Emma Lee saying she wants to be a marriage broker without ever having had a serious committed relationship.

"I t'ink it sounds like a grand idea. Sure, a grand idea," she says, reaching for a new pot to scrub. "And don't ya worry, luv. I would tell ya if I thought it sounded like biscuits to a bear."

Biscuits to a bear has been one of Mrs. McGregor's favorite phrases for as long as I can remember. It means *a waste of time*.

"Thank you, Mrs. McGregor." I hurry around the counter and throw my arms around her. "You're better than butter. You know that, don't you?"

"Go on with ya," she laughs, waving her salt covered hands at me. "Go fetch your cookbooks and I will pour ya a cuppa."

I hurry down the hall, energized by Mrs. McGregor's enthusiasm. Instead of heading to the pantry, though, I head to the Steward's Room and press my ear against the closed door. Sin is speaking Japanese.

Sin speaks Japanese?

Sweet Gary Stu! Is there nothing this man can't do? Manderley taught me about Mary Sues and Gary Stus, seemingly perfect characters in novels, when we were reading a bestseller about a centerfold model/helicopter pilot/covert agent who disarmed an explosive device with a hairpin after hacking into the Pentagon's computers to stop a Chinese-fired nuclear weapon from obliterating London—while wearing six-inch heels! Sin, with his model good looks, financial acumen, and multi-linguistic abilities, is proving to be a Gary Stu.

Sin switches to English and says goodbye to the person on the other end of his line. I wait a few seconds before knocking on the door.

"Yes," he says. "Come in Mrs. McGregor."

I open the door.

"Actually, it's me," I say, peeking around the door.

"Good Morning, Tara." He smiles, pulls his ear piece out of his ear, and tosses it on the desk. "This is a lovely surprise."

"Good Morning, Sin," I say, trying not to look directly into his model/business wizard/linguist beautiful eyes. "I was wondering if I might beg, borrow, or steal a few office supplies."

"Of course," he says. "What do you need?"

"A pad of paper, pen, highlighter, and some of those little colored sticky things you use to mark a passage in a book."

"Flags?"

"Yes, Sir!" I laugh. "Flags."

He opens a desk drawer and pulls out a new yellow legal pad, pens, highlighters, and flags.

"Here you are," he says, handing me the supplies. "Good luck with the novel."

I stare blankly.

"Cookbook?" He says, trying again. "New recipe? Epic tic-tac-toe battle with Mrs. McGregor?"

I laugh.

"Close," I say, taking the supplies. "I am working on a potential new venture that could help raise the money to keep Tásúildun in the black."

"Bloody intriguing." His phone rings and he smiles apologetically. "Sorry, but I have to get this."

"No worries." I turn to leave. "Thanks for the supplies."

"Wait," he says, putting his hand on the door. "If you're free, would you like to go to dinner with me tomorrow night? I would love to hear all about your new venture."

If I am free? Hmmm. You mean, if I am not cuddling up with a box of Mrs. McGregor's Butter Cookies or listening for Lady Margaret's rasping death rattle?

"I would love to go to dinner with you."

"Capital." He grabs his earpiece off the desk and pushes it back into his ear. "Cheers."

And just like that Sin goes back to looking gorgeous and rescuing the world's ailing businesses (in multiple languages).

I walk back down the hall, grab a stack of cookbooks from the pantry, and carry everything back to the kitchen table. Mrs. McGregor has set some logs to fire in the fireplace and arranged a lovely tea tray on the table.

The book at the top of the stack is *Mrs. Beeton's Every Day Cookery*. I flip through the foxed pages, working around the discolored spots to read various tips on how to run a proper Victorian household. I set it aside and open a brown leather book with faded blue print. *Commonsense Cookery* by Colonel Kenney Herbert proves to be an entertaining gastronomic read, offering examples of elaborate dinner menus and concise recipes for complex dishes, like pickled beef tongue and mutton saag.

Some of the books offer advice unrelated to cooking. For instance, in one book I learn that putting an eel in a bottle of whiskey and drinking from it will "cure frequent and prodigious inebriation."

In *The Lady's Handbook and Household Assistant*, circa 1886, I find notes scrawled in the margins by a Mrs. Mairead E. Cumiskey. Some of them humorous. Some of them emphatic. Some of them inexplicable.

"Mrs. McGregor?"

"What is it, luv?"

"What is a tallywag?"

Finished polishing the copper pots and pans, she pours herself a cup of tea and joins me at the table.

"Is it listed as an ingredient in one of those old cookbooks?"

"No, ma'am," I say, sliding the book over to her. "Someone named Mrs. Cumiskey wrote in the margin beside a recipe for oxtail soup, 'Tougher than tallywags.'"

"I believe a tallywag is an Atlantic sea bass."

"Sea bass? What does a fish have to do with oxtail soup?"

"Why don't ya giggle it?"

"Giggle?"

"Search for the answer on the inter-webs."

"Oh," I say, laughing. "You mean Google."

I grab my iPhone and google tallywag.

Mrs. McGregor was right. A tallywag is an Atlantic sea bass—but it is also Victorian slang for testicles! *Mrs. Cumiskey! You naughty girl.*

"You were right," I say, quickly putting my phone down. "It's a sea bass."

Mrs. McGregor sips her tea and flips through yesterday's *Irish Times*, while I finish perusing the cookbooks.

In the slender, red leather bound *Breakfast, Luncheon, and Tea*, I find another handwritten note from Mrs. Mairead E. Cumiskey, this one a recipe for potato and Irish cheddar rolls to be served with stew to be served with *neck oil* (beer). I imagine a bitter winter day, the potato rolls fresh out of the oven, served on a pretty hand painted platter with pats of Irish butter.

In the last book I find a yellowed sheet of paper stuck between the pages. It is a hastily written recipe for Barmbrack, a traditional Irish fruitcake made with dried sultanas and raisins that have been soaked overnight in spiced whiskey.

I know Barmbrack is the first recipe I want to try. I will dry Aidan's apples and plums in the oven and then soak them in Bushmills whiskey overnight. Tomorrow morning, I will make my first loaves of Barmbrack.

I carry the books back to the pantry and return to review my copious notes. I can't remember the last time I felt so motivated and creatively inspired! In just a few hours I have collected over a dozen new recipes, learned Victorian food preservation techniques, and added tallywag to my repertoire of testicular slang.

Mrs. McGregor folds her paper and stands up.

"I will leave you to it, then, luv," she says, carrying our empty teacups to the sink. "I have a dental appointment in Dungloe at half-two. If ya give me that list, I'll

stop at the market on my way back and pick up everything ya need."

"Thank you."

I rip the page with my grocery list off the legal pad
and hand it to her.

"Do you need a ride? I would be happy to take you
in Aunt Patricia's Rover."

"Have ya driven in Ireland, then?"

"Never."

"Thanks a million, luv, but I'll take me chances with
old Mrs. O'Kelly. She's got cataracts and she's deaf as
a broomstick, but she knows how to manage these
Donegal roads."

How old is Mrs. O'Kelly, I wonder? If Mrs. Mc-
Gregor is calling the woman old, she must be positively Jurassic.

"You're sure?"

"Stop fretting and start baking."

Mrs. McGregor grabs her handbag and sweater off
the hook behind the door, gives me a cheery wave, and
is about to leave when I remember something I forgot
to add to my grocery list.

"Mrs. McGregor, wait!"

She turns around.

"Would you please add bottles of cider to the list?"

"How many bottles did ya need?"

"Three or four."

"Did ya want Bulmers, then?"

"No," I say. "I would like a craft cider. I believe it is
made locally. Bánánach Brew. Have you heard of it?"

An intriguing, enigmatic Mona Lisa smile stretches
across her face. "Of course I've heard of it."

"Great," I say, smiling.

"But ya can't buy it at the SuperValu."

"Oh."

"Aidan left a few bottles in the fridge." She walks back to the table, picks up a pen, and jots something down on the legal pad. "The brewery isn't too far from the castle. I drew a map in case ya want to go there and get more cider."

Outside, Mrs. O'Kelly honks her horn. Mrs. McGregor waves again and hurries out the door, leaving me with one more Nancy Drew mystery to solve: the reason for her strange, secretive smile when I asked if she had heard of Bánánach Brew.

Chapter Seventeen

Is drinking two bottles of hard cider alone in the middle of the afternoon the sign of a drinking problem? Have I traded my comfort eating for comfort drinking?

After Mrs. McGregor left, I diced the plums and apples for the Barmbrack and put them in the oven on a low temperature to dry. I got to thinking about desserts I could bake that would be referential to traditional Irish recipes, but original enough to make them my own, and I came up with the idea of making a Bánánach Brew inspired cookie. I opened a bottle of cider just as a reference, but the tart apple aroma seduced me, and before I knew it, I was sitting on the counter, eating a ham sandwich, and drinking straight from the bottle.

No chilled glass.

Not even a straw.

Just straight from the bottle.

In the middle of the day!

I feel like a sinner in Sunday school.

I am now sipping my second bottle of cider while

waiting for the first batch of Bánánach Brew cookies to finish baking in the oven. The logs are still crackling and hissing in the fireplace. The air in the kitchen is perfumed with the comforting, homey scents of burning wood, cinnamon, ginger, and apples. Raindrops patter against the windows in a steady, soothing rhythm.

When the timer goes off, I walk over to the oven, stick my hands in a pair of mitts, and open the oven door. A blast of hot, spicy air hits my face, reminding me of summers in Austin, stepping out of the culinary institute into the scorching Texas heat.

I carry the cookie sheet to the counter, inhaling the aroma with a critical, assessing nose. Too much cinnamon, not enough apple. My Bánánach Brew cookie recipe will need to be reworked. I know this even before I break one in half and pop it in my mouth.

The consistency is good, soft, sweet middle with crunchy, slightly salty edges, but the flavor is too weak. The cookies just don't pack the same tart punch as the cider. These would be perfectly fine cookies to serve at a church social or an afternoon tea for the Charleston Junior Woman's Club, but I wasn't aiming for *my, how nice* mediocre. I don't want to bake plain, mealy-mouth cookies, the sort of cookies Melanie Hamilton would have served at Twelve Oaks. I want to bake the sort of cookies Scarlett O'Hara would have served to Rhett if he were to visit her in her bedroom, sassy, seductive cookies that leave you wanting more even though you know they are just plain bad for you.

So, I open another bottle of cider *(Why yes, that does make three and, yes, ma'am, I know I am a shameless sinner.)* and begin again. With the first batch, I shredded fresh apples and used standard flour, white sugar, and apple pie spices. This time, I use fresh and dried apples, an oat and flour mixture, a dash of cinnamon and ginger, and apple sugar, which I made by pulverizing dried apple peels with sugar in a spice grinder. I tip in some cider and a splash of Longueville House Irish Apple Brandy.

While the cookies are baking, I make more apple sugar using the dried apple peels and a combination of muscovado and demerara sugars. I sprinkle the dark apple sugar on top of the cookies a few minutes before I take them out of the oven and the result is spectacular, soft golden brown cookies with a dark, crunchy topping. Best of all, I can taste the cider in this batch. Tart apples, punchy alcohol.

I am so excited! I want to share my Bánánach Brew Bites with Aidan. After all, he inspired my creation, with his bottles of craft cider hidden away in his rucksack. I would take him a plate of cookies if I knew where he disappeared to each day.

I grab my iPhone and snap a picture of my failed first batch of Bánánach Brew Bites beside the second, seriously successful batch and upload the picture to my new Instagram account, @WhiskfulThinking.

> My first batch of Irish Hard Cider inspired cookies didn't make my mouth water, so I tried again and—voila—apple cookies to drool over. Just goes to show, when it comes to baking, you shouldn't be afraid to take whisks. #instafood #pubcrawl #foodpuns

Chapter Eighteen

Sin strolls into the kitchen the next morning as I am mixing whiskey-soaked fruit into Barmbrack batter. He sniffs the air and presses a hand to his flat abdomen.

"What smells so good?" He looks around the kitchen. "Has Mrs. McGregor made more of her gingerbread?"

I tuck an errant hair into the bun at the back of my neck and grin. "Mrs. McGregor has abandoned the laboratory. There's a new scientist in the mix and she's madder than Victor Frankenstein. Beware!"

Sin laughs.

"Mad, perhaps, but you are no Victor Frankenstein," he says, leaning against the counter. "That is, unless old Victor was utterly charming and beautiful."

"Flatterer."

"Guilty."

He watches me fold more whiskey-soaked apples and raisins into the batter, his lips curved in a dangerous, flirty smile. *Lawd! I feel naked. Nekked as a jay bird walking from one end of the prison to the other.* I self-consciously run a hand over my apron, wishing I had dressed in something more sophisticated than boots, black leggings, and a soft denim shirt with the sleeves rolled up. Sin reaches over and brushes my cheek with his finger.

"You have flour on your face."

"Th . . . thank you."

Why, why does this man make me jumpier than a nun in a sex shop? Why can't I just relax and be myself around him? Why is he staring at my lips? Do I have something stuck in my teeth? Please, sweet baby Jesus, tell me I don't have a raisin stuck in my teeth. So I had one little whiskey-soaked raisin . . .

"Will you let me have a little taste?"

"Excuse me?"

"Your biscuits. I would like to try your biscuits."

He's talking about my cookies, right? The cookies I just took out of the oven, not my lady bits. He's not asking to put his *tallywag* near my . . . *hoo-hah*.

"Of course." I stop mixing my batter, grab a spatula, and scoop three cookies onto a small plate. "I hope you like them."

"I'm sure I will."

His phone begins vibrating in his pocket and a wicked little voice in my head whispers, *"Is that your phone or are you just happy to have my biscuits in your hand?"* His phone vibrates again and it takes all of my self-control not to look down at his bulging, pulsating pocket.

He pulls his phone out and looks at the screen.

"I better get this."

"Absolutely."

"See you tonight, six thirty?"

"Sure. Yes. Six thirty."

He strides out of the kitchen, the plate of cookies in one hand, his vibrating phone in the other. A second later, I hear him say, *"Ohayou gozaimasu."*

I feel a pang of disappointment—not because Sin has gone, but because I had hoped it would be Aidan strolling through the door, pressing his hand to his stomach and sniffing the air appreciatively. I didn't see him yesterday, even though I waited up to give him some of my cookies. I heard him moving about his room early this morning, but he was gone before I got up.

The cakey, fruity Barmbrack is cooling on the counter and I am pulling another batch of Bánánach Brew Bites out of the oven when someone knocks on the back door. I slide the cookies off the baking sheet and onto a wire rack on the counter to cool, before answering the door.

I expect a deliveryman or a curious tourist to be standing on the step, but it's a beautiful, leggy blonde with a long fishtail braid hanging over her slender, sweater-clad shoulder. She has sparkling blue eyes the same shade and shape as . . .

"Catriona Gallagher!"

"Tara Maxwell, as I live and breathe," she says, in a lilting Irish accent. "Will ya be givin' me a hug, then, or are ya too important for the Gallaghers now that you're Lady Tásúildun?"

"We don't do hugs, but we will permit a single, chaste kiss pressed to the back of the royal appendage," I laugh, holding out my flour-dusted hand.

"La-dee-da! I'll tell ya what to do with that bloody appendage, Tara Maxwell."

We fall into each other's arms, giggling and squealing like two schoolgirls, the time and distance that separated us for the last ten years instantly vanishing.

In the kitchen, we sit at the table beside the fire, a

fresh pot of tea and plate of cookies between us, filling each other in on the important details of our lives, peppering each other with questions.

Catriona, I learn, handles public relations and events planning for a luxurious castle hotel and spa down the coast. She lives in a cottage just outside the village with her boyfriend—despite her Catholic granny's frequent, embarrassing protests—and has no plans to get married.

"What about ya? Do ya have a fella pining away for ya back in the States?"

"No."

"What do you think of our Aidan?"

"What do you mean?"

"Ya know what I mean, ya divvy cow." She takes a cookie from the plate. "Do ya still fancy me brother or not?"

I think about Aidan, bare-chested and covered in tats, muscles bulging as he exercises, and my cheeks flush with heat.

Catriona laughs. "Ya do!"

"I don't fancy Aidan."

"Ya don't? Me bollocks!" She takes a bite of her cookie. "Ya fancy our Aidan, ya do. I'd wager he still fancies ya something chronic, too."

"Go on with ya, Catriona Gallagher," I say, waving my hands in a spot-on imitation of Mrs. McGregor. "Himself hardly knows I exist."

"Hardly." She rolls her eyes. "He hardly knows you exist." She finishes her cookie and takes another off the plate, breaking it in half and dipping it into her tea. "Did ya be making these biscuits, Tara?"

"Yes," I say, smiling. "Do you like them?"

"Like them? I fecking love them." She finishes the

other half of her cookie and wipes her mouth with her napkin. "Are they an American recipe? What do ya call them?"

"They're my creation. I call them Bánánach Brew Bites."

Catriona covers her mouth with her napkin and looks at me through wide, unblinking eyes.

"Bánánach Brew Bites?"

"Yes," I say, confused by her strange reaction. "Bánánach Brew, after the locally made craft cider. Have you heard of it?"

"I have." She lowers her napkin, revealing a toothy grin. "It's not very well known, that cider. How did ya come to hear about it?"

"Aidan gave me a bottle the other day."

"Our Aidan gave ya a bottle of Bánánach Brew? Did he now?"

She chuckles.

I feel like I missed the punchline of a joke.

I tell Catriona about running into her brother when I was hiking in the hills, the sudden rainstorm, the abandoned cottage, and his rucksack filled with apples and cider.

"Did our Aidan tell ya how he came to have the cider?"

"No."

She presses her lips together as if she is trying not to laugh. "Did ya use the cider in the biscuit dough?"

"Yes."

"This is gas!" She laughs and claps her hands. "Does our Aidan know about the biscuits?"

"No," I say. "He got home late last night and was gone before I got up this morning. I wanted to take him a tin, but I don't know where he works."

"Grand idea, that one. Take yer man some of these biscuits." She drops her folded napkin on top of her empty plate and stands. "Let's go."

"You'll drive me?"

"I will indeed, Tara Maxwell. In fact, there's nothing I would rather do."

I find two tins in the pantry and fill them with the freshly baked cider cookies, untie my apron, grab my jacket off the hook behind the door, and follow Catriona down the gravel drive to where her car is parked. We climb inside. Catriona turns the key in the ignition and we are off, flying down the drive in a spray of gravel.

"Where does Aidan work?"

"It's not too far from here." She turns left out of the drive onto the road leading north. "I saw Rhys Burroughes in the village a few days ago. I hardly recognized him. I can't believe the little boss-eyed fella with the thick Harry Potter glasses and wheezy breath has grown up to be . . . If I wasn't in love with Cillian I could have a glad eye on Rhys."

"He's certainly changed."

"Do ya fancy him, then?" She looks over at me. "More than our Aidan?"

"No!" My cheeks flush with heat again. I look out the window. "I mean; I don't fancy either of them."

Catriona laughs. "Ya might want to tell that to your face then, because it is saying something different. Ya know what I think?"

"Lawd help me! Do I really want to know the answer to that question?"

"Aidan hasn't been himself since he returned from Afghanistan."

"Afghanistan?"

"Our Aidan did two tours over there."

"Was he wounded? I noticed the scar behind his ear."

"Yes."

"That explains it."

"Explains what?"

"He seems different, more intense. The Aidan Gallagher I remember loved the craic."

"What has Aidan told you?"

"Nothing. Why?"

She draws a breath, sucking the air between her teeth so it makes a whistling noise. "It's not my place to tell me brother's tales. He'll tell ya, when he is ready." She turns off the road onto a dirt track lined with fruit trees. "Until then, try not to take his moods personally. Our Aidan is haunted by ghosts he can't exorcise."

I think of that day in the cottage, when I asked Aidan if he believed in ghosts, the sad, faraway look in his eyes, and my heart aches. I don't know what happened to Aidan in Afghanistan—I'm not sure I want to know—but it must have been dreadful to have made such a profound impact on him. How strange. I've listened to the news reports about the problems in the Middle East, watched footage of soldiers fighting insurgents in places like Kandahar, Kabul, and Mazar-i-Sharif, but they always seemed like scenes from a gritty movie. Flickering scenes that shock, sadden, then fade away. In my mind, I put Aidan in one of those scenes. I see him crouching behind a crumbling mud wall, bullets whizzing over his head, and I feel sick, even a little panicked.

We have reached the end of the dirt track. Two stone barns lie straight ahead, separated by an asphalt parking lot. Ailean, Aidan's great beast of a dog, is stretched out in a patch of grass between the two buildings, sound asleep despite the pervasive, drizzly rain.

"Here we are," Catriona says, parking beside the first barn. "Are ya ready?"

"For what?"

"We have come to see your man, remember?"

"Aidan is not my man. Stop calling him that!"

She looks over at me, grinning. "Ah, but he will be, to be sure. And if I am wrong, I will eat an entire tin of those biscuits."

I roll my eyes.

We climb out of the car and walk toward the barn. A heavy wooden door opens and a man in orange coveralls steps out.

"Catriona! Didn't expect to see ya here today."

"Hiya Billy," Catriona says. "This is my friend, Tara. She's brought a little something for Aidan. Is he inside or is he acting the maggot in the ring?"

"Johnny is putting him through the paces."

Catriona shakes her head. "*Bowsie eejit.*"

"You know the way."

"Ta Billy."

Billy smiles at me.

"Pleased to meet ya, Tara."

"Nice to meet you, Billy."

Catriona links her arm through mine and we walk in the drizzling rain to the second barn, a big, beautiful modern building designed to look like an old, traditional Irish barn, with arched doors painted glossy red and steep slate roof.

"So Aidan works on a farm?"

"Mmmm," Catriona murmurs.

Aidan. A farmer. He always said he wouldn't be like his father, toiling over a patch of earth to eke out a humble existence. Now, there isn't anything wrong with being a farmer. After all, my six times great-grandfather started Black Ash Plantation with only a handful of rice seeds. It's just, well, I always imagined Aidan working as a deep-sea fisherman, police sniper, Coast Guard rescue swimmer, or covert operative. An adventurous, testosterone-heavy job. I look at the rolling countryside, hear the wind rustling the leaves of the apple trees, and I think I get it. After surviving two tours to the war-torn Middle East, Aidan's soul probably craves the peace and quiet of the country. Solace and the softer things in life. That's what he's after.

Chapter Nineteen

"Ready?"

We are standing at the entrance to the first barn. Catriona's hand is on the door pull.

Ready? For what? Pitchforks and bales of hay?

"Sure."

Catriona opens the door and we walk inside. I was expecting a dimly lit, musty barn, littered with tractor parts and farming tools. I was *not* expecting a bright, airy gymnasium, with weight benches, barbells, and cardio equipment. A massive circular playpen stands in the middle of the barn—or is it a trampoline enclosed by a chain-link fence? I can't tell. Aidan is inside the pen, shirtless, sweaty, and barefoot. He is wearing headgear and boxing gloves and facing an opponent double his weight, an ox of a man with a big head and no neck. They are circling around each other, warily. The ox lumbers forward, throwing a punch that lands on Aidan's cheek like a battering ram. Aidan's head swivels violently to the right. I hold my breath and wait for him to hit the mat, but the punch doesn't knock him out. It doesn't even bring him to his knees.

Suddenly, Aiden charges at the ox. Crouching low, fists moving with stunning, blurring speed, he pummels his opponent's ribs again and again. The ox is driven back, back, his meaty body pressing against chain-link fence. My heart is thudding fast, as fast as Aidan's punches. Thud-thud, thud-thud. Then, just as fast, inexplicably, Aiden stops punching and moves back.

"He had him. Why did he stop?"

"It isn't sporting to pin a fella."

Even though there is a lot of mat between them, the ox throws a double jab and lands them both.

"Get out of his strike zone, ya fecking eejit!" Catriona yells at Aidan. "Avoid the clinch!"

The ox jabs, slides right, jabs, slides right. Aidan moves with his opponent, even though each jab is landing.

"Jaysus," Catriona mutters.

It's a terrible, perverse thing to watch, Aidan following his opponent around, taking brutal blows, blows that would make most men claw their way across the mat and hurl themselves over the fence to get out of the cage.

Catriona cups her hands around her mouth.

"Stop chasing him. Make him come to you."

Aidan moves in close, sweeps his left leg out, and knocks the ox off his feet.

I have never enjoyed boxing. It's too bloody, too barbaric. This doesn't look like boxing, though. It's faster, less structure, like something you would see if two highly trained fighters got into a bar brawl. They're on the ground, grappling like wrestlers.

"They're on the ground. I didn't think that was allowed in boxing."

"This isn't boxing, Tara; it's MMA."

"MMA?"

"Mixed Martial Arts," she says, her gaze fixed on the men in the cage. "It's a mixture of martial arts and hand-to-hand combat. It's fecking brutal and our Aidan is savage, he is."

The men are up again, jabbing and weaving, jabbing and weaving. Some blows glance or miss completely, but most land with bone-jarring force. My chest aches from holding my breath each time the ox throws a punch.

"I can't watch anymore," I say, turning away.

"Don't ya be worrying about our Aidan, Tara. He comes from a long line of warriors who fought for Ireland, scrappers who fought for freedom."

I take a peek back at the men exchanging blows in the cage and a wave of nausea rises in my throat.

"I can't," I say, turning to leave. "I am sorry, but I can't stand here and watch Aiden get hurt. I'll wait outside."

"Suit yourself," she says. "But ya might want to wait in the other barn, out of the rain."

I leave without looking back. Ailean is waiting outside, his grizzled coat beaded with raindrops, his long, mop of a tail sweeping back and forth over the wet asphalt. I open one of the tins and take out a cookie, holding it on the flat of my hand in offering to the beast, half-expecting him to bite off a finger. He nudges my hand with his nose and then gently, ever so gently, takes the cookie, his whiskers tickling my skin.

I put the lid back on the tin and walk to the other

barn. Ailean trots close behind me, my shaggy shadow.
I open the door and step inside. Ailean sits like a sentry
just outside the door, his stony gaze fixed straight
ahead. I motion for him to follow, but he doesn't budge
or blink a feathery gray lash.

"Stoic and stubborn," I say, petting the damp fur on
his head. "Just like his master."

This barn isn't filled with exercise equipment. This
barn is a factory, with large steel tanks and wooden
shelves filled with oak barrels. The steel tanks are the
same type I saw when I went on the Austin Brewery
Tour with some of my fellow students from the culinary institute. Fermentation tanks for aging ingredients
that will eventually turn into an alcoholic beverage—
like Irish hard cider.

Bánánach Brew.

No wonder Aidan always has apples and bottles of
cider in his rucksack. He works in a cider-making factory.

Orange lines painted on the ground form a path. I
follow the lines, like Dorothy on the Yellow Brick
Road, until I arrive at a tasting area, with a long refec-
tory table and stools fashioned from old oak barrels.
An iron sign hangs over the table, suspended from the
ceiling by chains.

BÁNÁNACH BREW
AIDAN GALLAGHER, PROPRIETOR
FOUNDED 2016

Aidan is the owner of a cider mill? And a Mixed
Martial Arts fighter? Here I thought he was a farm
hand, picking apples, and seeking solace in the hills of
Donegal. I thought I had him all figured out, but now I

realize I don't know him at all. At some point, Aidan Gallagher went from being a person I knew very well to a person I used to know. It makes sense, but it also makes me sad.

I don't know why I am so surprised to discover he has changed, grown up and away from me. So many life-shaping events occur between the ages of eighteen and twenty-eight. High school graduation, leaving home, going off to college, making new friends, first love, second love, college graduation, first job, complete financial independence.

In Aidan's case, he left home to join the military. I can't imagine the experiences he had while he was a soldier, the character building and defining experiences that transformed him from an easygoing, craic-seeking boy into this . . . this intense stranger. Something happened. Something powerful and, most likely, tragic.

Waves of sadness and longing wash over me, building, crashing, pushing me down, down, until I feel as if I am drowning in grief. Why do things have to change, without warning or consideration? I thought my daddy would live a long life and Black Ash would remain in our family for generations to come. I thought Aunt Patricia would live to see my children running around Tásúildun. I thought I would always live close to my sisters, and we would walk into each other's houses without knocking, and gather for Sunday dinner. I thought Aidan . . .

If I am being perfectly honest, I thought about Aidan a lot through the years. Not just when Grayson and I were on a break, either. It sounds cliché, but I always thought of Aidan as the one that got away. He was the boy who made me laugh, made me sigh, but never, not once, made me cry. When Grayson worked my last nerve with his severely right-leaning political views, I would think of Aidan and remember how we would sit on the beach below Tásúildun and talk about anything, about everything, until the moon reflected on the ocean. Aidan was the best companion because he didn't just talk, he listened, he really listened.

Lawd Jesus, how he used to make me laugh!

What happened to that boy? Where did he go? Is he lost to me forever, like Daddy and Aunt Patricia?

Sure, I am sad for myself, for all of the people I have lost, but I am sad for Aidan, too. I saw the look on his face when he talked about his ghosts, the weary, haunted expression in his eyes, as if he was carrying a terribly heavy burden.

People exorcise their ghosts, their grief and guilt, in different ways. Some turn to the bottle, some turn to the Lord, and some turn to baking. I think Aidan turns to fighting. I think he climbs into a cage and risks grave bodily injury as a way to exorcise his ghosts.

I don't know much about PTSD or traumatic brain injury—only what I have gleaned from television news soundbites—but the little I do know has me mighty concerned for Aidan. He has a scar behind his ear that looks like a war wound. Catriona said he returned from Afghanistan a changed man, moody, intense, less so-cial. I know he suffers from insomnia because I hear him moving about the old school room. Then there's the Mixed Martial Arts, an extremely dangerous sport. Isn't self-destructive behavior another of the signs of PTSD?

A thick, salty lump has formed in my throat. Poor Aidan. I just want to hug him up, hug him something fierce.

I am sitting beneath the sign, sniffling like an over-wrought fool, when Aidan arrives. He's put on a pair of shoes and has a towel draped over his head and shoulders like a hood. He looks at my cheeks, wet with tears, and his brows knit together, his lips pull down in a frown.

"I suppose ya don't approve of fighting?" he snaps.

His face is hard, his eyes angry, defensive, as if he's still in the cage and I am his opponent. My daddy always said the best way to pierce a calloused heart isn't with a sharp gesture, but a soft word.

"I couldn't stand there watching while some ox pummeled you senseless," I confess. "It made me sick. What if you had been seriously hurt? What if he had killed you? I don't want to think about . . ."

. . . *what it would be like to live at Tásúildun, to climb the hills we climbed as children, knowing I would never see you again.*

"What don't ya want to think about?"

I can't tell him what I was thinking. We just aren't that close anymore—not deep-feelings-and-secrets close.

"I don't want to think about losing another person I care about."

He pushes the towel off his head and sits down beside me, putting his legs on either side of mine so I am trapped, forced to look at him. His blue, blue eyes. The sprinkling of freckles across his nose and cheeks, faintly visible beneath his fading tan. His bare chest.

"Ya care about me?" he asks, his voice gravelly.

"I've always cared about you, Aidan Gallagher."

"Ya didn't answer my letters."

"What letters?"

"I wrote to you when I joined the military."

"I never got any letters. I swear."

We look into each other's eyes—searching for answers to questions we aren't ready to ask. I want to
know what he said in those letters and how he really
felt about me that summer, because I went home thinking our kisses meant little to him. He was an outra-
geous flirt, a scandalous charmer with a long line of
sighing, lovesick girls trailing behind him wherever he
went, and I was a naïve skinny girl with a massive fat-
girl complex who found it difficult to believe any boy
could love her, truly, forever and ever, Amen love
(*Thank you, Grayson On-Again, Off-Again Calhoun*).

"Ya could have written to me." He presses his bare
knees against my legs. "Why didn't ya?"

I want to tell him I didn't write to him because I was
terrified he wouldn't answer and his rejection would
have been too bitter a pill to swallow. I left Ireland
with memories of my perfect summer romance with a
boy who seemed to like me, really like me. I cherished
those memories. What if I had written to him and he
ignored my letters? Or, worse, wrote back to tell me I
had misunderstood what happened between us, that it
was just a thing, a silly, meaningless thing and I was
being a silly, lovesick girl. No, Aidan was the perfect
boy in my perfect summer romance. The one that got
away, not the one who ran away (to Crawdad Cravath).

I am plumb out of words. I don't want to lie and my
pride won't let me tell the truth. So, I just slap a Band-
Aid on this painful situation. I hide my pain beneath a
smile.

"Ah, I see," he says, crossing his arms over his chest
and smiling back at me. "Ya didn't want your fella to
know about me. What was his name? Gaylord?"

"Grayson," I say. "His name was Grayson."

"Grayson. I knew it was a poncey name."

"He isn't a ponce!"

"Ya told me he took ya to a dance and got well fluthered after drinking something called a Furry Navel." He laughs. "If that's not a ponce, I don't know what is."

"It was the prom and the drink is called a Fuzzy Navel. It's made with peach schnapps."

"Peach schnapps?" He shakes his head. "Ya could crawl to every pub in every county in Ireland and ya wouldn't find a single Irishman drinking peach schnapps. What self-respecting man gets *fluthered* drinking peach schnapps?"

"Leave it to an Irishman to judge another man's masculinity by how much he can drink," I say.

"I question his masculinity because he chose drinking *girly* cocktails with the lads over dancing with you . . . and he made ya cry once when he said he thought ya needed to lose weight. *The fuck?*"

The last bit comes out as a confused exclamation, which I assume is Aidan's way of saying, *what is up with that?* I'm not gonna lie, y'all, the sentiment behind his profanity makes me absurdly happy.

"I can't believe you remember that story."

"I remember everything about ya, Tara." He smiles— not the half-teasing, half-mocking grin he flashed me a few seconds ago, but a smile so sweet it makes my teeth ache. "I don't remember ya being such a worrier, though. The Tara I knew back then would have climbed in the cage and challenged me to a fight."

I laugh. Aidan always brought out my feisty, fearless side, the side that didn't worry about spilling tea on my dress, or running barefoot, or scandalizing the neighbors with my tom-girl tree climbing. Maybe that's one of the reasons I liked coming to Donegal, because I could let my perfectly coiffed hair down and forget about my perfectly proper Southern roots. I could just be . . . me.

"I like knowing ya were worried about me," he says, pressing his knees against my legs.

"Of course I was worried about you. How could I not worry? And I'll be sick with worry if I ever see you in that cage again."

"Are ya planning on staying in Ireland for a while?"

"Yes."

"Then ya will definitely see me in that cage again."

"Great!" I look down at my legs, at Aidan's knees pressing against my legs, at the fine sprinkling of blondish hairs on his knees. "I can hardly wait."

"Ya don't need to worry about me, luv," he says, tilting my chin up until I look into his eyes. "Bet on me. Bet on me and I promise ya won't lose."

I am not sure if he is talking about betting on him as a cage fighter or something else? Is he charming me, like he did ten years ago? Is seducing me part of a plan to get me to name him as co-owner of the castle?

I look at the thick fringe of blonde lashes around his cobalt blue eyes, the dangerous glints of silver hidden in their depths, and hope he is trying to seduce me. I am twenty-seven years old and I have only slept with two men. Grayson Calhoun and Mason Haywood. Mason was from a respectable Southern family, attended Ole Miss on a football scholarship, belonged to Sigma Nu, and checked all of my daddy's boxes for the perfect son-in-law. Aidan doesn't check many of my daddy's boxes. Maybe that's why I find him thrilling, because he is different from the seersucker-wearing, polo-playing men I know back home.

"I'll bet on you, Aidan Gallagher, but that doesn't mean I'll watch you win that bet for me."

"Fair enough." He reaches for one of the tins sitting on the table between us. "Cat said ya brought me a wee gift. Is this it, then?"

"I wouldn't call it a gift," I say, suddenly embarrassed. "It's nothing, really. Just something I baked."

He lifts the lid.

"Biscuits? You baked me biscuits?" He looks at me with an expression of disbelief. "Are ya telling me the American princess took off her tiara and sparkly shoes to slave away in the kitchen for a lowly Irish lad?"

"Never mind," I say, reaching for the tin. "Give them back."

"I was only slagging," he says, nudging me with his knee. "Ya need to stop spending so much time with Oxford. He's thumping the humor out of ya with all of his dry shite numbers and financial talk."

"Try a cookie or I'll be giving you a grand thumping, Aidan Gallagher," I say, nudging him back.

"There's me lass," he says, laughing. "That's the Tara I remember."

He takes a cookie out of the open tin and bites it in half. He finishes the first cookie and reaches into the tin for a second.

"Do you like them?"

"Are you slagging me? These are the best biscuits I've ever had, even better than Mrs. McGregor's gingersnaps."

"You're serious?"

"They're deadly biscuits, lethal."

He breaks his second cookie in half and sniffs it.

"Working around cider every day must be affecting me sense of smell because I could swear these biscuits smell like Bánánach Brew."

"Your smelling is fine," I say, beaming. "Remember

that bottle of cider you gave me the other day? Well, I liked it so much, I replicated the flavors in a cookie. I used your cider in the dough. Of course, I didn't know until I got here that it was really your cider, that you own Bánánach Brew. Why didn't you tell me?"

"We haven't seen each other in ten years. I didn't think I should start with, 'Hiya Tara. I run a small craft cider business.'"

"You've created something really great here, Aidan. You deserve to brag."

"I don't brag." He smiles and the blood rushes to my head. "I would rather brag about these biscuits."

"You really like them?"

"I fecking love them."

"I call them Bánánach Brew Bites."

"Brilliant."

He puts the tin down and leans close, just like he did all of those years ago on the rocks below Tásúildun. Only this time, he doesn't kiss my chin.

Chapter Twenty

Aidan Gallagher is kissing me.

Again. His first kiss was innocent, a sweet, fleeting brush of lips over lips, a sincere promise of kisses to come. His second kiss—*lawd have mercy*—his second kiss is mature, fervent, urgent. *His second kiss is making good on the promise of the first one.*

He coaxes my lips apart with his tongue, deepening our kiss. I taste the cider from the cookies on his tongue, feel the grains of sugar on his lips grazing my lips, and the world around me sways, tilts, spins faster, faster, until I have to close my eyes and hold on to Aidan, anchor myself to his solid body.

"Jaysus, Tara," he whispers against my lips. "Ya taste so fecking good."

He kisses me again and again. Sweet cider kisses. Hot, heady kisses. Delicious, dizzying kisses that have me leaning closer, yearning, craving more.

Aidan breaks the kiss and leans back so abruptly I almost fall off my barrel. I open my eyes. Catriona must have decided to join us because she is standing at the end of the table, a smirk on her pretty face.

"Fair play!" Catriona laughs. "Whatever ya put in those biscuits did the job, Tara. Think I could get a batch for my fella? He hasn't snogged me like that in months."

"Feck off," Aidan says, whipping the towel off his head and tossing it at his sister. "I have a mind to tell Cillian what ya said."

Catriona sticks her tongue out and suddenly we are children again, chasing each other down the beach, laughing and teasing easily. Only we aren't children. I look at Aidan's muscular chest, the tattoo over his heart, and experience another one of those disorienting time shifts. Everything is the same. Everything has changed.

"I am sorry to tear ya away from our Aidan, Tara," Catriona says. "I have to get going. I'm meeting me fella for dinner."

"Of course."

Catriona isn't looking at me, though. She's staring pointedly at her brother, conveying some private message with her gaze. Aidan stares back. This goes on for several uncomfortable seconds.

"Aidan!" Catriona cries.

"Cat?"

She narrows her gaze. It's the look mothers give their children when they're acting up in public. Aidan seems oblivious.

"Ya fecking thick-headed eejit," Catriona huffs.

Aidan laughs.

"Tara," he says, turning to me. "Our Cat would like us to join her and her fella for dinner. She fancies herself a matchmaker and will probably spend the evening planning our wedding and naming our wee ones. I've painted a bleak picture of the evening, I have, but what do ya say? Would ya like to go out with me?"

Yes. Yes, yes, yes!

"I would love to—"

"You would?" Catriona cries. "She would! There ya have it. Me work here is complete."

"—but I already made plans."

Aidan looks at me. The light fades from his eyes. His expression is the same, but I feel the shift in his emotions, sense the annoyance building just below the smiling surface.

"Oxford?"

"He asked me to dinner this morning." And then I feel a need to minimize, to mitigate the damage my news might cause. "It's no big deal. I think he just wants to talk about castle business."

"Castle business," Aidan repeats, his lips quirking. "Right."

"Another time, then?" Catriona says, backing away from the table. "We can do it another time, right Aidan? Tara?"

"Absolutely," I say.

Aidan doesn't say anything.

The sky is as dark as my mood when Catriona drives away, beeping her horn and flashing her taillights. The drizzly rain has turned into a downpour, a relentless icy deluge with raindrops that feel like accusing fingers jabbing at me.

Logically, I know I am not doing anything wrong by going out to dinner with Sin. Emotionally, I feel guilty as a whore in church. I keep seeing the look on Aidan's face when I declined his dinner invitation, the frozen smile, the dark gaze, and it's paining me something fierce.

Mrs. McGregor is waiting for me when I walk into the kitchen. She's sitting at the table, holding a bag of frozen peas to her jaw.

"Gums still hurting?"

"Me gums and me gammy tooth."

"Why don't you go back to bed," I say, shaking my jacket out and hanging it on the hook behind the door. "I will make a milkshake with those berries you brought back from the market and bring it to you with a fresh ice pack."

"That sounds grand. Thanks a million," she says, standing. "Oh, I almost forgot. Rhys left a note for ya on the counter there, luv."

Mrs. McGregor tosses the bag of peas back into the freezer and shuffles out of the kitchen. I unfold Sin's note and look at his neat, precise handwriting.

> *Tara,*
> *Forgive me for cancelling our dinner plans. I have to return to London on important business. I will be gone for a few days, but would like to take you to lunch when I return. Raincheck?*
> *Fondly,*
> *Sin*
> *P.S. Your biscuits were quite good.*

I look at the note again, focusing on the salutation. *Fondly*. What a nebulous word. Fondly falls in the hazy no-man's land of salutations, between *Love* and *Sincerely*. It doesn't inspire passion, nor does it quash hope.

I toss Sin's note back on the counter and walk over

to the refrigerator, gathering the ingredients I need to make Mrs. McGregor's milkshake. I pour milk and scoop vanilla ice cream into the blender, making a basic vanilla milkshake. When the consistency is right I pour two-thirds of the mixture into a clean pitcher. I add fresh blueberries and blackberries to the milkshake left in the blender and pulse it until the mixture is purple. I pour the purple mixture into a tall glass. Next, I blend frozen strawberries and amaretto together with the rest of the vanilla milkshake and then layer the pink, booze-infused strawberry milkshake on top of the purple berry shake already in the glass. I slice a frozen strawberry in half and slide it onto the rim of the glass before delivering the concoction to Mrs. McGregor in her room.

She's sitting up in bed, watching TV.

"I added some amaretto," I say, handing her the glass. "I hope you like it."

"Isn't this grand?" she says, taking the glass. "*Moone Boy* and a milkshake! Aren't I the pampered one?"

"*Moone Boy*?"

"Haven't ya heard of *Moone Boy*, then?"

I shake my head.

"Sit down," she says, gesturing to the chair beside her bed. "Watch an episode with me. It's about the adventures of Martin Moone, an Irish lad, and his imaginary friend, Sean Murphy. Chris O'Dowd plays the imaginary friend. Have ya heard of Chris O'Dowd?"

"I don't think so."

"He's gas!" She aims the remote at the television and pushes a button. The volume increases. "It's starting."

A cartoon drawing of a boy playing the guitar appears on the screen and loud punk music blasts from the television's speaker, throbbing drumbeats, screeching guitars, and someone singing about Karl Marx and dancing in a disco and losing their jumper. The chorus of the ridiculous song is just one line, repeated over and over and over, *Where's me jumper? Where's me jumper? Where's me jumper?*

I look at Mrs. McGregor and she laughs.

"Isn't this song gas? I've heard it dozens of times and it still makes me laugh."

The episode turns out to be about young Martin enduring the humiliation associated with a particular symptom of male puberty, a symptom his chubby friend referred to as "flying the flesh flag" and "pitching the tent." Despite the uncomfortable subject matter, I laugh out loud throughout the episode. With the credits rolling, and the earwig theme song playing in the background, I make plans to watch more reruns of *Moone Boy* with Mrs. McGregor.

"You were right, Mrs. Mac," I say, collecting the empty milkshake glass. "Chris O'Dowd is hilarious."

"A treasure he is, a treasure."

I leave Mrs. McGregor in her room, return the milkshake glass to the kitchen, and head upstairs so I can take a bath before I make dinner (for one) and climb into bed to watch Netflix (alone).

I am soaking in a tub of bubbles, a Glam Glow charcoal mask slathered on my face, singing *Moone Boy's* beseeching theme song about the lost jumper, when the bathroom door opens and Aidan walks in.

I squeal. Literally squeal.

Aidan takes one look at my black-goop-covered face and bursts out laughing. I can feel my face heating up beneath the mask, my body flushing from the roots of my blazing ginger hair to the tips of my cranberry painted toenails.

"What are you doing here?" I slide down, hiding under the bubbles. "I thought you were going out to dinner with Catriona and her boyfriend?"

"Was that the Sultans of Ping?"

"What?" I snap.

"What were ya just singing?"

"It's the theme song to a television show I watched with Mrs. McGregor, *Moone Boy*."

He laughs again.

"*Where's Me Jumper* is a song by the Sultans of Ping. They're a punk band from Cork." He crosses his arms over his chest, grinning. "You're full of surprises, you are, Tara Maxwell. Combat boots and punk music."

"Yes, well"—I carefully lift my foot out of the water and use my toes to grab at the towel on the commode—"I would like to keep a few surprises hidden, if you don't mind."

The towel falls off the commode.

Aidan picks it up and hands it to me.

I snatch the towel out of his hand.

"Get out!"

"I knocked."

"Out!"

"Ya couldn't hear me over all that keening."

"Get"—I throw the towel at him but it misses, landing in a pool at his feet—"out!"

"I'm going. I'm going"—he backs out the door—"to look for your jumper."

He closes the door, but I can hear his deep, rolling laughter echoing in the hallway.

* * *

When I walk into the kitchen a little while later—sans bubbles, charcoal mask, and pride—the last person I want to see standing at the stove is Aidan Gallagher.

There he stands, though, a dishtowel tucked into his jeans waistband like an apron and a wooden spoon in his hand. The air is spiced with the aroma of garlic and bay leaves.

"I didn't realize you were still home," I say, turning to leave. "I'll grab something to eat after you've finished."

"Sit down," he says. "I am making dinner."

"I need to get my hearing checked"—I stick the tip of my finger in my ear and wiggle it around—"because I could have sworn you just said you are making me dinner."

"That's right."

"I didn't know you could cook."

"There's a lot ya don't know about me, *banphrionsa*."

"Are you trying to seduce me, Aidan Gallagher?" I say, twisting a lock of hair around my finger and batting my eyelashes at him.

"Seduce?" He laughs. "I am taking pity on ya."

"Pity?"

"I saw the note Oxford left for ya. I thought ya might need a wee bit of sympathy."

"Why would I need sympathy?"

"Sure, rejection is murder."

"Sin didn't reject me."

"Sure, he didn't." He stops stirring the pot (on the stove) and looks at me, grinning. "He stood ya up, didn't he?"

"He had work."

"Like Graylord had Fuzzy Navels?"

"Gaylord." I growl. "*Grayson*. His name is Grayson!"

"Relax," he says, laughing. "Can't ya see I'm just winding you up?"

"Sin didn't stand me up."

"Okay, okay," he says, holding up his hands as if deflecting blows. "Oxford didn't leave ya sitting at home, alone, so he could spend the night entering numbers into his spreadsheets."

"Sin doesn't care about me, is that it?"

"Oxford cares for you," he says, chuckling. *"Fondly."*

"Haven't you ever canceled a . . ."

"A what? A *date*?"

"I was going to say *dinner*."

He crosses his arms over his chest and looks at me. He's still smiling, but his gaze is focused, intense.

"If I were to be asking you out on a date, Tara Maxwell, I wouldn't be canceling and I sure as shite wouldn't leave ya sitting at home, alone, with a sorry excuse for a love note."

The air leaves my lungs in a sudden, reflexive exhalation. So this is what it feels like to stand opposite Aidan, to be the focus of his intensity, to feel the staggering effects of his lethal, manly charm. I try to tell myself his flirtatious banter and intense gazes are merely the moves of a man skilled in the sport of seduction, that they mean nothing, nothing at all, but I keep remembering the taste of his lips, the feel of his legs pressing against mine.

"I'm not alone. I have you."

"Not yet," he says, winking. "But it's still early."

"Ooh!" I stomp my foot. Literally stomp my foot. "You are the most egotistical, big-headed man I have ever known, Aidan Gallagher."

He laughs. "I love it when ya whisper sweet-nuttins to me."

Like the bell at a boxing match, the oven timer starts ringing. *Ding. Ding.* Aidan grabs a potholder and opens the oven. A wave of hot, floury air flows into the kitchen. I walk to the other side of the counter, wanting to put a barrier between me and the lethally hot Irishman.

"You know how to make soda bread?"

"I know how to do a lot of things, love," he says, putting the hot bread on the counter. "Making soda bread is the least of those things, but I'm glad it impressed ya."

I should be mighty irritated with him—barging into the bathroom while I was soaking in the tub and giving me the piss (or is it *taking the piss*—either way, it's a revolting phrase) over Sin—but I am finding it difficult to keep my anger fires burnin' when he speaks to me in his thick Irish accent. Truth y'all? I like the way he drops the *h* from *th* words, pronouncing *those* as *toes* and *things* as *tings*. Even so, I am not going to let him off that easy.

"Here"—I pull an apron out of the linen drawer and hand it to him over the counter—"an apron might work better than that little dishtowel."

Aidan flicks his gaze from the apron dangling from my fingers to the innocent smile on my face.

"Ya must be taking the piss out of me."

I feign ignorance, thrusting the pink ruffled apron at him. "What's the matter? You're not going to let a frilly little apron threaten your masculinity, are you?"

He stares at me.

"Grayson wore an apron whenever he cooked."

"No shite?" His lips twist in a sardonic smile. "Did he wear it while he was mixing his Fuzzy Navels?"

"I'll bet Sin would wear an apron if he were cooking me dinner," I say, unable to resist teasing him.

"But he's not, is he? I am here, cooking ya dinner, and I have more self-respect than an American ponce and a rawny Brit."

He looks so fierce, so genuinely affronted, I can't hold back my laughter. I laugh until my stomach hurts. I laugh until I can't catch my breath. I imagine Aidan in a pink ruffled apron as wide as a tutu and I start laughing again, hooting like a barnyard owl.

"I am sorry, but I imagined you in one of Mrs. Mc-Gregor's aprons and . . ." I wipe tears from my cheeks. "I haven't laughed that hard in a long time."

His gruff, grumbly, bear-like mask slips. His lips twitch, his eyes sparkle, and he is that craic-loving boy again, the one who made me laugh with his stories and sigh with his devilish smile.

"Are ya done taking the piss out of me?"

"I think so."

"Ya think so?" He snatches the apron from my fingers and flicks it at me playfully. "Go on or I'll take me pot of chowder and soda bread and leave ya with nuttin but Mrs. McGregor's butter biscuits."

"That would be bad, right?"

He flicks me again and I hop back, laughing.

We carry our bowls of steaming chowder and plates of bread to the kitchen table and sit across from each other, the steady patter of rain against the windows and the amber glow from the fireplace creating a cozy, romantic ambiance. I ask Aidan about Bánánach Brew. He tells me about the challenges of growing apples in

Donegal's waterlogged soil and salt-laden air, his efforts to grow multiple-budded and hybrid fruit trees,
and his desire to create a second line of keeved cider.

"What is *keeved* cider?"

"Keeving"—he slices off another piece of soda
bread and puts it on my empty plate—"is a traditional
artisan method for making cider sweetened naturally,
using only apples."

"What's the difference?"

"Modern cider is made by crushing the fruit and immediately extracting the juices, resulting in a clean,
sparkly brew. Keeved cider is earthier, pulpier, and
naturally sweeter because the fruit is crushed and then
left to ferment before the juice is extracted."

"The longer a crushed apple is left to ferment, the
more pectin leaks out of its membranes." I tear a piece
of bread off and dunk it in my stew. "It seems like you
would have a thick jelly layer in your tanks."

"That's right." He looks impressed. "That's what
gives the cider an earthier flavor."

"Keeving must take longer than modern methods."

"Keeving does take longer, a lot longer, which is
why most cider makers opt for the modern methods.
Faster fermentation means greater production."

"And greater profits."

He nods.

"You don't care about maximizing your profits?"

"Some things are more important than profit."

"Like what?"

"Like respecting tradition and the pride that comes
from knowing ya created something extraordinary."

I think of Sin and his bottom-line mentality and
wonder what he would say if he could hear Aidan right
now.

"It's not a popular business model, I know."

"It's an admirable one, though."

Our gazes meet and a frisson of excitement, a thrilling sexual current, passes between us. I feel myself falling into his gaze, plunging deeper and deeper, becoming hopelessly lost in his unfathomable blue-eyed gaze. A woman could swim in those eyes . . . or find herself perilously adrift. Drifting, drifting, drifting ever closer to heartbreak.

We linger over our empty chowder bowls, the conversation flowing like the Santee after a summer storm, freely, easily, sweeping away any debris of awkwardness.

The tall-case clock is striking eleven as we dry the last washed dish. We lock the back door, turn off the kitchen lights, and climb the stairs to our rooms side-by-side, as if we've traveled this path together hundreds of times.

Aidan stops at my door and the awkwardness returns. We aren't lovers traveling a well-trod path of intimacy. We are strangers who once had a . . .

A what? A juvenile flirtation? A summer romance? I still don't know what we had that summer. I don't know how Aidan felt about me or what he feels for me now.

I wish my deeply instilled Southern reticence would disappear so I could muster the courage to grab Aidan by his shirt front and pull him into my room. I wish I could be the bold, brazen woman I've always wanted to be. That woman, that fearlessly scandalous woman, would already be rolling around in bed, nekked as a jaybird.

My daddy always said, *Tara, dahlin', the most piti-*

ful soul you'll ever encounter is the one who grew a wishbone instead of a backbone.

Daddy probably didn't intend for me to use my backbone to seduce an Irishman, but we can't always control our wishes and wants, now can we?

"Thank you for dinner," I say, avoiding his gaze. "It was delicious. Just what a body needs after a long day in the cold Irish rain."

Kiss him. Just kiss him, you poor, pitiful, backbone-wishing woman.

So, with a wicked little voice urging me not to lose my backbone, I press my palms against Aidan's muscular chest and stand on my tippy toes. I mean to kiss his cheek, to give him an *amuse-bouche*, a tantalizing sample of what he could have, but he's obviously hungry for something more. At the last second, he turns his face so I end up kissing his mouth instead of his cheek. He wraps his arm around my waist and pulls me against him with a strength that is positively primeval, a strength that says, *Me, man. You, woman.* It's like no embrace I've ever felt. Confident, commanding, with a barely restrained intensity that has me clutching his shirt to keep from swooning like Jane in Tarzan's arms.

Breathless, feeling my backbone like never before, I thrust my tongue between his lips while reaching back, fumbling for the doorknob. Aidan growls low in his throat, a sexy, emboldening groan that has me fumbling, frantic to open the door, to unleash the vixen that has been living inside me, that has been desperately trying to claw her way out.

I finally feel the cold iron doorknob against my palm. I grasp it, twist, listen for the telltale click of the lock tumbling. The door opens and I lean against Aidan's arm. He tightens his hold around my waist, lifting me off my feet. I hear the door close and then we are falling on my bed, arms, legs, tongues entwined. I don't know how it is possible to be terrified and aroused at the same time, but I am. I imagine it's the way skydivers feel before their first jump.

I am sick with fear, regretting the folly that has brought me to the brink of disaster, but exhilarated at the possibility of cheating death. Part of me wants to shuffle backward, seek the safety of solid ground, while another part fears the scathing self-recriminations I will endure if I do.

Kissing Aiden is like skydiving. I'm floating through the clouds, looking at the world far, far below, and wishing this euphoric weightlessness could go on forever.

If I have learned anything in the last year, though, it's that nothing good can last forever and gravity has a nasty way of sneaking up on you.

When Aiden finally stops kissing me, it feels as if a big old chute has suddenly deployed and is jerking me back to reality, violently.

Reluctantly—with painful awareness of my ragged breaths, my wet, bruised lips—I open my eyes to find Aidan staring down at me, his lips still close enough to kiss.

"I need to know this is really what ya want, Tara."

Of course I want him here, in my bed, kissing me senseless. Can't he feel my heart beating, thudding against my ribs something fierce?

"This is what I want," I say, sliding my hand between us and unbuttoning my blouse.

"I'm no Prince Charming, *banphrionsa*. I won't be promising ya happily-ever-after. In fact, the only promise I can make is that if ya let me stay tonight, I will make love to ya like there's no tomorrow. If ya be needing something more from me, I will go now and we will pretend this never happened."

"You sure know how to woo a girl." I twist another button open, and another, exposing the narrow space between my breasts, driven by a reckless desire to feel his lips on my skin again. "Fortunately, I'm not looking for roses and heart-shaped chocolate boxes."

I twist the last button and my shirt falls open. Aidan looks at my nipples straining against my thin, lacy bra and lowers himself down, pressing his chest against my chest, dragging his lips over my lips.

I close my eyes, shivering as his whiskered cheeks graze my chin, my throat, the tender, thin skin of my collarbone.

I will make love to ya like there's no tomorrow . . .

Aidan uses his chin to push my bra aside, his beard creating pleasure-pain sensations on my skin, and then his lips are on my nipple, gently coaxing it into his warm mouth.

After seeing him in the cage this afternoon—aggressive and amped up—I expect his lovemaking to be equally aggressive, but it's not. His moves are slow and subtle, his touches deliberately designed to obliterate any resistance, to reduce me to a helpless, trembling . . .

. . . and they're working.

I reach around and pull his shirt over his head, itching, aching, to feel his skin against my skin, to kiss that tattoo over his heart. He smells like . . . like Aidan. Manly, clean, hot.

My iPhone starts ringing on the nightstand. I keep my eyes closed and will it to stop, stop, stop ringing. Why—why Lord—why didn't I turn the ringer off? It finally stops ringing, but it's too late. The mood is shattered.

I won't be promising ya happily-ever-after.

My phone chimes and I realize I am getting a text.

Aidan lifts his mouth from my breast, leaving it exposed, vulnerable to the cold air, to the encroaching shame. He pushes up on his elbows and looks at me.

"Do ya need to answer it?"

Do I? Is Emma Lee's latest matchmaking scheme or Callie's latest Happn hookup more important than letting Aidan finish making love to me like there is no tomorrow?

Supporting himself with one arm, he reaches over and grabs my iPhone off the nightstand. He hands it to me without looking at the screen.

"Thanks," I whisper, taking it.

I look at the screen.

Text from Rhys Burroughes:
Business meeting a complete wash. All your fault. Kept thinking about how beautiful you looked walking through Dublin Airport. Make it up to me? Sunday roast and a drive through the country?

"I hope it's nothing serious."

"It's not," I say, keeping my tone light. "Sin just wanted to check in."

Aidan rolls off of me onto his back. We lie side by side, staring up at the ceiling, and I know, with ice-cold certainty, that we won't be making love tonight, maybe any night.

"This isn't going to happen, is it?" he says.

I pull my shirt together and roll onto my side so I

can look at him and my heart aches for what could have been, for what might never be.

"I'm sorry," I say, reaching out to run my fingers through his hair. "I want this to happen. I swear I do. It's just . . ."

"Sin?"

"What? No." I pull my hand away. "It's just . . . I might say I don't care about roses and chocolates, but deep down, I do. I want my Prince Charming. I want a man who wants, truly, madly, deeply wants to give me happily-ever-after, not happy-for-a-night."

"I hope ya find him." Aidan stands up, grabs his shirt, and tosses it over his shoulder. "I wish I could be that man, *banphrionsa*, but I am not."

He kisses my forehead and leaves. A second later, I hear the lock on the connecting door turn.

Chapter Twenty-one

I am standing in the herb garden, watching the setting sun cover the castle grounds and distant hills in gossamer golden light, and listening for the sound of my aunt laughing with the fairies, when Mrs. McGregor joins me.

"The gloaming," she says, pulling her shawl around her frail shoulders. "When the day takes its last gasp before slipping into night. The ancients believed the time between sunset and darkness was magical. *An t-am mianta agus iontas*. The time of wishes and wonder."

"Wishes and wonder. What a lovely thought."

A skein of black-necked barnacle geese flies overhead, their mournful honks shattering the quiet of the gloaming. We watch their silhouettes move across the sky toward the ever-darkening horizon.

"If ya could make one wish, Tara, what would it be?"

"Just one?" I bend down and pluck a leaf off a peppermint plant, bruising it between my thumb and pointer finger, inhale the minty oil, and a memory sparks to life in my brain of Aunt Patricia serving me peppermint tea to calm an upset stomach. "If you had asked me that question a few months ago, I would have wished for Daddy and Aunt Patricia to be alive."

"And now?"

"Now," I say, tossing the bruised peppermint leaf onto the gravel and wiping my fingers on my jeans. "I accept the cycle of life as one of the more painful details in God's grand design. I don't have to like it, but I would be a damn fool to try to change it. No, now I would simply wish to live a life of purpose and passion, one that would make my family proud."

"She was proud of you, love." She reaches out and laces her fingers with mine. "She used to say she loved each of her nieces and nephews, but felt a special kinship with ya. Soul connection is what she said it was."

My throat tightens. "I loved her something fierce."

"I know ya did."

"I used to count the days until summer break. I had a calendar stuck to the back of my bedroom door and I would mark off each day with a big old red X." I blink back tears. "My sisters never understood why I was in such an all-fire hurry to leave South Carolina. They loved Charleston summers. Mandy curled up on the divan on the back porch, sipping sweet tea with lemon slices and reading, reading, reading. I swear the only time she left that porch was to go to church or to take Emma Lee to the beach. Mandy loves swimming almost as much as she loves reading. I never did like swimming much. All that sand in places where sand shouldn't be!"

Mrs. McGregor laughs.

"If Mandy would have spent a little less time curating her book collection and a little more time cultivating her social circle, she would have been the belle of every ball. She's our momma's daughter, sweet, soft spoken, and effortlessly pleasing. I reckon that's why she was daddy's favorite," I say without bitterness. "Emma Lee is the true Charlestonian, though. Charming, clever, and extraordinarily magnetic. People are just naturally attracted to her, like hummingbirds to honeysuckle. She couldn't wait for summer and her dizzying swirl of social activities. Pool parties, barbecues, clambakes, paddle boarding at Folly Beach . . . A body could get exhausted just listening to Emma Lee rattle off her summer schedule."

Mrs. McGregor laughs.

"What?"

"I seem to recall feeling knackered watching ya run around with the village kids when ya visited."

"That was different."

"How was it different?"

I peer at the distant hills as if the answer to Mrs. McGregor's question is hidden somewhere in the shadowy valley between them. How do you explain a vague and baseless feeling you've had all your life? It's like trying to hold fog in your hand. It's there. You know it's there. You can see it, feel it, but as soon as you try to grasp it you realize it has no real substance.

"I had loads of friends and a family that loved me, but I never felt like I belonged in Charleston." I let go of Mrs. McGregor's hand and wipe a tear from my cheek. "You once told me a story about a baby who was stolen from her crib and replaced by a fairy child."

"The Changeling."

"I've always felt like a changeling, like I was in the wrong place and living a life not intended for me. In the story, the changeling eventually loses her fairy features and learns how to behave like a human. I have learned how to behave like a proper Southern lady, but I don't feel like a proper Southern lady." I sigh. "Shoot, I don't want to be a proper Southern lady. I don't want to spend three hours putting on my face just so I can sit on the front porch and gossip with my neighbors. I don't want to conceal my backstabbing knife behind a plastic smile. I don't want to burn a hole in my gut worrying I won't make the perfect match, raise the perfect kids, amass the perfect shoe collection."

"What do ya want?"

"I'm still trying to figure that one out."

"Will ya forgive an *auld* woman with a gammy tooth if she tells ya something ya might not like hearing?"

"Yes, ma'am."

"People are people, whether they're from South Carolina or South Cork. Do ya think the villagers don't gossip about their neighbors or fret about their kids?" She turns her watery blue gaze on me. "It wasn't fairy magic that turned ya into a changeling, Tara love. Ya became a changeling by convincing yourself ya were different and that being different was a bad thing."

She pats my cheek before shuffling back into the kitchen.

Chapter Twenty-two

Text from Manderley Maxwell de Maloret:
FedEx delivered the box with your cookies twenty minutes ago and already the tin is half-empty! Xavier thinks they are delicious. So do I. Have you thought about selling them at the local markets?

Text from Emma Lee Maxwell:
Ooh! Thank you for the cookies. You know how much I love surprise prezzies! I gave one to the FedEx guy and he asked if they were gourmet. Of course, I said yes. We got to talking and . . . Guess what? He asked if I would match him with someone. FedEx delivered your cookies and my first client. Sweet!

I think it was Julia Child who said, *Find something you're passionate about and stick to it like taffy to teeth.* That might not be verbatim. I might have seasoned it a bit, but I think Julia would have appreciated the additive.

I am passionate about baking, so I have been sticking to the kitchen like taffy to teeth. I have tested recipes from the old cookbooks and created a few new ones. Dark chocolate cake with Guinness frosting, granola bars made with Irish oats and golden syrup, Mrs. Cumiskey's booze-infused Porter Cake, and my own creation, Feckin' Faddle, popcorn and peanuts coated in Bush-mills Whiskey Caramel. It's like Fiddle Faddle, but with an Irish twist.

I am making a custard sauce to go with an apple cake cooling on the counter when Catriona arrives, her thick blonde hair scraped back in a bun.

"Mmmm," she says, shaking the rain off her coat. "It smells like me gran's house in here."

I remember visiting old Mrs. Gallagher's cottage, eating blueberry crumble in her cramped, cozy kitchen, helping her press buttery shortbread dough into wooden decorative molds.

"Thank you. That's the nicest compliment I've received in a long time," I say, taking her coat and hanging it over the back of a chair near the fire. "What are you doing here, Cat?"

"That's a fine *how do you do*," she laughs. "Is that the way you greet people in South Carolina?"

"I'm sorry," I say, giving her a quick hug. "I'm just surprised to see you here. Shouldn't you be at work?"

"Do ya know what time it is, then?" She narrows her gaze, taking in my messy top knot, flour-dusted flannel shirt, and old Abercrombie sweats. "Jaysus! It looks like ya haven't been out of this kitchen in don-key's years."

"Thanks a million," I say, laughing. "Is that the way you greet people in Ireland?"

"Sorry," she says, lifting the lid off a container of

Feckin' Faddle. "Ya look a little rough around the edges though."

"I've been baking."

"I see that," she says, grabbing a handful of the popcorn mix and popping it into her mouth. She chews. Her eyes widen. "What am I eating?"

"I call it Feckin' Faddle."

She snorts.

"Brilliant! I bloody love the name." She grabs another handful of the mix, staring at the golden brown cluster of popcorn and peanuts. "But what is it?"

I tell her about my addiction to Fiddle Faddle, the sweet, salty popcorn treat in the bright, happy blue box, and my grown-up take on it.

"Whiskey? Ya put whiskey on your popped corn?" She shakes her head, laughing. "You've definitely got Irish blood in your veins, Tara Maxwell, but if ya tell me you're putting it in your morning oats, I'll be staging one of those interventions, I will."

"You know," I say, stroking my chin. "That's not a bad idea."

"Go away with that." Catriona laughs. "What else have ya got brewing and baking? I'm Lee bleedin' Marvin."

"Lee Marvin? The actor who starred in those old Westerns?"

"The same," she says, dipping her finger in my pot of custard. "I dated a fella from Dublin who used to say he was *Lee bleedin' Marvin* whenever he was hungry. I don't know what a cowboy has to do with being hungry, but it sounds better than saying I could eat a nun's arse through the convent gate."

"Ew! Who says that?"

"Never mind," she laughs. "I stopped by to see if ya

want to go to the chipper and grab a pint at the Red Horse after. Fancy a night out with your old friend?"

I look at my reflection in the copper pot hanging from a hook in the ceiling and grimace. What would stinky old Crawdad and the Cravath set say if they could see me now, holed up in the kitchen on a Friday night?

"Come on, Tara," she says, grabbing my hand. "It'll be great gas!"

"Are you kidding? I could murder a bag of fish and chips, anything that isn't Guinness soaked cake and cider cookies."

"Guinness soaked cake, ya say?" She sniffs the apple cake cooling on the wire rack. "Is that what this is, then? Do ya mind if I help meself to a wee piece while you're changing out of those sad rags?"

"Help yourself," I say, pouring the custard into a bowl. "But that's not the Guinness cake. That's my version of an Irish Apple Cake, a vanilla-bean-flecked cake filled with apples and topped with a crunchy sugar crust. Pour some custard on top of your slice before you eat it."

I rinse the custard pan out in the sink and leave Catriona to satiate her Lee bleedin' Marvin with a giant hunk of apple cake.

I'm not gonna lie, y'all. Julia's sage advice isn't the only reason I've been sticking to the kitchen like taffy to teeth. A passion for baking is only part of it. The other part of it, the downright humiliating part, is that if I don't keep busy I just know I will sit and ruminate on what happened in my room the other night, replaying over and over again the scene where Aidan said he couldn't be my Prince Charming. Burying pain through baking has become one of my trademark moves.

I am not saying I want Aidan to be my Prince Charming. I swear. It just smarts a little to know we were in the middle of a hot and heavy make-out session, with my hoop-dee-hoops exposed before Jesus, and he got up and walked away.

Catriona showing up and inviting me out feels like a blessing from above. I wasn't looking forward to spending another night tiptoeing around my room like a panty thief stealing his neighbor's knickers.

A night out, laughing and drinking in a pub, is just what I need to forget all about Aidan Gallagher. Who knows? Maybe I'll meet my Prince Charming over a pint of Guinness.

Two hours later, my belly full of the freshest, flakiest fried cod, a foamy pint of Guinness in my hand, I realize I am probably not going to find my Prince Charming at the Red Horse pub. Unless, that is, my Prince Charming is an old man with more hair in his ears than under his flat cap. To say the pickings at the most popular pub in the village are slim is like saying Julia Child was a little fond of butter.

I am about to ask Catriona if we could try another pub when the door opens and a crowd of newcomers enters. They're young and boisterous, dressed in cool, edgy clothes. A few of them are toting musical instruments.

"You're going to love this, Tara," Catriona says. "The Red Horse hosts trad sessions every Friday night. Live music played by musicians from all over Ireland. The band playing tonight is from Cork and they're class. Really, really good."

The door opens again and another group enters the bar. All of them know Catriona and greet her with hugs or *hiyas*. Within minutes, the Red Horse is filled to standing room only, people packed in from wall to wall like butter beans in a can. Catriona introduces me to her friends. There's Rory, a red-haired fisherman with an infectious laugh, and his girlfriend Mary, a Sligo-based graphic designer. Michael owns several restaurants around the county and Sorcha, a raven-haired beauty with startling green eyes, is a hospitality specialist.

Catriona managed to snag one of the few tables in the pub, perfectly situated near the musicians. It's one of those tall tables meant to be paired with stools, but there are no stools, so we all crowd around it.

"Michael," Catriona says, opening the container of Feckin' Faddle she insisted on bringing with us. "You have to try this. It's deadly."

Michael looks at the container skeptically.

"Go on you," Catriona says, thrusting the container at him. "It's deadly."

Rory reaches into the container, grabs a handful and shoves it into his mouth as if he is Lee bleedin' Marvin (Cat's right; it is a catchy phrase). He barely swallows his first handful before he is reaching for seconds.

"Mmm," he murmurs.

"Deadly, right?" Catriona says.

Michael grabs a handful. And another. And another.

"This is deadly," he says. "Did ya make it, Cat?"

"Me?" Catriona laughs. "And when have you been knowing me to cook anything worth eating, Michael

Donovan? I could burn cold cereal. Tara made it. She's a brilliant chef." She turns to me, grinning. "Go on, tell 'em what you call it."

"Feckin' Faddle."

Rory laughs so loud the sound carries over the noise of the musicians warming up their instruments.

"That's a bleedin' brilliant name."

"What's in it?" Michael asks.

"Popcorn and peanuts coated in caramel made with Bushmills whiskey and cream."

"Jaysus!" Mary cries. "Whiskey covered peanuts. That does sound deadly."

She grabs the container from Rory, takes a handful of Feckin' Faddle, and passes it on to Sorcha. Before I know it, the container is empty and Catriona's friends are slapping me on the back and buying me pints.

The musicians start the session off with a cover song, Gaelic Storm's "Johnny Tarr," about the hard-drinking son of a preacher who, ironically, keeled over dead from thirst. It's one of those upbeat songs that makes you want to clap your hands and tap your feet. They play several more songs, some original and some modern interpretations of traditional Irish ballads. When they take a break between sets, Catriona leans over and whispers in my ear.

"Ya better watch out or you're going to make our Aidan pure jealous, ya are. That fella playing the fiddle has been looking at ya like he wants to shift ya."

"Hush your mouth," I laugh, remembering that Aidan told me shift means kiss.

"I am serious, Tara. See for yourself."

I wait a few seconds before casually looking over at the musicians. My cheeks flush with heat, a heat so fierce I reckon I could set a pot of water on my face and boil myself some peanuts right here in the Red Horse. Catriona is right. The fiddle player is looking at me.

And he's cute. Like cute enough to shift.

He's shorter than the guys I am usually attracted to—shorter than Aidan—but he has broad shoulders and a wild thatch of dark curly hair that could make a girl's fingers itch to touch. He's wearing jeans and a black Henley. He's pushed his shirtsleeves up, exposing muscular forearms and wrists covered with leather bands.

"I was right, wasn't I?" Catriona crows.

"You were right about him looking at me, but not about it making Aidan jealous," I say. "Aidan doesn't care if I shift a fiddler—a thousand fiddlers."

She snorts and rolls her eyes.

"What are ya on about? I saw the way he was shifting ya in the barn the other day."

"Believe me, that meant nothing to him. You know how that old song goes, *a shift is just a shift . . .*"

Catriona frowns. "Did something happen?"

My cheeks flush again. I grab my glass and finish the thick, black Guinness in one swallow. I am a lightweight. This is my second pint and I am feeling the effects.

Catriona is staring at me, but I don't know what to say. *Cat, your brother offered to make love to me until the heavens wept and I heard the Hallelujah chorus playing in my head . . . and then he walked out and left me lying there holding my hoop-dee-hoops.*

"No," I lie. "Nothing happened. I just don't think either one of us is ready for anything serious."

She narrows her eyes and I know she doesn't believe me. When subterfuge doesn't work, try evasion.

"I think it's my turn to buy a round," I say, grabbing

the empties and pushing my way through the crowd to the bar.

I haven't been standing at the bar long when someone touches my shoulder. I knew Catriona wouldn't be satisfied with my answer.

"What do you want to hear? That I am going to leave the pub right now and climb into your brother's bed? Would that make you happy?"

I spin around, but it isn't Catriona standing behind me. It's the fiddler.

"It wouldn't make me happy," he says, his eyes twinkling with humor. "But it would sure as feck give me something to rib the jammy eejit about."

I stare at him, all slack-jawed and wide-eyed.

"My brother's a priest, don't ya know?"

He grins and waggles his black eyebrows. All I can do is laugh, laugh until I am sure everyone at the bar thinks I am an eejit American who can't hold her Guinness.

"What's your name?"

"Tara."

"Tara is it?" He reaches around me and drops some money on the bar. "Tara's Halls. Where the kings met and the bards sang ballads about Irish heroes. A name fit for a queen. Are ya a queen then, Tara?"

I hear Aidan's voice in my head, calling me a princess in Irish.

"My mom named me Tara after the plantation in *Gone with the Wind*."

"A plantation? Bollocks," he says. "Look at ya. You're a queen, ya are."

"And you're a smooth talker."

"Guilty," he says, laughing. "I'm Jer, by the way."

"Nice to meet you, Jer."

"Nice to meet ya, Queen." He reaches around me again, his leather-clad wrist brushing against my arm. "Excuse me, will ya?"

"Of course."

I step aside and he lifts two pints off the bar.

"Here ya go, Your Highness." He hands me a pint of Guinness. "I hope ya like Guinness."

"You didn't need to buy me a drink."

"Sure I did," he says, winking. "Do ya not know the rules that govern this country? If a fella buys ya a pint, ya can't leave the pub until ya return the favor."

"Is that so?"

"God's honest truth," he says, pressing his hand to his heart and looking at me through wide, innocent eyes. "So I'll see ya after this next set, yeah? Don't be slipping out the back door, like. Ya don't want to start an international incident."

He turns around and disappears into the crowd. I lift a tray of pints off the bar and work my way back to the table. I put the tray down and try not to look at Jer.

"I need to make a call," Catriona says, pulling her phone out of her pocket. "Be right back."

She returns a few minutes later, her cheeks flushed from the cold, her braid beaded with droplets of rain. She doesn't make eye contact and I wonder if she is upset with me for chatting up Jer.

The music starts again and I am forced to look at the musicians. I say forced, but it's not exactly hard-time labor, y'all. Jer is extremely good looking and watching him play the fiddle is doing things to my lady parts. Mighty fine things. *Lawd have mercy.* Did I really just think that? It must be the Guinness.

. . . *Or maybe your lady parts have been revving like*

*Jimmie Johnson on a NASCAR Speedway ever since
Aidan took you in his arms and kissed you stupid.*

Aidan! Aidan! Aidan! I am plumb worn out of
thinking about Aidan *bleedin'* Gallagher. I make an
apple cake and remember him kissing in the cider
house. I watch *Moone Boy* with Mrs. McGregor and
blush remembering Aidan walking in on me in the tub.
A handsome guy calls me queen and I think of Aidan
calling me princess. Well I am done thinking about
Aidan. Done, you hear?

I smile at Jer. He winks and I feel my lady parts
revving up. By the time he plays his last song and
packs his fiddle away, I have finished my third pint. I
close my eyes and imagine my body is glowing like a
lightning bug. I'm just so darned happy. Happy and
warm.

I am swaying to the music still playing in my head,
my eyes closed, a stupid-happy smile on my face,
when I hear a voice in my ear, feel a hand on my arm.

"How about that pint?"

I open my eyes and find the fiddler standing there.
What's his name again? Jimmy? Jerry? Jer.

"Hiya, Jer," I say, throwing my arm around his
shoulder. "These are my friends. Cat. Rory. Mary.
Michael, and Sorcha. This is Jer, y'all. His brother is
a priest."

"Hiya Jer," Catriona says.

"Are you ready, cowboy?" I say to Jer. "Let's see a
man about a pint."

"Wait!" Catriona grabs my arm. "Tara, do ya think
that's wise?"

"Wise-schmise," I say, pushing her hand away.
"Who needs wisdom when the Guinness is still flowing and the fiddlers are still fiddlin'? There'll be time

enough for wisdom when I'm as old as Mrs. McGregor, too old to drink and too old to dance."

"Hurrah!" Rory cheers.

"Hurrah!" Michael says, raising his pint.

I buy Jer a pint and we find a dark, cozy corner in the back of the pub. I stand with my back to the corner. Jer sets his pint on a ledge and leans in close so I can hear him.

"Did ya like the music, Tara?"

His hot, Guinness scented breath ruffles the hair around my ear.

"Are you kidding? I loved it!" I say. "I could listen to you play your fiddle every darn day and twice on Sunday."

"Keep talking like that and I am going to snog ya right here in this pub."

"That's all it takes?" I giggle, batting my lashes at him. "You're an easy one, Jer the Fiddler."

He grins.

"I'm easy and you're a ride. We're a grand pair."

"A ride?"

"Super sexy."

My breath catches in my throat, reminding me of the time Manderley talked me into jumping off the high dive. I was fine, filled with piss and vinegar, until I got to the top of the platform and realized I didn't have the guts to make the leap. I am feeling like that now—short on guts to make the leap.

"This pub is jammers," he says, twisting a lock of my hair around his finger. "Whaddya say we get out of here? Would ya like that?"

"I wouldn't like it one fecking bit."

Sweet baby Jesus and the sheep in the manger!
That isn't . . .

It couldn't be . . .

Jer pushes himself off the wall, turns around and . . . sure enough, there is Aidan *bleedin'* Gallagher, standing not four feet away, arms crossed, looking like he wants to crush Jer beneath the heel of his boot.

Or is it me he wants to crush? I can't tell.

Jer looks over at me. "Is this your fella, then?"

I snort, but it comes out as a messy, wet raspberry. "Aidan bleedin' Gallagher is not my fella. He might could have been my fella, but he doesn't like women in that way."

Might could have? Did I really just say that? Lawd, I must be drunk. I thought I had the *might could haves* beaten out of me in broadcasting school by Mr. Rhunda, a tyrant of diction.

Aidan looks at me with murder in his eyes and I suddenly realize the unintended implication in my statement. A bubble of laughter floats up my throat, tickling my tongue, until I can't contain it anymore.

"T . . . that sounded like I was s . . . saying you are"—I scrunch up my face trying to think of the word—"a p . . . ponce! Trust me, Jer, Aidan is not a ponce. He likes women. He just doesn't like me."

Jer looks from Aidan to me and back again.

"Feck off," Aidan growls.

Jer doesn't even stop to collect his Guinness from the ledge. He just mumbles something to Aidan and walks away.

"What is wrong with you?"

"What's wrong with me?" Aidan stalks closer until I can feel the heat of his body, smell the smoky scent of peat fire clinging to his clothes. "You're the one making a holy show of yourself over some feckin' eejit fiddle player from Cork. Jaysus, Cork!"

"I am not making a holy show of myself . . . whatever that is," I say, pushing myself off the wall and swaying as a wave of dizziness washes over me.

Aidan picks me up and tosses me over his shoulder like a bag of potatoes. People in the bar hoot and holler. The floor spins around and around until I think I might be sick. *No! I will not be sick.* I am clutching onto a tiny scrap of dignity and I will not let it go by losing my fish and chips all over the Red Horse. I close my eyes and take several deeps breaths. When I open my eyes again, I am standing beside a shiny black Range Rover. The rain has stopped and a fat, silver moon hangs low in the sky—so low I feel like I could just reach out and grab it. Aidan keeps one hand clamped around my arm as he opens the passenger door.

"Get in," he says.

I climb inside. Aidan reaches around me and secures the seatbelt around my lap. I close my eyes, and rest my forehead against the cool window. I am vaguely aware of Aidan opening the driver's side door, the sound of the engine starting, my head bumping against the glass as we hit a pothole.

"Where are you taking me?"

"Home."

"What?" I open my eyes and sit up. "You can't take me home. I don't want Mrs. McGregor to see me like this. Please. Can't we go somewhere else? *Please?"*

I try to focus on his face, but the Range Rover is swaying like we've driven onto one of those carnival Tilt-A-Whirls. We tilt to the left, then the right. Centrifugal force moves me away from Aidan, spins me around and around, moves me closer, then away again. I close my eyes and let my head fall back against the headrest.

"Fine."

He turns into an Esso and pulls into a parking spot.

"Stay here," he says, opening the door and climbing out. "I will be right back."

He raises his hand and pushes the button on a small black remote. The doors lock with a startling click.

I close my eyes again and am drifting off to sleep when the locks click again and he climbs back into the driver's seat.

"Here," he says, handing me a steaming Styrofoam cup. "Drink this."

I take the cup from him and lift it to my mouth. Wispy tendrils of coffee-scented steam tickle my nose. I take several sips of coffee and then slide the cup into the cup holder between our seats. Aidan hands me a sack. Inside, I find a bottle of water, a pack of peppermint-flavored gum, and a small package of Buplex— Ireland's equivalent to Advil.

My throat suddenly feels lumpy and tight, like I swallowed the wrong way, and hot tears fill my eyes. I sniffle. Aidan looks over at me.

"What's the matter?"

"Y . . . you bought me gum!" I cry. "That's the sweetest, most considerate thing anyone has d . . . done for me in a long time."

"Jaysus!" He pushes the ignition button and the engine roars to life. "How many pints did ya have, then?"

"Three."

"Three? Is that all?" He laughs. "Ya know how to bake, but ya sure don't know how to hold your Guinness."

"I like the way you say three."

He frowns at me.

"T'ree." I hold up three fingers. "I had t'ree feckin' pints of Guinness."

"Jaysus."

He backs the Range Rover out of the parking spot and we are off, speeding down a dark, winding road. I sip my coffee whenever we hit a straightaway. When the cup is empty, I twist the lid off the water and swallow the Buplex. I feel myself sobering with each mile and with sobriety comes a deep, mortifying humiliation. I open a piece of peppermint gum and pop it into my mouth—eager to erase the evidence of my shame.

Aidan turns down onto a dirt track and we bump along for several miles. Finally, he stops driving and kills the engine.

I look out the front window, at scrubby bushes that seem to be glowing in the quicksilver light of the moon, at a lone tree, its bare white branches stretching up to the black sky, like a skeleton reaching for the heavens, and I have the strange feeling I have been here before.

"Where are we?"

"Somewhere special." He looks softer in the moonlight, the sharp edges of his face blunted. "I come here when I want to be alone."

But you're not alone. You're with me.

He gets out of the SUV. I hear the lift gate open, feel a rush of cool air, see him through my side mirror, rifling around in the trunk. He opens my door and holds his hand out. A thick blanket is rolled up and tucked under his arm and his trusty rucksack is flung around his shoulder.

I put my hand in his and let him help me out of the vehicle. An adrenaline-like burst of excitement quickens my pulse. I am alone with Aidan. It is the middle of the night and we are alone, in the middle of nowhere. I should be frightened remembering the homicidal look on his face when he saw me flirting with Jer. I should be frightened over my own nonsensical reactions to this man.

I like him.

I hate him.

I lust him.

I hate him.

I love him.

I love him . . .

My hand feels cold and so very, very small in his, like I am a lost child he found wandering around in the dark. Aidan has always made me feel that safe and protected, even when we were both children. He is only a year older than me, but he exudes such strength, such confidence that it's easy to forget we are contemporaries.

Maybe that's why I've always loved him.

Hush up, girl. What's wrong with you? Stop saying you love Aidan Gallagher. You don't love him. You don't know him.

Hand in hand, we start climbing up hill while I wage a heated debate in my head.

I can't love Aidan.

Why can't I love him?

Because I love Grayson.

Do I? Really?

Okay, maybe I was just comfortable with Grayson. Maybe Grayson is like that worn-out, tattered robe of Momma's hidden in a box under my bed back home in Charleston. I have kept that robe all these years even though it doesn't fit and has more holes than a block of Swiss cheese. I kept it because it felt wrong not to keep it.

Grayson was my security blanket, a tattered, worn-out relationship I held onto because I was too afraid to let it go. Is that what I am doing now? Clinging onto this remnant of my past because I am too afraid to be alone? Too afraid to feel the discomfort and loneliness that comes with the unfamiliar? Maybe I should pump the brakes on my speeding, out-of-control, soap-box-derby wreck of emotions until I am certain they're not heading me down a road to nowhere.

That's it then. I will listen to my logical side, that eloquent, persuasive side that knows, just knows, falling in love with Aidan Gallagher would be the same as disaster courting folly.

We reach the top of the hill and stop walking. The moon is so bright it reminds me of the lightning bugs I used to catch and keep in an old mason jar. I would fall asleep watching those bugs glowing in the dark, their light reflected through the glass creating a soft blue halo on my bedside table. I always put a slice of apple and wet grass in the jar because Daddy said it would keep the air moist and help them live longer in captivity. Even so, I cried when I eventually let them go.

I guess I've always struggled with letting things go.

I shift my gaze away from the moon to the lake shimmering and rippling like molten silver in the valley below.

The lake.

I look at Aidan.

"This is your special place?"

He nods.

"This is *our* lake."

This is the lake where Aidan kissed me that last summer beneath a moon as big and beautiful as the moon hanging over our heads right now.

"Come on," he says, grabbing my hand. "I'll row ya to the middle of the lake and by the time we step on dry land again, ya will be sober as a nun."

I'm already sober as a nun.

I follow Aidan along the spongy shore until we arrive at a flat-bottomed rowboat beached amid willowy grass. Aidan tosses the blanket and his rucksack onto one of the wooden seats and pushes the boat over the grass. When the stern of the boat slides into the water, Aidan stops pushing. He walks over to me, sweeps me up in his arms, and carries me to the rowboat.

I feel seventeen again. Seventeen and, *deep sigh*, in love, love, love with a beautiful Irish boy, with eyes as blue as the sea, and a smile that makes my heart skip several silly beats.

I won't pay my silly beat-skipping heart no mind, because I am not, not falling in love with Aidan Gallagher. It's only the pints of Guinness, the romantic moonlight, the way I get all dizzy headed when he wraps his arms around me.

Chapter Twenty-three

I sent Manderley a postcard from Ireland once. It was a scene of a cloud-ringed mountain reflected in a glassine lake. I bought the postcard at a roadside gas station somewhere in Connemara, during one of my outings with Aunt Patricia. Manderley kept the postcard, probably hidden away in the Georgian-era tea box with the cracked lid she used to store her treasures. She sent the postcard back to me during my first semester in college, when I was having a difficult time adjusting to life in a place as strange as Austin. She attached the postcard to a piece of expensive stationery, upon which she had jotted a poem by William Butler Yeats in her beautiful, loopy script. I've never been one for poetry, too many confusing, highfalutin' words, but that one resonated because it talked about a person in search of peace. *A peace that dropped like the veil of morning and glimmered like the moon at midnight*—or some such thing.

Three lines stuck in my memory and I recall them now, sitting in a rowboat on a lake in Donegal.

"*I hear lake water lapping with low sounds by the shore,*" I say, reciting the lines aloud. "*While I stand on the roadway, or on the pavements gray, I hear it in the deep heart's core.*"

We are in the middle of the lake now. Aidan stops rowing and secures the oars. He is sitting on the center bench, across from me, facing me.

"'The Lake Isle of Innisfree'," he says.

"You read poetry?"

I don't mean to sound so surprised, so supercilious, but Aidan Gallagher spends his free time training to be a Mixed Martial Arts fighter. I never imagined someone so rough around the edges would like something as soft and refined as poetry.

"I don't read poetry," he says. "I read an article about Yeats in a magazine when I was waiting to be deployed to Afghanistan. 'The Lake Isle of Innisfree' was printed at the end of the article. I liked it, so I ripped it out and stuck it in my *caubeen*."

"Caubeen?"

"Cap."

"You carried a Yeats poem in your hat band when you went to war?"

"It stayed in my cap until . . ."

Aidan looks away, fixing his blank, dead-eyed gaze somewhere in the distance. I hear Catriona's voice in my head.

Our Aidan is haunted by ghosts he can't exorcise.

Silence descends over our little boat, like the veil of morning descending on the shore, as Yeats would have said. I want to ask Aidan what he thinks about when he drifts away from me, when his eyes get that sad, haunted look in them, but I am afraid. Afraid my poking and prodding will be like picking a scab. So, I sit real still like and listen to the gentle, soothing sound of the water lapping against the side of the boat. I sit still and silent until I can't take sitting still and silent, until I feel my heart will twist itself into a knot if I don't say something to bring him back to me, to sooth the invisible wounds paining him.

"I don't like poetry." My voice sounds too loud against the hush of night. "All of those obscure words and incomplete thoughts and misplaced punctuation marks. Shakespeare is the worst. Lawd! I hated having to read his poems in Lit Class. To me, they were gobbledygook."

Slowly, surely, my pointless prattle leads him out of the hazy labyrinthine he has become lost in, out of the mist of his memories, and back to me. He smiles and I know I have his full attention again.

I tell him about my decision to attend college in Texas, about how I knew, just knew, I would die if I kept on living the life my daddy expected, the life of a well-bred Southern girl.

"All of my friends went to Clemson because that's what their parents expected them to do," I say. "Every good Southern girl knows she will leave home to attend a good old Southern college, where she will meet a boy from a good old Southern family. She'll get married, have babies, and the cycle will repeat itself. It felt like the important milestones of my life had been decided for me, picked and stacked up like bales of cotton." My throat tightens remembering the fear, the desperation I felt back then. "I knew if I didn't do something bold, all of those bales wouldn't amount to much and I would die an old, unhappy, unremarkable woman, one of thousands of old women who travel from cradle to Clemson to grave without pausing to wonder if there's a world beyond the Mason-Dixon line."

I don't bother telling him about my relapse, about how I moved back to Charleston after college and slipped right back into my old life of vying for my daddy's attention and Grayson's fidelity.

"Anyway," I say, picking up the dropped thread of conversation. "I thought I was too exotic a bloom for Charleston, that I would grow and thrive somewhere outside of South Carolina."

"Did you?"

I crinkle my nose and he laughs.

"The transplant turned out to be more difficult than I imagined it would be," I say, shivering. "I was lonely and confused and depressed. My sister, Manderley, found an old postcard I sent her from Ireland. She mailed the postcard to me along with the Yeats poem. I think it was her way of reminding me that I could visit the places and people I loved just by remembering them, by tapping into my heart's core."

I cross my arms over my chest, as a shield against the cold and my suddenly vulnerable, exposed heart. Aidan grabs the blanket off the spare bench and stands. The boat sways with his movement, but Aidan remains sure-footed, steady. He squats down in front of me and wraps the blanket around my shoulders.

"I was in love with ya, Tara Maxwell," he says, still holding the ends of the blanket. "Did ya know it?"

I shake my head because I am too afraid to speak, too afraid words will break this wonderful, magical spell and I will find myself back in Charleston, standing at my kitchen counter eating day-old Cain's chicken, and wondering why, *why* Grayson Calhoun chose Maribelle Cravath over me, and why, *why* nothing ever came of my summer romance with Aidan Gallagher.

He pulls the ends of the blanket, bringing me closer,

closer, until I am on my knees, kissing him, touching him, pleading with him to satisfy ten years of longing.

"Jaysus, Tara," he says, groaning against my lips. "I want ya so bad it hurts."

I slide my cold hands under his shirt, follow the thin trail of hair from his belly button up his flat abdomen to his muscular chest. He pulls back.

"If ya don't stop touching me," he says, grabbing my wrists. "I'll take ya right here in this boat."

"I can't think of a better place for you to *take* me for the first time"—I kiss him softly—"can you?"

He reaches around me, grabs his rucksack, pulls an army blanket out of the main compartment, and spreads it on the bottom of the boat.

And then he takes me . . .

. . . beneath a midnight moon, in a boat, on a lake, in Donegal.

After, we lie under the heavy woolen blanket, our limbs tangled together like the roots of the old magnolia that grew back behind Black Ash.

The roots of a magnolia need to be strong, strong enough to keep an eighty-foot tree standing through centuries of torrential rains and hurricane winds. Lying in Aidan's arms, I feel magnolia-root strong, like nothing, not the rains or winds of life, could knock me over.

I doze off and wake a few hours later, when the rising sun is a pink stain against the watercolor gray of dawn. My muscles ache from the cold, but I don't want to move. Aidan is still sleeping, his chest rising and falling with a slow, easy rhythm I find comforting. I ease onto my side and look up at him, at the whiskers covering his chin, reddish in the light of dawn, and flush as I remember the way they felt brushing against my bare breasts.

"Good morning, love."

My breath catches in my throat. "How long have you been awake?"

"All night."

"Why didn't you sleep?"

"A sentry doesn't sleep when he's guarding a princess."

He kisses my forehead and I hear Taylor Swift's *Love Story* playing in my head. He is Romeo, throwing pebbles at my window, and I'm Juliet, running barefoot through the castle to meet him in the garden. A kiss and a sweet word and I'm a lovesick teen again, daydreaming about a white dress and happily-ever-after.

I pull my hand out from under the blanket and run my fingertip over the puckered mark behind his ear. *Use the sense the good Lord gave you, Tara, and let it be. Just let it be.*

I know I should let it be, but the irrational, over-wrought teen in me wants proof that Aidan feels this connection as deeply as I am feeling it.

"Will you tell me how you got this scar?"

His body tenses beside mine. "I will tell ya, but not now, not here," he says. "I don't want to spoil this moment talking about it."

Aidan hasn't moved. I can still feel the rise and fall of his chest under my arm, the warmth of his leg beneath mine, but I have the feeling that a part of him has retreated. I stop tracing his scar and shove my arm back under the blanket, suddenly chilled to the bone.

I say I understand, but I don't.

Chapter Twenty-four

Aidan drops me off at the castle. I don't see him the rest of the day, but I wake the next morning to find a CD on the floor in front of the connecting door, a folded piece of paper taped to the plastic case.

I remove the note and smile when I see the CD is a copy of "Casual Sex in the Cineplex" by the Sultans of Ping—an original copy, from the look of the cracked, scuffed jewel case. I flip the case over and, sure enough, "Where's Me Jumper" is listed as one of the tracks.

I open the note. I have never seen Aidan's handwriting, but the bold, energetic scrawl seems familiar somehow. Maybe not familiar, but fitting. Bold, energetic handwriting for a bold, energetic man.

> *Tara,*
> *I found this CD in one of my old trunks and thought you might like it since you're already a huge fan of "Where's Me Jumper." I was always*

fond of "Kick Me with Your Leather Boots," *but I think you'll enjoy* "Karaoke Queen." *I lost the liner notes ages ago. You can google the lyrics to learn the words. I look forward to another of your Bathtub Concerts—less bubbles this time, yeah?*

Affectionately—which is a wee bit more than fondly,
Aidan

I am back in bed, reading Aidan's note for the third time, when someone knocks on my door. I practically leap out of bed when I hear Miss Belle's rolling voice in my head.

Grace and poise, Miss Maxwell, the anchors that keep a young lady from drifting into disgrace.

I am still wearing my pajamas—a silky, see-through chemise I bought at a lingerie boutique in Charleston called Bits of Lace—so I pull my robe out of the wardrobe and slip it on. It's a fluffy white fleece robe like the kind they have at fancy spas, with a big cursive T embroidered in pink thread. Emma Lee gave it to me last Christmas along with a pair of lipstick-pink faux-fur slippers. I left the slippers at home, because I have an extremely low tolerance for the color pink. I can only stomach so much of the nauseating color before I'm reaching for the ipecac.

I take several poise-restoring breaths before I pull the door open, slow and graceful-like. I expect Aidan to be standing in the hallway, but it's Sin. He's wearing a gray flannel three-piece suit and a slow-burning, dimple-coaxing smile. The top two buttons of his crisp gray shirt are open, revealing a sexy V of smooth tanned skin, and he has one arm behind his back.

"Good morning, Sleeping Beauty," he says, looking at my bed-head hair and bare feet. "Are we still on for lunch or has another Prince Charming swept you off your feet in my absence?"

He pulls his arm out from behind his back revealing a giant bouquet of frail, paper-thin pale pink peonies wrapped with a white velvet bow and my heart skips a guilty beat.

Tell him. Tell him you spent the night with Aidan.

Hush! A lady doesn't kiss and tell. Besides, spending the night with Aidan didn't change one damn thing. Didn't he say—just as plain as day—that he couldn't be your Prince Charming?

"Are those for me?" I say, stalling for time.

Sin looks around, frowning in confusion.

"Did another fairytale princess move into Tásúildun while I was in London?"

I laugh. "Be careful Rhys Sinjin Burroughes. I'm Southern born and raised, which means I have a genetic deficiency making it damn near impossible for me to resist flattery."

"Flattery?" He slaps his hand to his chest. "You wound me. Mortally. Flattery is insincere praise, while my praise is quite sincere, I assure you."

Damn you, Miss Belle! For all your schooling on grace and poise, you didn't teach me a thing about how to respond when a fan-your-face gorgeous man shows up at your door wearing a Dolce and Gabanna suit that hugs him in all the sinful places, or what to do when you find yourself the object of affection for not one, but two dashing beaux!

I thank Sin for the flowers and promise him I will be ready to go to lunch in an hour—an hour and a half, tops. Then, I close my door and lean against it before I fall to the floor in a fit of vapors.

I grab my phone off the nightstand and dash off a group text.

To Emma Lee Maxwell; Manderley Maxwell de Maloret:

Hypothetically speaking, let's say you were attracted to two men. Let's say one of them was named Aidan, a sweet, strong, silent type who made you think of picket fences, even though he made it clear he wasn't the marrying type. Now, let's just say the other one was named Sin, a tall, dark charmer, who brought you expensive bouquets and made you think of naughty nights. If you were stuck smack dab in the middle of two men, which one would you choose?

Showered and delicately spritzed with my favorite perfume, I am putting the finishing touches on my face when my iPhone chimes.

Text from Emma Lee Maxwell:

Need more information. What kind of flowers? What color?

Text to Emma Lee Maxwell:

Pink peonies.

Text from Emma Lee Maxwell:

Pink peonies? Ooh, choose Sin.

I laugh. Leave it to my baby sister, the professional matchmaker, to get to the very center of a perplexing matter of the heart. I send her a kissy face emoji and go back to applying my second coat of mascara.

I take a cue from Sin in choosing my outfit—a black Raf Simons for Dior sheath dress and matching jacket. With the jacket on, it looks almost prim. The perfect Sunday dinner ensemble. Without the jacket, it's all curves and cutout back. I finish my look with the two carat diamond stud earrings my daddy gave me as my high school graduation gift and slip my feet into the black Louboutins I wore when I filmed news segments for WCSC (an impulsive first-paycheck splurge, back when I foolishly believed Daddy would always be around to supplement my income).

I look in the mirror and feel a queasy kind of sickness, the queasy kind of sickness I used to feel before Grayson would pick me up to take me to the Carolinian Debutante Ball or the Charleston Rose Ball. I smooth my jacket and tell myself it's only nerves. Just a pesky old case of the nerves, that's all.

Maybe it's your body's way of telling you that you're acting as phony as stinky, old Maribelle Cravath, with her fake as Splenda greetings and false smiles, because, let's face it, dahlin', you are not a lady-who-brunches-in-Louboutins kinda girl. Never have been, never will be. What was that your daddy used to say about people trying to be something they weren't? Oh yeah. You can put pearls on a pig and call her Miss Petunia, but she's still a pig.

The thing about hateful little voices inside your head? They're just like pigs in pearls, you can't trust 'em one darn bit.

I stick my tongue out at the girl in the mirror, just in case the hateful little voice in her head is looking, then grab my iPhone and purse and head out the door.

I am halfway down the stairs when my phone chimes again.

Text from Manderley Maxwell de Maloret:
Aidan. You have to respect a man honest enough to tell you what he's willing to offer, even if it's less than what you hope for. A well-tailored suit and expensive bouquet can hide a multitude of sins (excuse the pun).

Chapter Twenty-five

We eat lunch at a posh restaurant located in a hotel on the banks of Lough Eske. Traditional Sunday Carvery—tender roast beef with a slightly blackened, peppery crust, whipped potatoes, fresh vegetables, and thick, brown gravy. Sin called ahead to reserve a table by the fire and we sit there long after our plates have been cleared away and our champagne glasses refilled, basking in the warmth of the flames and the glow of friendship.

The conversation flows as freely as the champagne, and is equally sparkling thanks to Sin's charm and wit. He is open and direct, possessing none of Aidan's reticence.

Even so, I find myself wishing I was with Aidan and not Sin. Does that make me a shameless hussy, accepting flowers and eating lunch with one man while wishing I was with another? Apparently, even a hussy has a conscience, because mine is pricking at me to be honest with Sin. Better to let him down soft and easy now than crush him later.

"Right then." Sin pushes our champagne glasses aside, rests his forearms on the edge of the table, and forms a steeple with his fingers. "Shall we talk business?"

"Business? What sort of business?"

"Castle business."

I frown. "You want to talk about the castle?"

"I do."

When I told Aidan I thought Sin invited me to lunch to talk about castle business, I was just playing at being humble. *Shoot, y'all.* I didn't really think he invited me out just to talk about lead eavestroughs and glazing windows. Now, I realize I let all of Sin's heart-holding and compliment-giving ways go straight to my head. *It's not the first time I've let myself get too big for my britches.*

"What do you want to talk about?"

"The crippling cost of keeping a country house."

"Be still my heart," I say, drawling my Southern out.

"I am serious," he says, holding my gaze. "I have a story I would like to share with you."

"Do tell." I smile sweetly and rest my hands in my lap. "I am all ears, Mister Burroughes."

"My parents have a friend in Sussex, the heiress of a remarkable estate built by one of Henry VII's most loyal subjects. It's a massive house, filled with all of the treasures one would expect to find in a historic country house. Antique furniture, sculpture to rival the Eglin Marbles, loads of pricey bric-a-brac." He leans forward and narrows his gaze. "Nithercott Park has more assets than Tásúildun, but the heiress is still struggling to keep it from crumbling around her. She spent one million pounds last year on roof repairs, eighty-four thousand pounds on oil for the Aga and heating, five-hundred pounds on firewood, and forty-nine thousand pounds for maid service."

"Did you say forty-nine thousand pounds?"

"Yes," Sin says, narrowing his gaze. "What do you think about those numbers?"

"What do I think?" I widen my eyes all innocent like. "I think we should give Mrs. McGregor a raise."

"I don't think you are grasping the precariousness of this situation."

Emma Lee uses some slang word to describe when a man condescends to a woman. What is it? *Manalyze? Manustrate.* Mansplain! That's it! Mansplain. Sin is mansplaining like I am a few crawfish short of a Low-Country Boil.

"We have a saying back home." I lean forward and rest my forearms on the table. I'm about to do a little mansplaining myself, y'all. "*Too poor to paint, too proud to whitewash.* It harkens back to the days just after our Civil War, when so many plantation owners were feeling the pinch of poverty. You see, paint was expensive back then. Whitewash was a cheap alternative. I might be too poor to paint Tásúildun, Mister Burroughes, but I am not too proud to whitewash. So, if you have some suggestions on how I might economize, I would be happy to listen to them."

"Now we are getting somewhere," he says, shrugging out of his coat and rolling up his sleeves. "We need to do more than economize, Tara. We need to develop a revenue stream, a steady income to offset the expenses."

"A revenue stream? We could open the castle to the public and charge an entrance fee."

"I am afraid that would generate a trickle, instead of a stream."

"Don't be such a negative Nelly!" I say, warming to the idea. "I am sure there are loads of people who would pay five, maybe even ten pounds to tour a haunted Irish castle."

"Have you heard of Dunluce Castle?"

Dunluce is a stunning medieval castle perched on the very edge of a plunging cliff on the coast of Northern Ireland.

"I visited it with Aunt Patricia once."

"In 2009, Dunluce attracted over eighty-thousand paying visitors. By 2015, the number of paying visitors to Dunluce had dropped to less than forty-five-thousand."

"That can't be right," I argue. "Wasn't Dunluce used as one of the filming locations for *Game of Thrones*? The show is one of the most popular series on television. Surely—"

"The popularity of *Game of Thrones* helped boost tourism in Northern Ireland by nine million pounds, but Tásúildun was not used in the filming."

I have been holding my breath but now I let it out in one slow, controlled exhalation, like air leaking from a punctured tire. Dunluce is in ruins, but they're massive, breathtaking ruins.

"If Dunluce is struggling to attract visitors, Tásúildun doesn't stand a chance." I sit back. "We're doomed."

"Not necessarily."

I sit up again, encouraged by Sin's optimism.

"True, Tásúildun is much smaller than Dunluce and

it doesn't have the allure of having been a filming lo-
cation for a popular television series, but it has a fasci-
nating history and is located on some of the most
stunning land along the Wild Atlantic Way." He smiles,
the way my daddy used to smile when he felt a fish tugging on his line. "The renovations Aunt Patricia made to
Tásúildun were brilliant. She modernized while maintaining as much of the architecturally historic details as
possible. For that reason, I think Tásúildun is a prime
candidate to become Ireland's next luxury country
house hotel."

"*Hotel?*"

I imagine children sliding down the banisters and
playing ball in the porcelain room, tourists rolling their
suitcases over the centuries old wooden floors and
spilling their drinks on Aunt Patricia's prized Indian
rugs, and I want to cry.

"Hear me out." He grabs my hand across the table
and squeezes it. "A luxury country house hotel."

"There must be hundreds of country house hotels in
Ireland."

"Bang on," Sin says. "In fact, we are sitting in one
right now. This was once the home of Red O'Reilly, a
nineteenth-century mining expert who made his fortune in India. When his descendants couldn't afford
the upkeep, they sold the estate to a hotel chain."

The waiter arrives with our bill and Sin hands him a
black American Express card. I look around the room
with fresh, critical eyes, at the floor-to-ceiling doors
that open onto a slate terrace, at the sweeping mani-
cured lawn, perfect for hosting larger scale events, and
wonder how we could hope to compete with such a
space.

"This place was built hundreds of years after Tásúildun and has obviously undergone a major, expensive renovation, how can we compete with them?"

"True, this hotel is beautiful and modern. Beyond that, it is unremarkable from the dozens of other castle hotels scattered around Ireland. Tásúildun could compete with them by offering the sorts of amenities modern travelers desire."

"What sorts of amenities?"

"I am glad you asked," he says, reaching into his front jacket pocket and pulling out a piece of paper folded in half. He unfolds the paper and slides it across the table to me. "I have done the research and come up with a list of the top projected trends in the hotel industry for the next ten years. You can take that with you and read it later. If you would like, I would be happy to paraphrase."

"Okay."

"Travelers are becoming more sophisticated and tech-savvy. They expect luxury, efficiency, and innovation. It's not enough to offer designer soaps and turn-down service with Belgian chocolates. Travelers have higher-expectations."

"What does that mean?"

"I predict the most successful hotels will offer unique experiences. Hotels with a persona, a brand that sets them apart from the Hilton and Marriott clones."

"A persona?"

"Absolutely," he says. "A hybrid with a persona. Travelers want the comfort of the familiar—room service, maid service, concierge—combined with the thrill of the unexpected. They want to be pleasantly nudged out of their comfort zone so they have something unique to share when they go home."

"So, a luxury hotel with a hook, like underwater

rooms or staff that dress in period-correct costumes?" I laugh as I imagine Mrs. McGregor in kirtle and bonnet. "Are you sure you're not talking about an episode of *Fantasy Island*?"

"Fantasy Island?"

"Cheesy old American television series about people who travel to a tropical island to live out their wildest fantasies."

"Less gimmicky, more tailored."

I can't imagine anyplace being more tailored than *Fantasy Island*, but this is Sin's ball and I'm just here to dance.

"So how do we tailor the experience?"

"By capitalizing on Tásúildun's most unique and impressive features. Our entire brand must be built around that which makes Tásúildun unusual. That is how we will distinguish ourselves as a truly remarkable hotel *experience*."

Sin is such a persuasive speaker; I almost forget he is talking about turning our aunt's beloved home into a hotel. A hotel! I couldn't save Black Ash from the indignity of being wantonly and cruelly transformed from a family home into a . . . I don't know what Black Ash will be transformed into but I'm guessing it's going to involve a Japanese hotel conglomerate and a tacky neon sign.

"I don't know, Sin." I stare at the fireplace as if the answer to our very real problem is hidden in the flames. "What do you think Aunt Patricia would say if she knew you were thinking about turning Tásúildun into a hotel? Do you think she would be happy knowing that her home, her passion, was going to be transformed into a crass commercial venture? It makes me sad, down-to-my-soul sad, to even think about doing anything that would strip Tásúildun of her magic, her grandeur." I sigh.

The waiter returns with the charge slip and Sin's credit card. Sin signs the bill, slips his credit card into his wallet, and lifts his jacket off the back of his chair.

"Don't make your mind up just yet," he says, walking around the table to pull my chair out. "There's something I would like to show you first."

Sin takes my arm and leads me out of the hotel. We follow a snaking gravel path around the main lodge and the hotel's newer, modern wing, and continue following it through the gardens, until we arrive at a pier extending out over Lough Eske. A helicopter is waiting on a helipad built at the end of the pier.

"Have you ever seen Tásúildun from the air?"

I shake my head.

"Then you are in for a marvelous treat."

We board the helicopter. The passenger compartment is more luxurious than business class on most airlines, with wide, leather upholstered seats and plush, wall-to-wall carpet. Sin helps me adjust my lap belt before taking a seat in the chair across the aisle.

"This helicopter has advanced acoustics and vibration suppressors, which means the cabin will be much quieter than most helicopter cabins." Sin slides his seatbelt buckle in until it clicks. "That means we will be able to talk without having to wear headsets."

"Is this the way you always travel?"

He chuckles.

"Not always. My company has a contract with an executive aeronautical service, though this is definitely one of the nicer helicopters in the fleet."

The helicopter vibrates. I hear a muffled *thwack-thwack-thwack*. I look out the window and realize with a start that we are already lifting off. The lake is churning, capped with white peaks as the helicopter's blades spin around and around, pushing air down.

We climb straight up, up, up and then we are moving forward, speeding over the tops of trees, rolling hills, villages filled with crayon-box colorful cottages. We turn north and follow the coast.

"This is amazing." I can't look away. "I've never seen anything more beautiful."

Less than fifteen minutes later, two television monitors swing down from the ceiling and the pilot's voice fills the compartment.

"Mister Burroughes, Miss Maxwell," he says. "I have turned on the nose camera. Please direct your attention to the monitors as we are approaching Tásúildun."

I can barely contain my squeal of excitement as I watch the dark gray speck in the middle of the screen grow larger and take the shape of Tásúildun. The camera zooms in close enough for me to count each of the tall, octagonal chimneys.

"Look," I say, pointing. "Did you know there were cupid faces carved into the stone pediments over each of the windows?"

Sin squints at the screen.

"No." He smiles at me. "Perhaps we could have an artist do a rendering and use it as a logo for branding."

Logo? Branding? Who cares about logos and branding when you're flying in a helicopter over a glorious Irish castle?

The helicopter circles around and around, affording us the opportunity to see the castle from all sides. The oldest section with towers looming over the sea, towers too dangerous to inhabit but intact enough to spark the imagination of days of knights and female pirates. The front hall, the newest section, with the façade of a grand country manor home. The sides, where the old and new were cobbled together.

We are circling back around to the front when I spy Mrs. McGregor standing in the kitchen garden, her hand pressed to her forehead to shield her eyes from the sun. She waves at us.

"Look, Sin! It's Mrs. McGregor!"

I hold my iPhone against the window and start filming a video. A split second later, Mrs. McGregor comes into view. From up here, she looks like a dollhouse doll, with her teensy-tiny shawl wrapped around her shoulders.

I know she can't see me but I wave back anyway.

The helicopter follows Tásúildun's drive, whizzes over the standing stone, and then we are flying over furze-covered hills.

"This is what I wanted to show you," Sin says, leaning closer. "The estate extends over one hundred acres, far beyond these hills. Nearly one hundred untouched acres of that could be developed into luxury cottages, a five-star restaurant, a wellness center and spa, hiking trails. The possibilities are endless." He reaches across the aisle and grabs my hand, squeezing it. "Think about it, Tara. With the right financial backing, we could turn Tásúildun into a premier vacation destination and raise enough money to keep the castle in lead eavestroughs for the rest of our lives."

I look at Sin, see the sincere enthusiasm shining in his eyes, and the apprehension squeezing my heart like a vise-grip relaxes.

"It might work."

Sin is out of his seat, unfastening my seatbelt, and

pulling me into his arms before I've even finished talking. He kisses me full on the lips, hard and quick. So quick, there's no time for me to close my eyes or pop my leg, no time for my butterfly nerves to fully develop and start fluttering about inside my belly.

I sit back down and stare out the window, but the landscape is a blur. I pinch my leg good and hard just to make sure I am actually awake, that I am not dreaming this afternoon with Sin. I pinch harder.

Ouch. Yep, I am definitely awake.

Of course you are awake, you fool. Do you really think you would dream about a man as gorgeous as Sin Burroughes kissing you like . . . like a man who hates kissing?

Sweet Jesus! There's a terrible, awful, rotten, no-good, miserable thought: a sexy-as-sin man born without a libido. What would be the point?

No, God doesn't make those sorts of mistakes.

What about the pipefish? The starfish? They're fish, but they can't swim. What about the ostrich and the penguin? Are you telling me God meant to create flightless birds?

Since I refuse to believe a being powerful enough to create the sun, the moon, the earth, and each of the stars twinkling in the sky, could make a mistake, I have to assume Sin has the ability to muster passion—just not with me.

Sin isn't attracted to me.

I would have expected such a realization to feel like a shotgun blast to my ego, but the truth is my initial attraction to Sin has faded faster than a ten-dollar spray tan.

Chapter Twenty-six

By the time Sin maneuvers his sleek car off the main road and onto the drive leading to Tásúildun the sky resembles a deep purple curtain with just a ribbon of weak golden light peeking out at the bottom. Aidan is backing into a parking space as we pull up to the castle.

"Right," Sin mutters. "Perhaps it would be best if we didn't mention our plan to Aidan."

I look at him, but I must not do a good job of hiding my emotions because he starts talking faster than a Baptist preacher at a tent revival.

"Just until I have had time to fly to London to see if I can secure the financial backing necessary for such an ambitious endeavor." He smiles one of his smooth smiles. "Just give me two weeks."

"I don't know if I am comfortable keeping such a big secret from Aidan. It feels dishonest."

His smile fades. "Don't you trust me?"

I remember Manderley's text. *An expensive suit and a bouquet of flowers can hide a multitude of sins.*

"It's not a matter of trust, Sin."

"What is it then?" He looks out the window at Aidan's car and back at me. "Oh, I see."

"What? What do you see?"

"You're in love with Gallagher."

"What?" I snort. "In love?"

"Stupid me." He smiles again, only this time it's a sad smile. "I came here hoping I stood a chance, slender as it might be, to win your friendship and impress you with my business acumen."

"You have my friendship, Sin. As to your business acumen, I am extremely impressed."

"Really? Enough to choose me over Gallagher?" He shakes his head. "It's just like when we were kids. You will always choose running wild with Aidan over playing chess with me."

"That's not true!" My words sound forced, false, even to my ears. "I remember playing chess with you in the library several times. I always lost."

"I just want a fair crack at it, Tara. That's all."

Is he talking about winning my friendship or our aunt's castle, I wonder. Either way, it makes me sad to think of little knock-kneed Rhys, all alone, staring out the library window as I ran off with Aidan.

"Fine," I say. "I won't tell Aidan about your hotel scheme until you've had some time to see if it is financially viable. You have two weeks. No longer. Aidan deserves a fair crack, too."

"Brilliant!"

He climbs out of the car and hurries around to open my door. I get out and immediately look over at Aidan leaning against his Range Rover. My skin flushes with guilty heat.

Aidan takes one look at my body-con dress and nose-bleed high heels, Sin's guiding hand on the small of my back, and his face hardens.

"How are you, Aidan?" Sin says. "Sorry we didn't invite you along, but . . ."

Aidan skewers him with a stare so sharp, so point-edly hostile, I check to make sure he hasn't drawn blood.

"Right then," Sin says. "I'll just pop into the kitchen and start the kettle to boil."

Sin retreats into the castle faster than green grass through a goose. *Coward.*

"So, ya went out with Oxford?"

"He took me to lunch."

"After we spent the night together?"

"What does that mean?" Guilt sharpens my tone. "You walked me home from school so I am not al-lowed to sit beside anyone else in the cafeteria?"

"I did a whole lot more than walk you home from school, *banphrionsa*, but thanks for letting me know how little it meant to ya. *Thanks a million.*"

"That's not what I meant."

"What did ya mean, then?"

"Our night on the lake was"—my face flushes with heat because, well, it ain't fittin' to talk about what happens between a man and a woman when they're alone together, naked as the day the Lord made them, it just ain't fittin'—"special. Mighty special. But that doesn't mean you own me. You don't own me, Aidan Gallagher. If I want to spend the day with Rhys bleed-in' Burroughes, I will!"

"I never said I wanted to own ya, Tara," he says,

quietly. "Is that the sort of man ya think I am? The sort that would try to control ya?"

He's not yelling or pitching a big fit, though I almost wish he would because the calm, controlled Aidan feels far more threatening than the fists-flying, legs-sweeping brute I saw in the cage that day at Bánánach Brew Farms.

"That's not what I meant. Let me explain."

"Don't bother," he says. "I waited ten years to catch you between ponces. I won't be waiting another ten years."

"That's not fair."

"Fair? What are ya on about?" He looks incredulous. "I'll tell ya what's not fair. It only takes a bouquet of flowers to make you forget all about me. Am I really that unimportant to you, Tara?"

I want to cry out, *you're the one who said you couldn't be my Prince Charming*, but it sounds petulant and juvenile in my head.

"You are important to me, Aidan." I grab his sleeve, but he pulls it away. Gently. "I just didn't think I was that important to you."

"Are ya fecking kidding me? Why would ya think that? Because I don't leave ya alone at a dance to run off with me mates? Or tell ya to lose weight? Or is it because I don't play the fiddle and try to take advantage of you when you've had one too many pints of Guinness?"

"Well, you don't play the fiddle anyway . . ."

I regret the words as soon as I say them. Words are like bullets though, once they're out of the gun there's no sucking 'em back in.

"Is that what ya think, then? That I took advantage of ya? That I don't care about you?"

"I don't know how you feel about me because you haven't told me."

"Maybe ya don't know how to listen."

He shakes his head, the same way my daddy shook his head when I told him I was going to college in Texas, and it tears through my heart like a hot knife through butter. I hear my daddy's voice in my head, *Tara, dahlin', you're just too darned headstrong for your own good.*

Aidan climbs into his Range Rover, starts the engine, and drives away. No big dramatic scene. No spinning tires and spitting gravel. Just red taillights fading into darkness.

I see those taillights later, as I am lying in my bed, staring up at the ceiling, listening for the sound of Aidan's footsteps in the hallway. I see the disappointed look on his face, the broad expanse of his back as he is walking away, and the bright red taillights of his SUV driving off into the night, like a video clip stuck on a perpetual loop. Playing over and over and over.

Aidan was right. I don't listen. I hear, but I don't listen. I didn't listen to my daddy when he told me he loved me as much as my sisters. I didn't listen to him when he told me he thought I was making a mistake studying radio, television, and film. I got all defensive and defiant because I mistook his concern for my happiness as doubt over my abilities. I thought he was telling me I wouldn't be successful in radio, television, and film because I wasn't as clever as Manderley or as personable as Emma Lee.

I didn't listen to Grayson when he told me I wasn't the sort of girl he was going to marry. He told me, maybe not in those exact words, but he definitely told me. I thought I could stomp through life in my cowboy boots, dying my hair crazy colors and rebelling against the Old Guard, and Grayson would just chuckle and say, *That's my dahlin', Tara. Isn't she just precious?* The same way Rhett Butler chuckled over Scarlett O'Hara's antics.

I didn't listen to Aidan when he told me he liked me just as I was, pudgy-fudgy middle, frizzy hair, braces, and all. He told me he liked me when we were kids by spending his summers with me instead of his friends. He told me he liked me when he kissed me on the rocks below Tásúildun. He told me he liked me when he quietly listened to my silly childish woes and worries, never once laughing or teasing me. In dozens of quiet, meaningful ways, Aidan told me how much he cared for and respected me. I just didn't listen.

Worst of all, I haven't been listening to myself. I knew my daddy loved me—deep down in my bones, I knew. The day before I sent my enrollment deposit to the University of Texas, I was watching Super Soul Sunday on OWN and I had an epiphany. Oprah was interviewing this man who lost three of his limbs in a tragic accident. The man was talking about how nearly dying taught him about living, that he was lying up in his bed feeling sorry for himself when he suddenly had an epiphany that he was using his accident as an excuse not to look at what was really ailing him: lack of faith in himself and gratitude for what remained.

That's when I had my epiphany. I realized there was only one person to blame for my pitiful low self-esteem: Tara Grace Maxwell. Daddy never told me I wasn't as clever as Mandy or as sweet as Emma Lee. Daddy never said I wasn't pleasing enough to be a good Southern girl. I said those things, in quiet, destructive whispers.

You're too fat to be pretty.

Clever girls don't read cookbooks.

Proper, pleasing Southern girls don't wear overalls, catch frogs, go quail hunting, or eat the pecans out of a pecan pie with their fingers.

I knew then, on that Super Soul Sunday, that I was making Daddy my whipping boy, blaming him for the wounds I inflicted myself. I was running off to Texas half-cocked because I didn't have the courage to stay and admit I didn't know who the hell I was or what the hell I wanted to do with my life, really do.

I didn't listen to myself when I said, *Girl, what are you doing with a man like Grayson? He's never gonna make you happy, with his boring political aspirations and narrow worldview. He'll put you in a pretty little box on the shelf in his family's drawing room, another pretty little ornament in Grayson Calhoun's privileged world. Is that what you want to be? A useless ornament? To be valued for your beauty instead of your substance?*

I fall asleep, still listening for the sound of Aidan's footsteps, and vowing, sincerely vowing, to listen to Tara Grace Maxwell and the people who really, truly love her.

Chapter Twenty-seven

"I have changed my mind."

Sin is seated at his desk, pouring over spreadsheets. He leans back, pulls his stylish glasses off his handsome face, and frowns. "Sorry?"

"I don't feel comfortable keeping our plan from Aidan. I think we should tell him about your idea to turn Tásúildun into a hotel."

"I see." He smiles with his mouth but not with his eyes and I know he isn't pleased. "When did you want to tell him?"

"Now."

"*Now*?"

"He's in the kitchen," I say. "Why don't I put the kettle on? We can all sit down, have some apple cake, and talk about the situation openly and honestly. What do you say?"

"Is that a rhetorical question?"

"Of course not."

"Well, in that case, I think it would be a grave mistake telling Gallagher about the plan before we have performed a thorough due diligence."

"Why?"

"Gallagher strikes me as the sort of man who makes his mind up about someone—and something—rather quickly. Once formed, I suspect his opinion isn't easily altered."

"I disagree."

"Is that so?" Sin rests his elbows on the arms of the desk chair and forms a steeple with his fingers. "How long do you think it takes for someone to form a first impression? An hour? Five minutes? Thirty seconds?"

"Thirty seconds sound about right."

"What would you say if I told you recent experiments by Princeton psychologists suggest that people develop first impressions in a tenth of a second."

"I would say, I'm glad you were extremely far-sighted when we first met or we probably wouldn't be having this discussion today. Something tells me you wouldn't have taken me serious if you had been able to see that I was clutching a Furby."

"I would have taken you seriously, Tara," he says, his deep voice convincing. "Just as I hope you are taking me seriously now. If we are not prepared, if we do not arm ourselves with as much information as possible, Gallagher will dismiss our idea completely."

Our idea. Hearing Rhys describe the plan to save Tásúildun as *our idea* should make me feel as light and effervescent as a champagne bubble, but it doesn't. What's wrong with me? A handsome, intelligent, ambitious man wants to be my partner and I feel . . . flat. We left Aidan out of *our plan* and it feels wrong, just plain shady and wrong.

"I think you are wrong."

"Perhaps I am, but are you willing to risk jeopardizing the best plan, the only plan, really, for saving our aunt's castle?"

Sin might be right. Turning Castle Tásúildun into a hotel might be the only way to save our aunt's beloved home, but I truly believe, deep down in my bones, telling Aidan is the right thing to do.

"I am willing to risk it, but only because I believe you are wrong about Aidan. He's more open minded than you give him credit."

"Very well," Sin says, tossing his glasses onto the desk and standing. "Let's tell him."

Aidan is sitting on a stool at the counter when we walk into the kitchen, a half-eaten ham sandwich on a plate in front of him, a bottle of Bánánach Brew in his hand.

"Tara," he says.

He nods at Sin.

"We have something we would like to share," Sin says, wasting no time with pleasantries.

So much for apple cake and tea. It appears our cordial little chat is going to happen while we are standing around the counter, watching Aidan sip from a sweaty bottle of hard cider.

Sin tells Aidan his plan for transforming the castle into a luxurious resort in great detail—rattling off projected operating expenses and profits, offering a shrewd assessment of potential competition, and ideas for an aggressive, but thoughtfully tailored marketing strategy. By the time Sin finishes presenting his clear, convincing business plan, I am certain Aidan will be onboard.

"That sounds like a grand idea, Rhys."

"It does?" Sin says, his brows knit together.

"Sure." Aidan smiles at me. "What do you think, Tara? Isn't it a grand plan?"

"Yes," I say, fixing Sin with a smug, I-told-you-so smile. "Sin has thought of everything, hasn't he?"

"Everything?" Aidan looks confused. "I wouldn't say he has thought of everything."

My stomach tightens.

"Really? What did he forget?"

Sin presses his lips together in a thin, tight smile and a muscle begins to twitch on his jawline, just beneath his right ear.

"I'm just an apple farmer," he says, holding his hands out as if to show us his callouses. "I didn't graduate from a prestigious university. What do I know about big business? I am probably being a feckin' eejit, but don't ya need to own land before ya build a hotel?"

"We do own land," Sin says.

"Do we?" Aidan's question seems benign, but I have a sick, uneasy feeling in the pit of my stomach that he is about to deliver a swift jab to the heart of our plan. "Do *we* own that hill?"

"Tara owns it."

Aidan shakes his head.

Here it comes. Brace yourself.

"What does that mean?" Sin asks. "Why did you shake your head? What does that mean, Aidan? Tara owns the castle and the lands."

"Tara owns the castle, but I am the legal leaseholder of eighty-nine of those acres."

Sin curses and runs his hand through his hair.

"What is a leaseholder?" I say, looking from Sin to Aidan. "What does that mean?"

"It means, *banphrionsa,*" he says, smiling. "You can't

trade the keys to your castle without first consulting your serf."

"Serf?"

"I pay the owner of Tásúildun an annual rent in exchange for the use of eighty-nine acres."

"Am I right in assuming you possess a ratified, legally binding lease?"

"Right as Donegal rain, old chap."

"How long is the lease?"

"Twenty-one years."

"*Twenty-one years*?"

Aidan grins.

"Wait," I say, still confused. "Are you saying I am going to be your landlord for the next twenty-one years?"

"Grand, isn't it?" he says, winking at me.

Sin frowns.

"Would you consider . . ."

"Nulling my lease?"

Sin nods.

"Even if I wasn't negotiating a lucrative deal with an international restaurant chain, I wouldn't forfeit my right to the use of the land to a load of overweight tourists who would stomp around the hills in their ridiculous boots, trample the gorse, and litter the ground with their crisp wrappers." Aidan looks at me. The grin has disappeared from his face. "Is that what ya want then, Tara? To let a load of tourists destroy the peace and beauty your aunt worked so hard to maintain?"

"Of course I don't want to see Tásúildun destroyed," I say, my voice wobbling. "But what choice do I have? I don't have the money to maintain the castle, do you? No, you don't! Sin came up with a solid plan to save the castle and he has the expertise to make it happen. Can you say the same thing?"

"That's your problem, Tara." He tosses his empty cider bottle in the recycle bin and walks to the back door. "Ya don't have faith in me. You've never had faith in me. What's worse, you don't have faith in yourself."

Chapter Twenty-eight

Gaston Lenôtre.

Some women dream about movie stars. Some dream about male models. Others dream about athletes. I dream about a dead French pastry chef.

I started dreaming about Gaston Lenôtre when I was in college. I watched a documentary about famous chefs and the narrator referred to one of them, Gaston Lenôtre, as the God of Desserts. After that, the Dessert God would appear in my dreams as a portly elderly man with sparkling blue eyes and a tall, starched toque perched atop his balding head—almost like a Fairy Godfather, but brandishing a whisk instead of a wand.

The dream is always the same. I see him in the distance, dressed in a pristine white chef's coat, carrying a tray of pastries, and wreathed in clouds of flour. He walks up, smiles his radiant smile, and offers me a lavender-flavored macaron. I take the macaron, but it's so pretty, with a smooth, crumbly crust and thick, creamy center, I don't want to eat it. The Dessert God stares at me, his benevolent, wise blue eyes twinkling, and then says, *Allez-y, enfant. Allez-y.*

The dream mystified me until I typed the phrase into Google translate and discovered it means, *Go ahead, child. Go for it.*

Since then, I have accepted that the Dessert God's nocturnal appearance is simply a manifestation of my subconscious urging me to push myself toward change. When Gaston Lenôtre entered the culinary world, pastry making had become as dry and uninspired as a box of saltine crackers. The same boring macarons filled with the same boring flavors—chocolate, strawberry, vanilla—and the same cake, croissant, and *croquemboche* recipes. Lenôtre changed all of that with his brightly colored macarons flavored with kiwi, lime, pistachio, and passion fruit. He used less sugar and flour, more fresh ingredients, and whipped them into light, airy confections that seduced all of the senses. He was incredibly innovative and, as a result, elevated pastry making to an art form. The unknown, self-trained chef from a small village in Normandy, who used his life savings to buy a patisserie in Paris, revolutionized pastry making and inspired countless chefs around the world because he wasn't afraid to shake things up, to try something new. *Allez-y!*

I am thinking about Gaston Lenôtre and his fearless pursuit of his passion the next afternoon when Catriona drops by for a visit. I am in the kitchen experimenting with one of Mrs. Cumiskey's recipes for Bread and Butter Pudding—adding my own special Southern-influenced tweaks to an accompanying sauce—when she arrives. She takes one look at the golden Bread and Butter Pudding and smiles.

"Comfort food, is it?"

"Blame it on your Irish weather," I say, stirring the sauce. "These dark, rainy days make me want to hole up inside this kitchen and bake fattening desserts."

"Me gran says the same thing."

"Thanks a million!" I say, laughing. "So you think I am an old lady? Is that it?"

"That depends."

"On what?"

"Do ya like to knit tea cozies and *whinge* about your aching bones? If that's your idea of craic, then yes, you're an old lady."

"No knitting or *whinging* . . . yet."

"Well, then, there's that going for ya."

We laugh.

"This is a nice surprise." I take the saucepan off the heat and carry it to the counter to cool. "I didn't expect to see you until the weekend."

"You remember my friend Michael? You met him at the pub?"

"Of course."

"He hasn't stopped talking about your Feckin' Fiddle."

"Feckin' Faddle."

"Feckin' Faddle, Feckin' Fiddle," she says, raising her hands in exasperation. "Whatever it's feckin' called, he's off his nut about it. He begged me to ask ya if ya would consider making enough to feed two hundred people, about four hundred cups, he figures."

"*Four hundred cups?*"

"He wants to test it in one of his pubs. If Feckin' Fiddle does well, he wants to contract you to make larger batches to be delivered weekly and sold in all of his pubs."

"*Four hundred cups?*" I look at Catriona the way I would if she told me she saw Lady Margaret dancing a jig in the courtyard. "Are you crazy? I can't make that much popcorn."

"Why not?"

"Why not? Why not?" I am about to tell Catriona why I couldn't possibly make enough Feckin' Faddle to feed two hundred people when I hear the Dessert God's voice in my ear telling me to *go for it.* "Where am I going to find that much popcorn? Do you think the Tesco in Donegal would have enough?"

"Forget Tesco," she says, hopping up on the counter. "I called the hotel's snack food supplier in Wicklow. You can order all of your supplies through them—kernels, popping oil, scoops, bags—and they'll even ship overnight."

"That's incredible. *You're* incredible."

"Go on," she says, waving away my praise. "You'll do it then?"

"Sure. Why not?"

"Grand. Just grand. Michael will be well pleased." She dips her finger into the pot and tastes the brown syrupy sauce. "When do ya think ya will be able to deliver your Feckin' Fiddle?"

"Faddle."

"What?"

"It's Feckin' Faddle."

She frowns. "What's a faddle?"

"I think it means foolish."

"Like feckin' eejit?"

"Sure."

"I don't like it."

"Don't like what?"

"The name, Feckin' Faddle," she says, shaking her head. "Are ya calling the people who eat your popcorn eejits?"

"Of course not."

"Then why name it Feckin' Faddle?"

"It's a play on Fiddle Faddle, the name of the popcorn I used to eat back home."

"Hmmm," she says, wiping her finger on her jeans. "I like Feckin' Fiddle better."

Her mobile phone starts ringing. She reaches into her jacket pocket, pulls out her phone, looks at the screen, and rolls her eyes.

"Jaysus, Mary, and . . ."

She holds the phone up so I can see the caller ID. It's Michael. She pushes the talk button and presses the phone to her ear.

"Hello Michael . . ."

I leave Catriona to her phone call to start a pot of tea boiling on the Aga. By the time she finishes her conversation, I have arranged the tea tray and scooped servings of Bread and Butter Pudding into bowls. She disconnects the call and joins me at the table.

"I changed my mind," she says, collapsing into a chair. "Feckin' Faddle is the perfect name for your popcorn. It's certainly turned Michael into a big feckin' faddle. He must have texted me a dozen times. *Will ya ask Tara to make more of her popcorn? Did ya ask her yet? When will ya ask her? How soon do ya think she can deliver it?* What do ya put in it, Tara, crack?"

"No crack, just craic," I say, laughing.

"There's a class name for it, Craic Corn. *So addictive, you'll need a twelve-step program.*"

"That's quite a slogan."

"You're welcome."

I pour tea into our cups. We eat our pudding, laughing and chatting like old friends. Catriona tells me about her job, about how she is tired of the monotony of working in a hotel, about how she wants to try something new, something that will really challenge her marketing skills. I can hear her frustration.

"I know how you feel, Cat," I say, reaching across the table and squeezing her hand. "WCSC is a fantastic place to work and I was blessed, truly blessed, to get hired there right out of college, but I felt unfulfilled in my job. Maybe all you need is a little break. Take a vacation."

She brightens. "Like a road trip?"

"Okay, sure." I smile. "I was thinking of a week in a Swiss spa or sunning yourself on a beach in Mallorca, but if a road trip is more your speed, good on ya!"

"What about a road trip to a music festival?"

"That could be fun."

"Have you heard of the Béal an Muirhillion Music Festival?"

"No."

"It's great gas," she says, sliding her empty teacup aside. "It's held in a town just up the road, right on the beach. People come from all over the world to camp and listen to live music. Vendors and artisans sell all sorts of things. So, what if you set up a booth and sell your Boozy Bites, like Bánánach Biscuits and Craic Corn?"

"Feckin' Faddle," I say, pushing my empty dessert bowl aside. "Why would I do that?"

"Are ya taking the piss? A load of langered eejits listening to music would probably sell their front teeth to get to eat something as delicious as your desserts. Market them as being made with whiskey and craft cider and you will sell out before the first band leaves the stage."

"You think?"

"Absolutely." She grins. "It would be a great way to launch your brand."

"My *brand*?"

"Boozy Bites."

I frown.

"Hear me out," she says. "You need to find a way to make enough money to keep Tásúildun from becoming a pile of rubble, right?"

"Right."

"Do you know how many people have developed a revolutionary product in the hopes of becoming rich and famous?"

I shake my head.

"Millions," she says. "Mark Zuckerberg. Steve Jobs. Bill Gates. Thomas Edison. They are aberrations, geniuses, and visionaries, but some of the most successful entrepreneurs are of average intelligence. They succeed because they use their talents to improve upon something that already exists or supply an unfulfilled demand. They are passionate and persistent. Your unique skill is baking."

"Baking isn't a unique skill, Cat."

"I disagree." She pushes her empty bowl at me. "I devour your desserts even though I don't fancy sweets. You have a talent, Tara, and I believe you could be very successful with the right vision and marketing plan."

"You do?"

"Sure, I do!" Her voice is high and her eyes are sparkling with excitement. "The trick is to start small and create a loyal following. That will help generate a buzz. Meanwhile, we will refine our products and obtain the financial backing necessary to take the business to the next level."

"Do you really think selling my baked goods at a music festival will be the first step to my becoming Mrs. Fields?"

"Who is Mrs. Fields?"

"A famous cookie chain in America."

"Sure," she says, smiling. "Why couldn't you be as successful as this Mrs. Fields?"

From crab cook-off judge to cookie mogul. Why not? I can see it now. Boozy Bites franchises in all of the malls in America, from Seattle to Savannah. Moody teens queuing up to exchange their hard-earned allowance for whiskey flavored cookies. Maybe MADD will be a corporate sponsor. Maybe I will be so successful the *Today Show* will invite me to film a segment with Savannah Guthrie.

"I wouldn't even know who to talk to about renting a booth at the Belly Million Festival."

"Béal an Muirhillion," she says, laughing. "As it happens, my cousin is one of the festival organizers. I told her about your Bánánach Biscuits and how crazy Michael is for your Feckin' Fiddle and she said she will reserve a booth for us."

"Just like that?"

"Just like that! She has the glad eye for Michael, so that definitely helped."

"You keep saying *us* and *we*. Does that mean you plan on helping me launch Boozy Bites?"

"I sure as shite won't get rich planning events for a hotel. I plan on hitching my horse to your comet—or however that American saying goes."

"It's your wagon to my star, but close enough." I laugh. "You're serious about all of this? You'll really help me?"

"Yeah. No bother, no bother. I've been banking my overtime hours for the last year. I can afford the holiday."

"Why would you give up your time off to be my sous chef?"

"Why?" She frowns. "You're me mate, aren't ya?"

"Sure."

"There you go, then."

She says it in such a matter-of-fact way, as if it is perfectly natural for her to give up hard-earned vacation days to help a friend sell baked goods at a music festival. Except for Callie, I don't think any of my Charleston friends would make such a sacrifice, not even to help me launch a cookie empire. My throat tightens.

"Thanks a million, Catriona. Really."

"Go on with ya," she says, waving her hand. "The festival is the last weekend in October, it's a bank holiday. That means we have three weeks to design your brand and logo, order labels and marketing materials, buy supplies, secure a commercial kitchen, and implement a social media campaign."

"Is that all?" I collapse against the back of my chair, already overwhelmed with my mission to become a cookie mogul. "Brand? Logo? I don't know anything about branding."

"Relax, Tara," she says. "Marketing is my unique skill. I already have some ideas. Boozy Bites is a cute name, but I think it might strike the wrong note. A lot of your recipes are based on old Irish and American recipes, right?"

"Yes. I was inspired by some of the Victorian-era cookbooks I found here in the castle. I tweaked them by adding a little Southern flavor."

"Didn't ya say someone wrote in the books? One of the cooks who used to work at Tásúildun?"

"Mrs. Cumiskey."

"That's the note we need to strike. Play up the whole castle-Victorian-cook angle."

"You think?"

"I know!" Her eyes sparkle with the light of inspiration. "*Downton Abbey* has made people interested in life below stairs. I think I read somewhere that Mrs. Patmore, the cook, was one of the most popular characters on the show. Maybe we use Mrs. Cumiskey's name but add something to make it more current and a little irreverent."

"Like what?"

"We can brainstorm first thing tomorrow." She pulls her bowl back toward her. "Now, scoop me up some more of that pudding and let's talk about another aspect of your future."

"What aspect?"

"Me bleedin' brother."

"Aidan," I say, pretending my heart didn't just skip a beat. "What about him?"

"He bloody loves ya," she says, fixing me with a serious expression. "Ya know that, right?"

"What?" I sputter. "Aidan? In love with me? Now who's off her nut? Aidan is not in love with me."

She narrows her gaze and crosses her arms. "Don't ya know he's been in love with ya since ya both were wee ones? Ya were his first love, Tara Maxwell. Sure, he's dated other women, even loved them, but no love is as powerful, poignant, and enduring as a first love."

First love. Isn't that how I have always thought of Aidan? As my first love? I loved Grayson. I really did, y'all, but it was more of a kissing-cousins kind of love. I never pined for him, never felt a pulse racing kind of passion for him. I know that now. Grayson Calhoun is my Ashley Wilkes. He's the boy from the respectable family everyone expected me to marry, the boy I convinced myself I had to marry, just *had* to marry, because he was a good catch, a great match. But Aidan . . .

Aidan Gallagher is my Rhett Butler. He is dangerous and exhilarating. He is the sort of man who would flout propriety and tradition to get what he wanted. The sort who would ask me to dance while I was still wearing widow's weeds.

I love Aidan. I fell in love with him when we were teenagers, but doubts rolled in like the morning miasma that blankets a Carolina swamp. Doubts so thick, so disorienting, they made me turn away from the truth and cling to what I told myself was solid, real.

Like Scarlett, I have been a fool. A silly little fool chasing after a boy who didn't want me even though I had a man who did, a man who wanted me something fierce.

"Do ya love our Aidan, Tara?"

I look at Catriona's sandy blonde hair and startling sea blue eyes and the weight of her question hits me hard, knocking the breath from my lungs.

"I do," I whisper. "I really do."

"Have ya told him?"

I shake my head.

"Why not? Ya used to tell each other everything."

I think of the open, easygoing boy Aidan was and the guarded, moody man he had become.

"He's changed."

"Our Aidan is a changed man, Tara, but he is still a good man. Do ya know why he changed? Has he told ya what happened to him while he was in service?"

I shake my head.

Catriona exhales and sits back.

"He has a hard time talking about what happened to

him over there," Catriona says, softly. "Don't ya know our Aidan has always been a sensitive man; still is, beneath his tattoos and behind his fearful scowls."

I remember the tender way he held me close and kissed my forehead that morning on the lake and the stricken expression on his face when he saw me get out of Sin's car the next day. Both times I felt as if he was holding back, giving me only a glimpse of what he was really feeling.

"He is so guarded now."

"He is guarded, but he isn't unfeeling. Our Aidan has too many feelings, that's the problem, and every day he battles to keep his emotions from overwhelming him." Catriona's bottom lip trembles and I realize she is making a valiant effort to her emotions from overwhelming *her*. "Aidan was on a mission with his squad when they came across a wee lad standing in a mine field, keening pitifully. Aidan was the squad leader and he made the call to try to save the lad. He followed the tracks in the sand to the boy and was headed back, slowly, when the first shot rang out. It turns out the lad was a decoy for an ambush. One of Aidan's men accidentally trigged a mine. There was an explosion and our Aidan was wounded by shrapnel. He woke up in a field hospital days later to discover he had saved the wee lad, but lost three of his men, three of his friends. He blames himself for their deaths."

"What? Why?"

"He believes he made the wrong choice."

"That's ridiculous! What choice did he have? He couldn't have walked away and left that child in a mine field. Not Aidan."

"We know that, but he thinks he should have placed his squad's safety over the well-being of the child."

Catriona's face crumples and my heart breaks for her. The Gallaghers are a close-knit family, but Aidan and Catriona have always shared a special bond. "He blames himself. He says he let his emotions get in the way of logic and training."

"My God." I imagine him in a field hospital, wounded and wracked by guilt, and I can't breathe. I want to go to him, put my arms around him, tell him how proud I am of the man he has become. "He could have died that day. He could have been shot or . . . He risked his life to save another human being. What could be more logical, more right, than that?"

Catriona shrugs. We sink into silence, the rhythmic *drip-drip* of the leaky kitchen faucet suddenly amplified in the hush. To think, I took Aidan's quiet, guarded demeanor personally. I made it all about me-me-me when it had nothing to do with me. I have done that a lot throughout my life—allow my less-than-rosy self-esteem to color the way I perceived other people and their feelings for me. *It's about Aidan being in pain. Not me. He's afraid to trust, to love. He is right. He has told me how he feels, in quiet, meaningful ways, but I was listening for the honeyed words, the flamboyant declaration. I wanted profuse poetry that would convince me he loved me . . . and that I am worth loving. I have been so selfish, so absorbed in healing my wounds, I never stopped to imagine Aidan has wounds of his own.*

"He has a scar behind his ear," I say, remembering the way he flinched when I ran my finger over the mark. "Was it caused by the shrapnel?"

"It was."

"Is he okay now?" The question sounds ridiculous once I have spoken it. "Did he suffer permanent damage? Is he still in pain?"

"Physically?" She shakes her head. "Some wounds go far deeper than flesh, tissue, and bone. Our Aidan has made a full physical recovery, but he suffers."

So I was right. The moodiness. The insomnia. The dead-eyed stare. Aidan has Post Traumatic Stress Disorder. I want to grab my iPhone and google PTSD, but I already know what I need to know. PTSD is a deep, soul-lacerating wound that can't be seen and can't be easily cured. I think of Aidan—sweet, charming, ready with a laugh Aidan—suffering with a wound that might never heal and it kills me. *Kills me.* My neck suddenly feels too heavy to support. I drop my forehead into my hands and let the tears fall—drip, drip—onto the scarred wooden table. Catriona begins speaking again, but it takes a while for her words to sink into my consciousness.

". . . he wasn't our Aiden when he returned from Afghanistan. Sure, he looked like our Aiden, but his eyes were distant, as if he were trapped in a place far from Ireland. It was sheer murder watching him sit at the kitchen table with that vacant expression on his face, his cheeks hollow from weight loss. We were almost relieved when it was time for bed. Then he started having nightmares. Screaming and crying." She swipes a tear from her cheek with the back of her hand. "There's nothing more brutal than watching your big brother weep like a wee lad."

I nod sadly. "Growing up, I was taught to *smile and sweep it under the rug, dahlin'*. It's the Southern way. But some can't be swept under the rug, can they?"

"No, they can't."

"I am sorry, Cat." I squeeze her hand. "Truly, I am. I hear how much you have hurt—how much you're still hurting—and it breaks my heart."

I reach across the table and squeeze her hand. Then, I set myself to pouring her a fresh cup of tea and finding a clean napkin so she can dry her tears.

Steadier, fortified with hot tea in her belly, she tells me about Aidan's first days home after being wounded in Afghanistan.

"We were too much for him, coddling and nursing as if he were a wee lamb with a gammy leg. He used to come here, to Tásúildun, when our mamming became too much for him. And then, he came home one day and said he was moving to the auld shepherd's cottage up in the hills to manage Tásúildun's orchards for your aunt." She takes a sip of her tea. "Herself knew our Aidan would find his peace through purpose. He always loved this land and tending it gave him a reason to get up in the morning, a purpose."

"Is that how he got the idea to start Bánánach Brew?"

"The cider was your aunt's idea."

"It was?"

"Aidan grew up working on our farm and he used to make cider with our grandfather. Your aunt had loads of apples—more than poor auld Mrs. McGregor could turn into jams and cakes—so she told him to make cider."

A wave of grief washes over me. Living in my aunt's home, spending time with the people she loved, should make me feel more connected to her, but it only makes me feel her absence more keenly. It also makes me confused. Why did she leave Tásúildun to me? Aidan is obviously more worthy of the inheritance and Sin more capable of preserving it.

Chapter Twenty-nine

I don't like the ending scene of *Gone with the Wind*. Never have.

After telling Scarlett to be kind to poor old Cap'n Butler, Miss Melly Wilkes takes her last melodramatic breath. Ashley Wilkes is wandering around his shabby parlor all zombie like, clutching one of Miss Melly's orphaned gloves, and wondering how he will live without her.

While comforting Ashley—the unworthy and highly confounding object of her affection—Scarlett has an epiphany: Ashley's been toying with her all these years. He's nothing but a sly, genteel cat in a frock coat and starched collar, idly batting her about like a ball of worsted yarn when all along he had his sights set on that skinny old Melly Mouse. Scarlett realizes she has loved something that doesn't exist. The revelation doesn't upset her though, not truly, because she also realizes she loves Rhett Butler. She leaves the *honorable* Ashley Wilkes wallowing in a puddle of his own high Victorian tears to run through the fog-filled post-Antebellum streets of Atlanta to Rhett. *Oh, Rhett.*

Rhett kicks her to the curb, y'all. Scarlett professes her love for him and he looks at her like she's a sad old mangy stray and says he doesn't give a damn.

Not one damn bit.

Then, as cool as a cucumber with a pencil mustache and pinstriped trousers, he picks up his carpetbag, dons his hat, and walks off into the fog.

I hate that someone as shrewd and clever as Scarlett O'Hara couldn't see what should have been as plain as the arched raven brows on her pretty little face: that Rhett Butler loved her something fierce. Simple, simpering Miss Melly could see it—so why couldn't Scarlett?

I have been thinking about that scene all night and I am still thinking about it, now, as I sit in Mrs. McGregor's cozy room, zoning out on another *Moone Boy* rerun. Haven't I acted like Scarlett O'Hara? First, I imagined myself in love with Grayson Calhoun, my very own Ashley Wilkes. I was so blinded by my desire to capture the cat's attention, I couldn't see that I was just a ball of yarn, a meaningless diversion. I have been flitting between Sin and Aidan, flirting with them like Scarlett batting her eyelashes at the Tarleton Twins throughout the Wilkes's annual barbeque.

Sin pops his head in Mrs. McGregor's room.

"Sorry," he says, smiling. "I have a conference call in a few minutes. Would you mind turning the telly down just a notch?"

"Not at all, luv," Mrs. McGregor says.

Mrs. McGregor pushes a button on her remote until *Moone Boy*'s theme song is a soft drone in the background.

"What are you watching?" Sin's dark brows quirk.

"*Moone Boy*," I say. "Have you seen it? It's laugh-out-loud hilarious."

"No, I haven't," he says. "It's brilliant?"

"Absolutely."

"Great gas," Mrs. McGregor agrees.

"I guess you can't judge a program by its wretched theme song, can you?"

He waves and then he is gone. I look at Mrs. McGregor beneath raised brows, my mouth hanging open, feeling like someone just said my biscuits need more butter or my pecan pie has too many nuts.

"I like this song."

"So does Aidan," Mrs. McGregor says.

"How do you know?"

"He was whistling it last week."

I listen to Sin yammering in Japanese down the hall and have my own Scarlett-like epiphany. Why? Why, oh why sweet baby Jesus? Why have I wasted years pining over the wrong man? I must have been plumb out of my mind thinking I could spend the rest of my life with a man as boring and predictable as Grayson Calhoun. And I sure enough was plumb out of my mind for entertaining the notion that there was a choice between Rhys Burroughes and Aidan Gallagher? There's no feckin' choice.

"I have to go," I say, leaping to my feet. "I have to go right now."

"Now?" Mrs. McGregor glances out the window. "Are ya sure ya want to go now, luv? Me bones are—"

"God bless your wise, *auld* bones, Mrs. McGregor"— I move toward the door—"I don't doubt their ability to forecast weather, but I have to go. I just have to."

Her lips curve in an all-knowing smile.

"Go on with ya, then, and good luck."

I am almost out the back door when I remember I don't have a shiny Mercedes waiting for me in the courtyard outside the castle. I hurry back to Mrs. McGregor's room.

"Mrs. McGregor," I say, sticking my head into her room. "Can I borrow the keys to my aunt's Range Rover?"

"Borrow? What borrow? The Rover belongs to you now, luv. The keys are in the top drawer of the desk in the library."

"Thanks a million."

"Where are you going?"

"To Bánánach Brew Farms. I have to see Aidan."

"Like that?"

I look down at the blue flannel Nick and Nora pajamas Callie gave me as a Bon Voyage gift. The jammies were a good-natured gag gift meant to poke fun at what Callie called the *inhumane* Irish climate. They're a size too large and printed with cartoon images of breakfast foods like cinnamon swirl toast, waffles, slices of ham, and squat pots of tea with smiling cartoon faces. They're not very flattering, but they're cozy and warm.

Miss Belle would pitch a cardiac arrest-inducing hissy fit if she knew I was off paying a social visit to a gentleman friend wearing flannel cartoon pajamas, but I don't give a Fig Newton what Miss Belle thinks. I highly doubt old, prune-faced Miss Belle ever felt the way I feel right now, like I will die, just die, if I don't tell Aidan I love him. I swear I am not trying to be ugly, but can you honestly tell me a woman who spends hours each day pondering the proper angle one should raise their pinkie while sipping tea has it in her to feel a burning, yearning, all-consuming kind of passion?

I don't think so, y'all.

"Yes, like this."

"Take a brolly then. It's going to—"

"Thanks."

I run down the hall and into the library. I yank open the top desk drawer, grab the only ring of keys in the drawer, and run back down the hall to the kitchen. I stick my feet into my shiny green rain boots and grab the umbrella off the hook.

The drive to the farm takes an eternity, down narrow, rutted roads. I don't like driving on Irish roads on sunny days, so I sure as hell don't like driving on them on a dark, rainy night, slamming the brakes and gripping the steering wheel at each curve in the road, praying there's not a fat, wooly sheep around the bend.

By the time I finally pull to a stop between the barns, my flannel top is plastered to my sweaty back and my fingers ache as much as Mrs. McGregor's arthritic *auld* bones.

I try the door to the first barn—the gym—but it is locked and the lights are off. I am clomping across the parking lot in my boots when it starts to rain. Raindrops as big and fat as Irish sheep that drench my flannel pajamas and cause my perfectly curled hair to stick to my face.

I swing open the door to the cider barn, expecting to find Aidan doing whatever cider maker's do at ten o'clock at night, but he isn't perched on a stool, stirring a vat of fermented apple mush with a big wooden paddle.

The barn appears to be empty.

I follow the yellow markings on the floor to the tasting area and die, just about clutch my heart and fall to the ground in a Miss Melly death swoon, when I see Aidan sitting at the long wooden tasting table, a fan of cards in his hands, a group of big, burly Irishmen seated around him.

Aidan looks up. His brows lift in surprise and then he laughs. The poker-playing (fill in the blank) laughs!

The other men look at me and the conversation dies. A little part of me dies, too, dies from the sheer humiliation of it all.

Oh, Miss Belle! I am sorry I didn't heed your lessons.

Aidan leans back in his chair, crosses his arms over his chest, and stares at me.

"There's something I need to say to you," I whisper, painfully aware I am creating a scene. "Can we step outside, please?"

"Outside?" He stops smiling. "Ya must be joking. I'm not going out there. It's lashing."

"When have you ever been afraid to get wet?"

He smooths the hair on top of his head.

"I just had me hair done."

"Your hair?"

"Yeah, yeah." He flashes me a big toothy grin. "I have a fight tomorrow and I like to be clean on when I step in the cage."

The man sitting beside Aidan punches him in the shoulder and then the men are talking all at once.

"Can't be lookin' like a dope, boy."

"Yeah, yeah."

"That's no joke."

"Gorgeous Gallagher."

I ignore the other men and focus on Aidan.

"I am not leaving here until I speak to you."

"Can't it wait? I'm with the lads."

His friends snicker.

"No," I say. "It can't."

His friends start talking all at once again.

"Go on then, boy."

"Let her speak."

"She's a ride, that one."

"Go on, then," Aidan says, grinning.

"Excuse me?"

"Ya said ya want to speak to me so start talking. I'm listening."

"Here?"

"Sure."

He has that look on his face, that arrogant Aidan Gallagher look. It's the same expression he had when we were kids and he challenged me to race him from one end of the beach to the other and when he dared Sin to swim across the lake. It used to rile me up, but not tonight. Tonight, it makes my heart ache in a good way.

And just like that, staring at his toothy grin and twinkling blue eyes, I find the clarity and courage to say what I want to say to him, what I have wanted to say since we were kids.

"You don't have to wait until I am between ponces. You wouldn't have had to wait the first time, but you were too darn pig-headed to tell me how you really felt about me. So, I went home thinking I was one of your many girls."

The lads hoot and holler. Aidan holds his hand up and they stop cheering.

"Go on."

I take a deep breath.

"I love you. I know it must seem fast, but it's not, not really. I have loved you since I was twelve and you kissed me on the rocks below Tásúildun." The lads cheer and a prickly heat moves down my body. "I told myself I couldn't love you because you weren't the sort of guy my daddy expected me to marry. You weren't . . ."

"Gaylord?"

"You know darn well his name is Grayson," I say, gritting my teeth. "But, yes, you weren't Grayson."

Aidan's friends look at him questioningly.

"A ponce she nearly married."

"He was *not* a ponce," I say, defensive.

"He drinks fruity cocktails."

The lads practically explode with laughter. I wait until they're done having their laugh.

"That's not the point."

"What is the point?"

"The point is"—I look down at my feet, at my flannel pajama bottoms pooling around the tops of my rain boots—"I love you."

"Why do ya love me?"

I look at Aidan again and tears fill my eyes. Sweet Baby Jesus, this is not going the way I imagined it would. This is mortifying! I am a sad, sorry mess, sniffling like Scarlett saying goodbye to Miss Melly.

"I love you because you give me the safety to be my real self—even if that means singing 'Where's Me Jumper' in the bathtub or wearing Doc Martens instead of designer heels. You see me for who I really am . . ."

"That's it? Ya love me because I don't care if ya sing in the bathtub or stomp around in combat boots? No other reason?"

"You're honest and kind and funny . . ."

"And?" Aidan prompts.

The lads are riveted.

". . . when I look at you, I hear that Taylor Swift song playing in my head."

"Which Taylor Swift song?"

The lads answer before I do.

The one where she jumps around in a tutu?

. . . or the one where she's mad as a box of frogs burning her fella's clothes?

"Shut up," Aidan says.

I can't see the expression on his face through my tears, which is a blessing I suppose.

"'Everything Has Changed,'" I say, blinking back the tears. "I hear 'Everything Has Changed' playing in my head when I am with you, because looking into your eyes is like coming home. You used to be my friend, a silly boy who dared me to do stupid things, but not anymore."

Aidan is a big, broad-shouldered, blonde-headed blur that suddenly comes into focus. He wraps an arm around my waist and pulls me against him.

"I love ya, Tara Maxwell. Don't you know I've always loved you, that you've always been my princess in the castle?"

He kisses me and the lads go wild.

Chapter Thirty

With everyone's help—Aidan, Catriona, Mrs. McGregor, even Sin—I am able to deliver four hundred cups of Feckin' Fiddle (Catriona was right about the name) to Michael and bake enough Boozy Bites to keep a festival full of music lovers happily buzzed.

Catriona was right. There is definitely a market for alcohol-infused baked goods in Ireland. After the music festival, the word spread from Donegal to Dublin, Cork to Coleraine. Cat's friend Mary designed an eye-catching logo, which we are using on our various social media platforms and all printed material. Mary also designed a simple website with information about our baked goods, professional photographs, and a contact form.

It's only been three weeks and already we have had dozens of requests for samples from pubs, cafes, and hotel restaurants. We are keeping it simple though, supplying Feckin' Fiddle and Bánánach Bites to Michael's pubs and a few cafes around Donegal until we have the money to expand the business. Sin has even offered to help with the loan paperwork. Life is pretty sweet—if you'll pardon the obvious pun.

It's like a big old box of sunny yellow Lemonheads. You know the hard candy that tastes sweet, but then suddenly turns sour?

Life is like a box Lemonheads.

Sweet, sour. Sweet, sour.

Today, my life is as sweet as a Lemonhead.

Tomorrow, I reckon my life might turn sour.

Tomorrow, I must choose between Aidan and Sin. Aunt Patricia's solicitor is traveling all the way from London with paperwork for me to sign naming a co-owner of Tásúildun.

I am not gonna lie, y'all. I am torn.

Choosing Aidan as the castle's co-owner means cheating Sin out of his family's ancestral home. It also means losing an invaluable ally who could help me preserve our aunt's legacy for future generations to appreciate.

On the other hand, choosing Sin might mean losing Aidan. My fierce Irish fighter might take my decision as a mortal blow to his pride.

It's late when I finally climb into bed, mentally and physically exhausted from wrestling with my tough decision, and I still don't have an answer. So, I do what any good Southern girl does when she is struggling to find an answer to a worrisome situation: I give it to Jesus.

Chapter Thirty-one

Text from Callie Middleton:
So, who are you choosing? Aidan or Sin?

Text from Emma Lee Maxwell:
A good matchmaker realizes that a man is like a Louis Vuitton Keepall bag. Some women will look at him and see gauche LV logos embossed on drab brown leather, but others will see an iconic, hand-crafted travel bag. The trick is not to respect her response and refrain from influencing her to change her mind. Whatever you decide—drab brown leather duffle or iconic, handcrafted travel bag—I support you.

Text from Manderley Maxwell de Maloret:
Today is the big day, isn't it? The day when you must decide who inherits Tásúildun: Rhys or Aidan. I know you have been fretting over the decision. Stop fretting, Tara darling. Aunt Patricia trusted you to

make the right decision. I trust you, too, because you have a good, sweet heart.

Text from Emma Lee Maxwell:

Ooo! I don't care if what I am about to say influences your decision . . . Pick Sin!

"Thank you all for coming today," I say, folding my hands and placing them in my lap. "I don't know what Aunt Patricia was thinking when she came up with the unusual stipulation to her will, but I do know she was wise and generous and I was blessed to have had her in my life. Just as I am now blessed to have each of you in my life."

I take a deep, steadying breath and catch the scent of the lemon oil Mrs. McGregor used to polish the wood table earlier this morning. Aunt Patricia's lawyer is seated at the opposite end of the table. Aidan and Catriona are on one side, Sin and Mrs. McGregor on the other.

I look at Aidan. His expression is somber but he nods encouragingly.

"As far back as I can remember, I ached to find a place where I belonged, truly belonged. I finally realized—not too long ago—that Tásúildun is where I belong, where I have always belonged. This castle means more to me than a lucrative money-making scheme"— I smile softly at Sin—"and I know it means more to you than that, too. I also know we will lose Tásúildun if we don't devise a way to make it self-sufficient."

I stop talking and look at Aidan, silently pleading with him not to hate me for what I am about to say. He nods again.

"It is my sole aim to preserve this castle. I believe the only way I will be able to achieve that aim is by maintaining it as a private residence." I shift my gaze back to Sin, see the pain in his eyes. "However, keeping the castle as a home is just not financially feasible. I believe I have devised a scheme that might help us protect Tásúildun while allowing it to be a money-making business."

Mrs. McGregor pats my knee.

"I propose we make a few, minor renovations that would allow us to turn the castle into a boutique bed and breakfast. I propose a super high-end establishment offering the finest amenities for discerning travelers—in-house holistically trained massage therapists, farm-to-table meals prepared by a chef, unique cultural activities off the tourist track. When we have raised the capital, I recommend we hire an architect and designer to renovate the old groundskeeper's home to rent to wedding parties. Finally, I would like to turn the stables into an upscale restaurant complete with a large commercial kitchen that would allow us to offer cooking classes and bake Mrs. Cumiskey's Boozy Bites."

I pause to allow them time to consider my proposition and then I borrow a page from Sin's book and hit them with my research.

"There are already two large castle hotels within driving distance. Why would we risk throwing our cap into an arena already dominated by larger, successful ventures? Catriona"—I look at my friend—"you said the most successful entrepreneurs capitalize on that which makes them unique, right?"

"Sure, I said that."

"Tásúildun is unique because it is still very much a

home. It's historic and grand, but it is a home. The land is virgin, unspoiled. Do we really want to ruin it with helicopter pads and swimming pools? Do we really want to transform it into another generic castle hotel? In the future, when we are financially capable, we could close the bed and breakfast and concentrate on baking cookies and making cider. In the meantime, this plan allows for the preservation of the castle and land. It means Aunt Patricia's staff would remain employed at the castle. It's smaller scale, but more organic and far more exclusive. So, what do you think?"

Sin is the first to speak. "I think it sounds like an interesting plan. I will need to run the numbers, do some market comparison and analysis, but I like it, Tara. I really like it."

"So do I, luv," Mrs. McGregor says.

"It's a grand plan, Tara," Cat agrees. "Grand."

Aidan doesn't say anything. He just stares at me with his unreadable, intimidating expression.

Aunt Patricia's solicitor clears his throat.

"There's just one thing, Miss Maxwell," he says.

"Yes?"

"You haven't told us who you have chosen."

Sweet baby Jesus and the Apostles. This is it. This is the moment when I tell the world the answer to the biggest decision of my life.

"I choose"—I reach into my pocket, pull out a small leather ring box, and hand it to Aidan—"you Aidan Gallagher. I choose you to be my life long partner. If you'll have me."

He exhales and I suddenly realize that intense, intimidating expression was anxiety. I look away from Aidan, shifting my gaze across the table to Sin.

"And," I say, sliding the stack of legal papers on the

table over to him. "I choose you, Sin, to be my business partner and the co-owner of Tásúildun."

Sin signs the paperwork. The solicitor shakes our hands and Sin walks him to his car. Mrs. McGregor gives me a hug and hurries off to put a kettle on the Aga. Catriona tells me I am a feckin' genius, blows her brother a kiss, and follows Mrs. McGregor out the door, leaving me alone with Aidan.

He crosses his arms over his broad chest and stares down at me, his blue eyes twinkling.

"You did it, *banphrionsa*."

"Did what?"

He bends down and kisses me, a soft, teasing kiss that makes me feel as dizzy as the first time he kissed me.

"You found a way to have your cake and eat it, too."

"I don't know," I say, grinning. "Did I? You still haven't given me an answer. Will you marry me, Aidan Gallagher?"

"What do you think?"

That old blanket of doubt, the one I thought I packed away, rolls out, threatens to smother me. I can't move, can't breathe.

"Go on with ya," he says, laughing. "What do ya take me for, a feckin' eejit? Of course I'll marry ya."

"Grand," I say, losing myself in the depths of his sea blue eyes. "Just grand."

RECIPE FROM TARA'S KITCHEN

Tara's Bánánach Brew Bites

Ingredients

⅔ cup white sugar
2 large eggs
½ cup shortening
1 teaspoon ground
   cinnamon
½ teaspoon salt
½ teaspoon ground
   nutmeg
2 cups thinly sliced,
   cider soaked apples

⅔ cup packed brown sugar
½ cup butter, softened
1 teaspoon baking soda
1 teaspoon vanilla extract
½ teaspoon baking powder
3½ cups old-fashioned
   rolled oats
1 cup all-purpose flour

Directions

1. Slice apples and soak in Bánánach Brew Cider for 24 hours.
2. Preheat oven to 375 degrees.
3. Beat ingredients until well incorporated.
4. Drain apples and pat dry with paper towel.
5. Add apples to cookie batter.
6. Bake until lightly browned, 9 to 11 minutes.

Can't get enough of the Maxwell sisters' antics?
Keep an eye out for Emma Lee's story
Coming soon
And don't miss
DREAMING OF MANDERLEY
Available now wherever books are sold
From
Lyrical Press